Lucy Ashford studied English with History at Nottingham University, and the Regency is her favourite period. She lives with her husband in an old stone cottage in the Derbyshire Peak District, close to beautiful Chatsworth House, and she loves to walk in the surrounding hills while letting her imagination go to work on her latest story. You can contact Lucy via her website: lucyashford.com.

Also by Lucy Ashford

The Major and the Pickpocket
The Return of Lord Conistone
The Captain's Courtesan
The Outrageous Belle Marchmain
Snowbound Wedding Wishes
The Rake's Bargain
The Captain and His Innocent
The Master of Calverley Hall

Discover more at millsandboon.co.uk.

UNBUTTONING MISS MATILDA

Lucy Ashford

MILLS & BOON

First published in Great Britain 2019
by Mills & Boon, an imprint of HarperCollins*Publishers*
1 London Bridge Street, London, SE1 9GF

Large Print edition 2019

© 2019 Lucy Ashford

ISBN: 978-0-263-08190-9

This book is produced from independently certified FSC™ paper to ensure responsible forest management. For more information visit www.harpercollins.co.uk/green.

Printed and bound in Great Britain
by CPI Group (UK) Ltd, Croydon, CR0 4YY

Chapter One

London—June 1816

Jack Rutherford hauled himself up from the mattress on the floor, poured water into a bowl and began to wash. The water was ice cold, but he scrubbed his face and chest all the harder because he damned well deserved the discomfort. For the third morning in a row, he'd left it till nine o'clock to struggle out of bed—and what was more, he had a hangover clanging like a set of church bells inside his head.

You, he told himself, *are an almighty fool.*

He looked around the cramped attic room. Now, where on earth were his clothes? Lying in a heap on the floor, of course, exactly where he'd flung them before falling asleep at past three this morning. He began putting them on. Buckskin breeches and a frequently mended linen shirt. An old leather waistcoat and a pair of scuffed rid-

ing boots. After glancing at the mirror hanging
lopsidedly on the wall he ran one hand through
his tousled black hair, noting that his jaw was
dark with stubble.

He looked like a ruffian. *Felt* like a ruffian.
The morning sun pouring in through the high
window was hurting his eyes and his head—
and it was all his own stupid fault, because he'd
drunk far too much brandy last night at Denny's
gaming parlour.

He was twenty-six years old and his life was
going precisely nowhere. Yes, he'd made some
money at the card tables, but he needed to make
a lot more and fast.

He clattered down two flights of twisting
steps to emerge in a ground-floor room that
was crammed with relics of the past, all set out
on dusty shelves and counters. Then after pulling open the shutters and unlocking the front
door, he stepped out into the cobbled lane and
gazed back at the building from which he'd just
emerged. A faded sign painted with the words
Mr Percival's Antiques hung over the door, although 'Antiques' was, in this case, a polite way
to describe utter junk.

As for the rest of the street, it was crammed
on both sides with terraces of three-storeyed

shops and eating houses in various states of dis-
repair. His abode was distinguished by a window
displaying just a sample of the wares inside—
chipped chinaware, clocks that didn't work and
dog-eared books. Yet when Jack had taken on
the lease two months ago, he'd been assured by
Mr Percival himself that the business was a gold
mine.

Jack had been dubious. 'It's a bit off the beaten
track, isn't it? Paddington?'

'On the contrary! You'll find, my dear Mr
Rutherford, that the fashionable set from Mayfair and Westminster simply *love* to drive out
to west London in their carriages, so eager are
they for historic rarities with which to embel-
lish their town mansions! Now, we decided on
a six-month lease, did we not? And you are
to pay me twenty guineas for all contents and
fittings—are we agreed?'

'Agreed,' Jack had said warily, shaking Mr
Percival's hand. He'd had a splitting headache
that day as well—again, the result of too much
brandy and too little sleep the night before. He
hadn't a clue about antiques—still hadn't. But
he'd known he had to do something to earn his
living, something other than winning at cards,
because winning made you enemies.

So Jack became an antiques dealer and he had tried to make a success of it, he really had. For the first two weeks he'd opened every morning at eight without fail, dusting the displays of bric-a-brac and cheap jewellery, making valiant attempts to impose some kind of order. Prices? He hadn't a clue, but he took a guess and stuck on labels galore. He slept on a mattress in the attic, he bought lunch from the nearby pie shop at midday and drank his ale in the local public house.

He also acquainted himself with his neighbours. To his left was a furniture maker, though Jack saw him only rarely, since he appeared to spend his days drinking gin in a back room. To the right was the pie shop run by two lively girls called Margery and Sue, and they did rather better business, as did the noisy alehouse just beyond, which served the boatmen from the canal wharf close by.

All in all there were certainly plenty of people around, but as for the carriages of the rich rolling up, for the first two weeks there wasn't one—in fact, to begin with, Jack's only visitors were other dealers, all of whom glanced around and said something like, 'You've a heap of worthless stuff here, haven't you? I'll take it all off your hands for a few pounds and believe me, I'll be doing you a favour.'

Jack shook his head. But at the same time he was noticing that their rather greedy eyes always alighted on the items that actually were starting to sell. War relics.

It was almost a year since the long war with the French had come to an end and, in London, many unemployed ex-soldiers drifted around on the streets. Though they had little enough money in their pockets, quite a few still possessed relics of their soldiering days: items such as belts and knives, brass buttons from old army jackets, pistols and spurs.

Jack got talking to some of them one night in an alehouse. 'I've an idea,' he'd said. 'I'll see if I can sell these things for you.' So he paid for a small advertisement in *The Times*.

For Sale at
Mr Percival's Antiques Repository
in Paddington.
Military Mementoes of Wellington's
Campaigns

The day after that advertisement appeared, a smart carriage rolled up outside Jack's premises and an exceedingly well-dressed man entered. 'I've come,' he announced pompously, 'to see these military mementoes of yours, young fellow.'

Half an hour later, another rich man arrived, then another. 'Ah, the heroes of Salamanca and Waterloo!' they would declare as they gloated over the pistols and spurs. Each time, Jack nodded politely. Each time Jack concealed his silent contempt for their fascination for these relics of war, guessing that they'd faint on the spot were they to get one glimpse of the horrors of a battlefield. And he made them pay—oh, yes—in hard cash.

But his calculations told him he was making just about enough to cover the rent, no more, which meant that some time soon he'd have to make a major decision about his future. As for now, it was surely time for a belated breakfast— and just down the road he could see a girl selling fresh-baked bread from a laden basket. He went to buy a couple of warm rolls, then strolled on, eating as he walked, to where the narrow street opened out to offer a completely different view.

For here, in front of him, was the newly built canal basin—Paddington Wharf. Thanks to this fresh waterway link with the north, the whole area heaved with industry and commerce. Jack walked on almost to the water's edge, where boat after boat were moored.

This busy scene fascinated him. The canal was busy from dawn till dusk with boats arriving from the Midlands, mostly laden with coal which was rapidly—*noisily*—transferred on to the waiting carts and taken to be stored in the nearby brick warehouses. The bargees, he'd noticed, scarcely paused to draw breath because the minute their loads were delivered they set to work again—the men, their wives, their children—to scrub down their boats, refill the holds with timber or grain, then once more head north.

It was mighty hard work for the boatmen—hard work, too, for the horses who hauled the laden vessels, although those horses, he'd noticed, were tended with as much care as a cavalryman would lavish on his mount. As it happened, just then Jack's eyes were caught by a big grey horse that was being led right past him, its halter firmly held by a youth in a long coat and battered, wide-brimmed hat.

The horse stopped to look at Jack inquisitively and he reached out to stroke his neck. 'Hello there, old fellow,' he murmured. 'I'd guess you have some stories to tell.'

'Best watch yourself, mister,' the youth in the battered hat warned him. 'He doesn't take kindly to strangers.'

'Doesn't he, now?' Jack tickled the animal behind one ear until it gave a soft whicker of pleasure.

The lad's face was shadowed by that big hat, but Jack was pretty sure he looked irritated by the horse's evident delight. The lad tugged at his horse's leading rein and moved on, but called back over his shoulder, 'Hear that noise? You won't find those tar barrels quite as friendly as my horse.'

Indeed, there was an ominous rumbling sound getting louder and Jack spun round, jumping out of the way just in time to avoid being hit by some huge barrels that were being rolled along the quayside. Damn! *That* was close. Breathing rather hard, he took one last look at the grey horse and its slim owner both heading for the blacksmith's forge, from which came the clanging of hammers on hot iron.

The noise and clamour reminded him that everyone around here was busy except for him and slowly he set off back to his shop, but he was sorry to leave the wharf with all its bustle and energy. More than once he'd found himself envying the sense of community these people who lived around the wharf seemed to enjoy, the sense of belonging. They were also a watchful set and it hadn't taken long for the regulars to get to know where Jack lived—they called him Mr Percival, or sometimes just Mr Percy, the antiques man. Right now, a bunch of young women from the boats were walking back with full baskets from the local food market.

'All right there, Mr Percy?' one of them called. 'D'you need a hand with anything today?'

They were casting eyes of approval over his curly black hair, his leather waistcoat and breeches and boots. He smiled back. 'All right,' he said. 'I'm all right.'

But that wasn't entirely true.

Letting himself into the dust and disarray of his shop, he lit a couple of candles to highlight the debris and wondered what on earth to do next. For several years he'd served with the British army in Spain—in fact, he'd been an officer and Lord Wellington himself had valued him highly. 'You're my man for tactics, Rutherford,' Wellington used to say to him. 'You're my man for digging out the enemy's secret plans.'

And what were Jack's plans now? He was aiming to get back his inheritance, that was what. He was plotting revenge against the man who'd robbed him, while he'd been away, of his home, his heritage and his pride.

Who'd robbed him, in other words, of pretty much everything.

Chapter Two

'There. That's Hercules sorted for you, young Matty!' The blacksmith checked the horse's freshly shod hooves, then nodded his head in approval. 'He's a fine old fellow. Let me know if you're thinking of selling him off, will you?'

The blacksmith's forge, Matty always thought, was like a goblin's cavern, glowing with the heat of the furnace and the glitter of molten metal. In answer to the blacksmith's question, she shook her head. 'I'll not sell him, ever. He's an old friend, and we won't be parted.' Carefully she counted out some coins into the blacksmith's sooty palm and began to lead Hercules back to the wharf.

Of course, the blacksmith never suspected she was a girl. Nor had that man who'd nearly been felled by those rolling tar barrels a little earlier. She shook her head at the memory; he'd looked like some arrogant ne'er-do-well and he'd taken more notice of Hercules than he had of her. Like most people, he'd assumed Matty was just another local lad and she was fine with that. Yes, thank you very much—just fine.

As Hercules clopped along beside her, she stroked his neck. 'Pleased with your new shoes, are you, old fellow?'

He nuzzled her neck in reply and she smiled as they walked on past the warehouses to the canal basin.

She had never deliberately set out to deceive people and her long coat and big hat weren't intended as a disguise—it was just that she found men's clothes more comfortable, more useful. She was nineteen years old and her full name was Matilda Grey. She'd lived on the canals all her life and as she walked by the moored boats, people stopped what they were doing to greet her. 'Morning, young Matty! How's Hercules? Did you get him sorted out at the forge?'

'Hercules is fine,' Matty called back. 'He needed shoeing, of course. But the blacksmith said that now he should be ready for anything.'

Yes, all her canal friends knew she was a girl, but strangers didn't realise, not unless they got up too close. And she didn't normally *let* anybody get too close, no, indeed; she kept her chestnut-brown hair cropped short, she wore a shirt and trousers together with an old coat that reached past her knees and some strong leather boots—no dainty shoes for her. She found it so much easier to dress like that. It helped her to look confident and carefree.

Even though today she felt anything but, because the blacksmith's fee had reminded her that she only had enough money left for three or maybe four more months of this way of life. *This can't go on, Matty.* The bills came in regularly for berthing her boat as well as for Hercules's stabling and food and that nagging little voice of worry had been wearing away at her for days now. Some day soon either her horse or her boat would have to go. Then what?

She looked around for inspiration, noting that as usual at this time of day the canal basin was packed with boats being laden with grain and timber for the journey north. *'One boat drawn by a single horse can carry six times as much as a cart pulled by four horses,'* she remembered her father telling her when she was small. *'Canals are the future, Matty!'*

He had died two years ago and recollecting his voice rekindled her sense of loss, together with her fears. Yes, canals might well be the future—but perhaps not for her.

She realised a woman was calling out to her from one of the nearby boats. 'How's things, Matty, love? Getting ready for another trip, are you?'

Bess, one of her oldest friends, had a big soapy scrubbing brush in her hand. She was always scrubbing something—her boat, her laundry or her children. 'I'm making plans, Bess,' Matty replied. 'You know?'

'You and your plans!' Bess shook her head and tutted, but in her eyes was nothing but kindness. 'Just be sure to let me and my Daniel know if you need any help, won't you?'

'I will. My thanks, Bess.' And Matty walked on towards her boat, *The Wild Rose*, where she tethered Hercules close by.

She'd been only three when her mother died and Bess in particular had taken Matty to her heart, cooking meals for her and her father, offering company when it was needed and easing the pain of loss for them both. Matty counted Bess and her husband among her most loyal friends, but Bess would still be watching her, she knew, and just now she needed some privacy. Making for the solitude of her tiny cabin, she dragged off her boots and sat down on the narrow bed.

She still missed her father, so much. An Oxford graduate, he had earned his living by writing articles for historical journals and occasionally giving lectures. He could have made a comfortable living as a tutor, but he loved the canals as much as he loved history—and Matty always suspected that, well educated though he was, he enjoyed the company of the canal folk as much as that of the Oxford men. There was nothing he relished more than to sit by the waterside with fellow travellers on a summer night listening to their tales and he looked after *The Wild Rose* as well as any true bargeman, seeing to the tarring and caulking, retouching the paint and polishing the brass work all by himself. From an early age Matty would follow him around, saying, 'Let me help, Papa!'

'We'll do it together,' he used to say.

Of course, the loss of his wife was a sharp grief, but he'd found a kind of peace, Matty always believed, in travelling with his young daughter from one town to another along the waterways. And everywhere they stopped, he would explore the surrounding countryside for old battle sites or castle ruins. Sometimes, her father unearthed valuable relics—though since the last thing he wanted was to make money out of them, he often gave his finds to museums or to other scholars to assist with their research. 'Our treasure hunter,' the canal folk liked to call him proudly.

From time to time Matty heard strangers whisper that it was a lonely and unnatural way of life for her father to inflict on his daughter, but in those days Matty was never lonely, for she had all of the canal community as her family. The women took special care of her and did what mothers do, explaining about growing up, giving her dark warnings about men—and oh, how they yelled at their own sons if they were too familiar with her! 'Don't you try anything with our Matty! She's special, d'you hear?'

It was indeed a special life with her father on *The Wild Rose*. In the summer months he taught her all about the birds who lived by the canals, the flowers and the water creatures; while on winter nights, when often the water on the canals would freeze over, they'd sit snug in their cabin and he told her enthralling tales of times gone by. He taught her practical things, too, like how to look after the boat and navigate the locks or how to make sure she was never cheated by the innkeepers or blacksmiths. Matty had grown up both capable and knowledgeable—and it was just as well, because two years ago her father had suddenly died.

'A heart attack,' the doctor had told her gravely. 'You mustn't blame yourself in any way, my dear. There was clearly nothing you could do.'

Her friends had gathered round after the funeral and offered their advice. 'Maybe now's the time to give up the boat, Matty, and consider another life.'

They were anxious about her, she knew. *'A girl her age, on her own in a boat,'* she'd heard them whisper. *'It's not right. Not safe.'* More than anything, it was becoming unaffordable— but what other kind of life could she possibly consider, after living so long with the freedom of the waterways?

For the last two years, she'd earned occasional money by carrying light loads on her boat for short distances only, taking on parcels of fabric or chinaware or other delicate goods. Hercules might be old, but he was also well trained—he knew exactly how to plod calmly along the towpath without starting at a flock of ducks or shying at an oncoming barge, while Matty, manning the tiller, dreamed of travelling farther some day and finding the lost treasure her father thought he was close to discovering only days before he died.

'You're one of us, young Matty,' the canal folk were always telling her. 'You always will be, lass.'

But Matty knew that in reality she was alone, cast adrift somewhere between the world of the Oxford scholars and the community of canal people, yet belonging to neither. She also knew this way of life couldn't carry on for much longer without a regular income and some day soon—by the autumn, most likely—she would have to sell *The Wild Rose*. Already the sharp tang of loss was making her cold. She'd told Bess she had a plan—if only she did.

Slowly she went to fetch a tin cash box from under the bed and unlocked it. *The money won't have magically multiplied since you last looked, you fool.*

Inside were some things she'd carefully kept over the years—three bronze Celtic brooches, an Iron-Age amulet and two small silver candleholders, Tudor most likely. And, wrapped in a soft piece of cloth, there was a golden coin. A Roman coin.

Holding the coin up to the light, she thought

she would never, ever forget the reverence in her father's eyes as he'd brushed the dirt from it two years ago. 'Where there's one coin like this, Matty,' he'd said, 'there'll be more.'

The Roman coin she would never, ever part with. But perhaps she could sell the Celtic brooches to a collector, then maybe have enough for all the extra expenses involved in journeying to find her father's treasure, though there was yet another problem. It would take three days at least to get to the site where her father had found the coin and for that length of journey she needed someone to help with the boat. But since there were no women for hire on the canals, that *someone* would have to be a man— and her heart sank at the thought. Sighing a little, she carefully slipped the coin, the brooches and other treasures into a purse, then climbed back up on deck.

'Matty, lass!'

It was Bess again on the wharfside, waving a sheet of paper. 'Look,' Bess was saying, 'someone's just handed me this letter. And bless me, I can't make head or tail of it.'

'A letter? Let me see.' Matty scanned it quickly. 'Bess, it's from the corn merchant in Brentford.

He's offering you a new contract, for a whole year!'

'Really?' Her friend gave a whoop of joy. 'Wait till I tell my Daniel! And he pays well, really well. How about coming to dine with us tonight, girl? This deserves a celebration!'

'I'd love to.' Matty really meant it. 'But, Bess, I've an errand to make first. I've decided I need to sell a few of my father's things—some old trinkets he gave me—so you see, I might have to head into town.'

'Lass, if you're in money trouble, maybe me and Daniel can help...'

'No! Bess, I wouldn't dream of it. And I might not even sell them, but I would like some idea of their value.'

'Well, instead of tramping into town and back, why don't you call at that place just up the lane there?'

'Which place do you mean?'

'There's a sign over it that says "Mr Percival's Antiques". Now, it all seems a bit rundown, but we've seen the young fellow who runs it and my Daniel reckons *he* looks a clever one all right. Why not try him?'

It was indeed a long walk to the antiques dealers in the centre of London. 'I might just do that,' Matty said thoughtfully.

'Just make sure, though, that Mr Percival doesn't swindle you. And you'll come to us later on for your supper, won't you? Then…' Bess hesitated '…maybe we can have a little chat. You see, we've been thinking, me and Daniel, that maybe you should stop this travelling about on your own. You've got an education, and this just isn't the life for a girl like you.'

Matty faced her steadfastly. 'But this is the only life I know. The only life I *want*, Bess, truly—'

It was with a sense of relief that Matty realised two of Bess's children were running towards their mother, one of them carrying a kitten. 'Mama! Mama! Look what Joe the coalman gave us for looking after his horse for him! The kitten's called Sukey and she'll be as good as gold, Joe says. Can we keep her, Mama? *Please*, can we?'

And so Matty was able to escape Bess's forthcoming lecture and seek the solitude of her own cabin again.

But she didn't really feel any better for it at all.

Bess was probably right to say this was no life for a girl like her. But how could Matty abandon it, when she'd known no life other than this, ever?

She'd not expected her father to die so suddenly. Even now a fresh wave of sadness hovered close, but there was no time for grief or any other indulgence of emotions. Her father had taught her everything she needed to know to survive on the waterways—and survive she would. She would not sell her father's boat, she would *not* sell Hercules. And she would never, ever abandon her father's final dream.

Chapter Three

It didn't take Matty long to find her way to Mr Percival's Antiques. Just as Bess had described, the sign was swinging lightly in the breeze; but her heart sank as she drew close.

She'd realised, of course, that Mr Percival was unlikely to resemble the antique experts her father had loved to visit in Oxford, but neither had she expected his premises to have such a general air of dereliction. Squashed in between a furniture maker's and a bakery, it would in fact have escaped her notice altogether were it not for that faded sign. And as she drew closer to the grimy window, she could see a variety of junk—yes, that was the word, junk—littering every available surface inside.

Should she even bother? Yet her father used to tell her appearances could be deceptive. 'You never can tell,' he would say.

She could only hope so.

Since the door was already ajar, she pulled her hat down more firmly, pushed the door open farther, and squeezed her way in past racks of old brass pots and pans that clanked together as she brushed by. Inside, a single oil lamp cast its dim light over shelves that were full of dusty books and ornaments. On the walls were paintings, most of them hung crookedly. As for the counter, she couldn't even see it thanks to a clothes rail full of old coats; but the sound of raised voices was hard to ignore.

'You let go of my son Tommy's jacket, do you hear?' a woman was squawking. 'You great brute of a thing. Why, Tommy's not a quarter your size!'

'Then,' came a man's calm voice, 'your son should know better—madam—than to come in here and steal my goods.'

'He wasn't stealing, my Tommy wasn't. He was just looking!'

'Oh, was he?' The man sounded interested. 'A peculiar way of *looking*, to stuff those various items rather deep in those pockets of his, wouldn't you say?'

Matty could see that the man who held a small, squirming lad by his collar was tall and dark-

haired, maybe in his midtwenties. And she recognised him. He was the man who'd admired
Hercules down by the wharf and he spoke in
that calm, surprisingly educated voice that had
so startled her earlier.

The woman was far from calm. 'You leave my
Tommy alone, you villain, or I'll call the con-
stables!'

'You do that,' the man agreed. 'Save me the
trouble.' The woman hesitated. Meanwhile the
man went on, 'Tell your angelic little son to
empty his pockets, will you?'

Just for a moment Matty wondered if the
woman might try landing a punch on the man's
stubble-darkened jaw. *Most unwise*, Matty decided as she assessed the breadth of his shoulders
beneath his coat. All in all his shabby attire concealed, she guessed, some rather powerful muscles—and clearly the woman thought the same,
because she said, 'All right, then, our Tommy.
Clear out your pockets, you young fool.'

Tommy scowled, but out came the goods—a
pewter snuffbox, a brass signet ring and a silver-
plated spoon. Tommy handed them over sullenly,
one by one.

'Right,' said the man. 'Now clear off, the pair
of you. And listen, young Tommy—' he bent

down close to the lad's ear '—if I ever catch you in here again, you'll get a wallop on the backside and that's a promise. You hear me?'

Tommy's mother, with one last baleful glance at the man, dragged her boy outside and began yelling. 'Listen here, our Tommy. If I've told you once, I've told you a dozen times...'

As the sound of her voice faded at last into the distance Matty stepped forward, still careful to keep herself away from the light of that single lamp. She cleared her throat. 'Mr Percival, I presume?'

He almost jumped. 'Ah. Forgive me. Didn't see you there.' He'd been examining the spoon the lad had tried to pinch, rubbing it on his sleeve before putting it back on an already crowded shelf. Matty couldn't see any order at all to what was already there—it seemed a higgledy-piggledy mess to her.

Then he turned to look at her full on and she felt her breath hitch a little. There was just *something* about him, something about his hard cheekbones and jutting jaw that gave her a physical shock after the almost lazy calmness of his voice. 'I believe,' he said, 'that we've met before. Thank you for warning me about those barrels heading my way.'

She nodded briefly. 'I had no wish to see you flattened.'

He laughed, but she was confused because she sensed that behind those amused blue eyes there lurked something rather dangerous. Though perhaps that was her imagination, because now he was sighing and saying to her almost sadly, 'So. Welcome to my abode—though I don't suppose that by any chance you've come to *buy* something, have you? Or perhaps—like young Tommy—you're hoping to do a bit of pilfering?'

Matty felt an angry retort springing to her lips, but she answered him coolly, 'That's a rather careless assumption, Mr Percival.'

'I'm sorry, but I'm afraid I find myself growing rather cynical these days. And as it happens, I'm not Mr Percival—Mr Percival is in fact somewhat elusive, except, alas, when his rent is due. My name is Jack Rutherford. And you, young sir, are here because...?'

He was trying to peer down at her but Matty, glad of her wide-brimmed hat and the general gloom in here, kept her distance. He assumed she was a boy. Let him. 'I have some antique brooches I'd like valued, Mr Rutherford.'

'Let me guess.' He sighed again. 'They're worth a fortune, yes? They date back to Tudor times at the very least, but as a special favour you'll let me have them for a guinea. Am I right?'

'They're not Tudor!' Matty was stung out of her usual caution. 'The brooches are Celtic, and—'

'Now that's original,' he said, breaking in. 'I'll give you credit for that.' He put his hands together and gestured applause. *Well-shaped hands*, Matty noticed. *Elegant hands...* Suddenly angry with herself for even noticing, she jerked her attention back to what he was saying.

'But if these brooches of yours are genuine,' he went on, 'I'll eat my hat. I do grow rather weary of fraudsters. And now, if you don't mind, I'll have to turn you away, because I have a rather urgent appointment elsewhere—'

Matty interrupted calmly, 'You're the one who's a fraud.'

He looked rather startled. 'I beg your pardon?'

'You're the fraud.' Matty strolled over to point at one of the crowded shelves. 'You're selling overpriced rubbish. These vases you've labelled as early eighteenth-century Delftware are nothing of the sort—they were most likely made last year, not in Holland but in Stoke-on-Trent.'

She saw him looking rather bemused. 'Stoke? *Really?* But how on earth do you—?'

'Because I've had an education in antiques, which clearly you have not.' She gestured towards another shelf. 'Those bowls you've labelled as Chinese, from the Ming dynasty—they'll have been made in a factory in east London. They'll be two years old, not two hundred. And as for that piece of wood labelled "Egyptian Oar"—do you want to know what it *really* is?' She indicated a six-foot length of wood leaning against the wall.

'I'm not at all sure that I do.'

Matty told him anyway. 'It's an old barge pole. It's probably been rotting in the Thames mud for the last twenty years or so.'

'What a pity.' He looked a little sad. 'Though I thought the Egyptian bit was rather fanciful.'

Matty was growing exasperated. 'I can see, Mr Rutherford, that my visit is clearly a waste of time.' She was also realising it might be risky, too, because he suddenly appeared more interested in her than in what she was saying.

Normally strangers didn't give Matty a second glance—they just assumed she was a lad and that was that. But Mr Jack Rutherford was looking at her a little too closely for her comfort and frowning, too. Swiftly she turned to go. But he called out, 'Wait! Please.'

She swung round in spite of herself.

He said, 'I don't suppose by any chance you're looking for a job, are you?'

She was astonished. 'A job?'

'Yes. As my assistant. You see, I only took over this place two months ago and I've been trying my best to label and price everything, but you're absolutely right.' He shrugged. 'I don't know nearly as much as I should.'

'Then why on earth did you take the business on?' She really couldn't hide her scorn. 'You're clearly not making much of a success of it.'

'I'm afraid it was just a stupid idea of mine. I'm rapidly coming to the conclusion that the place should be run by someone who might know rather more about antiques than I do.'

'Finding someone of that description shouldn't be difficult.' She pointed to another table, laden with pistols and swords. 'Though I imagine you don't have any trouble selling these things? These mementoes from the war?'

A shadow had crossed his face. 'No,' he said in a quieter voice. 'Actually, I don't.'

'Cheating old soldiers.' Matty smiled up at him brightly from beneath the brim of her hat. 'My goodness, you must be really proud of yourself.'

Something dangerous flashed through his blue

eyes then and her heart skipped a beat. *You fool, Matty. Deliberately antagonising a rogue like him.* It was most definitely time to go.

She looked round to where the door beckoned temptingly. But then he smiled—and it was a smile that shook her badly, because there was something so very bitter about it. 'Proud of myself?' he echoed. 'Just the opposite, in fact. And as for you—you really are rather bold, you know. For such a young…fellow.'

She felt her throat go suddenly dry at that momentary hesitation. Had he realised she was a girl?

So what if he had? she told herself quickly. What did it matter? Though she was unsettled, because she guessed this man knew an awful lot about women one way and another. For a moment his eyes arrowed into her, surveying her from the top of her head down to her toes, but she met his blue gaze and retorted, 'So you think me bold because I happen to tell you you're selling items that are wrongly labelled and wrongly priced? Surely you know that already?'

He'd come from behind his counter—to do what? Punish her for her cheek? Kidnap her? *Don't be stupid.* But even so her heart hammered and her imagination whirled. Then—*then* he laughed. And there was something about the rich, sardonic timbre of his voice that was more dangerous than words.

'Then help me,' he stated calmly, 'why don't you? Get everything here priced and dated correctly and I'll pay you a wage that's pretty generous for a lad like you. How about it?'

So he hadn't guessed her secret. Relief flooded her, but she shook her head decisively. 'I think,' she said, 'that you should find yourself an occupation more suited to your talents.'

'The trouble is, I'm not exactly sure what my talents are.'

'How about smooth talking? Pulling the wool over people's eyes?' *Oh, Matty.* She silently groaned at her rashness. *Stop talking so much, will you?*

He was still smiling, but his blue eyes had narrowed again and she found that her blood was pounding rather hard. She needed to get out through that door right now but there was one slight problem. This man, nearly six foot of muscle and sinew, was still blocking her way.

Just when she was considering how best to make a run for it, she heard the sound of men's raised voices from outside. 'Here we are, lads,' someone shouted. '*Mr Percival's Antiques*—let's give this one a go, shall we?'

And in marched four roughly dressed men. When Jack Rutherford turned in surprise, one of the new arrivals pulled out a nasty-looking knife. 'Careful now,' the man growled. Another of them pounced on Matty and pinned her hands behind her back. 'Keep still, young 'un,' he hissed in her ear, 'or you'll find yourself at the bottom of the canal.'

She kept very, very still and she saw that Jack Rutherford was motionless, too—he didn't have much choice, with that man's knife pointed at his neck.

'Now, then,' said the man with the knife, who was clearly their leader. 'I didn't realise Mr Percy's place had a new owner. And *you*, my friend—' he leered at Jack '—perhaps didn't realise you owe us a fee for the privilege of running the place.'

'A fee? What the hell *for*?' Jack lunged forward, but two of the men grabbed his arms while the man with the knife waved his blade tauntingly. 'That was a bit silly, wasn't it? Now, listen. The money's for your own safety—you pay us ten shillings a week and in return we protect you from thieves and robbers. Simple, right? All the businesses round here pay up 'cos they're smart. So don't you try playing silly games with us.'

Matty had already guessed what they were up to. Most of the London districts had gangs like this who frightened the business owners into paying them a regular fee—*protection*, they called it. But Jack Rutherford didn't appear to quite understand.

'You say that everyone pays you?' Scorn etched his voice. 'Not me, my friend. The hell not me.'

Even as he spoke, Jack lashed out to free himself, then lunged at the man with the knife and chopped at his arm so hard that the knife went flying. At exactly that moment, Matty kicked the man who held her and darted sideways to heave over a display case full of vases. It fell with an enormous crash, bringing the other ruffians to their knees under an onslaught of heavy pottery.

Next Matty picked up the barge pole—*an Egyptian oar? I don't think so, Mr Rutherford*— and swung it against the legs of the man who was fighting with Jack. The man howled and fell to the floor. The others were getting to their feet, but Jack grabbed the pole off Matty. 'Great idea,' he said. 'Thanks. Keep well clear.' Then he swung the pole round with far more force than she could manage, catching the ribs, arms and knees of their attackers.

Soon all four were stumbling out through the door and limping off down the street. Matty heard their final words. 'A madhouse in there,' they were muttering as they glanced back. 'A damned madhouse...'

Jack, who'd put the pole down, rubbed his hands together in satisfaction. 'Well done,' he said to Matty. 'My thanks.'

She was assessing the wreckage of the room. 'Mr Percival should have warned you.'

'Warned me of what?'

'That there's a protection racket in this area. They're dangerous.'

'But this time they met rather more than they bargained for. Didn't they?' He grinned. 'You and me together, youngster. What a team!' He put his hand on her shoulder.

She pulled away quickly. By now he, too, was surveying the mess on the floor—he'd lost interest in *her*—but she was still unnerved, because when he'd touched her just now, she'd felt that touch ricochet all through her body. Matty spent her time avoiding men, not encouraging them. She didn't even like anyone to come near her. But something about this man made her wonder

what it might be like if he touched her again...
Ridiculous.

He was shaking his head as he looked round the room. 'I suppose,' he was saying rather regretfully, 'that I'd better start clearing up this mess.'

Matty shoved at the pieces of shattered pottery with her booted foot. 'You could look on the bright side, Mr Rutherford.' *In control again, thank goodness.* 'At least you know now that your pottery wasn't worth the shelf space you gave it.'

He put his hands on his hips and laughed outright. 'You've certainly received quite an education from somewhere.'

'I had an excellent tutor.'

'And did this tutor of yours teach you how to fight, too?'

'That? Oh, that comes naturally.'

Again he laughed, but this time she refused to allow herself to be distracted by his sparkling blue eyes or his merry grin; instead she straightened her hat and headed directly for the door. *Come on, girl. Get out of here while you can.*

'Wait.' His voice from behind stopped her in her tracks. 'Wait,' he repeated. 'Those brooches you were telling me about. I would be quite interested in seeing them, you know.'

She almost gave a snort of disbelief. 'Too late.' Her hand was already on the door.

'Very well. Though could it be—' and his voice softly pursued her '—that your so-called treasures are fakes? Just as you say mine are?'

This was a challenge she couldn't refuse, so she swung round and headed towards him once more, already extracting her silk purse from her pocket. 'I don't imagine,' she said with a fresh edge to her voice, 'that you've actually come across genuine objects like these. But here—' and she laid them on the counter '—are two Celtic brooches.'

He whistled under his breath. 'Even I can see these are quite something. So you weren't joking when you told me they're valuable?'

'I don't joke about matters that are important, Mr Rutherford.' She gathered up the brooches to slip them in her purse again. 'And I came here because I wanted an expert opinion on their value. A pity I came to the wrong person.'

'You certainly did.' He looked mildly regretful. 'But what's *that*?'

Because as she was putting away her brooches, the Roman coin fell from her purse. And before she could stop him, he'd picked it up and held it to the light. 'It's beautiful,' he said quietly.

'Yes.' Her eyes never left the coin as it winked between his fingertips. 'It dates back to the first century, when Tiberius was emperor of Rome. You can tell by the image—do you see?—which changed in the year of—'

'Stop. Stop!' He was almost laughing again. 'How do you *know* all this?'

'My father was a historian.'

'And where did he find this coin?'

'He dug it up in a field.'

'Dug it up in a field? But—'

Just at that moment the door opened again and they both turned quickly. This time, though, it wasn't ruffians, but two women with aprons over their plain brown gowns and merry smiles on their faces. And they weren't smiling at *her.*

'Jack,' they called, 'we need your help! Two days ago that thieving innkeeper down the road ordered five dozen of our pies and he's not paid us for a single one! The horrid man takes no notice of us when we ask for our money, so will you close up for the day and come to sort him out for us? *Please?*'

It was only then that they noticed the shattered

pottery lying on the floor. 'What's been happening in here?' Then they saw Matty. 'Who's this?'

Jack nodded towards Matty and began, 'Here we have a young scholar, who has certainly proved his worth—'

Only then he broke off and he was saying, '*No. Please, wait,*' because Matty grabbed back the coin and was heading for the door.

'I can see it's time for me to go,' she called over her shoulder. 'Goodbye, Mr Rutherford. This has certainly been an...*interesting* encounter.'

The girls were staring at her, open-mouthed. 'Ooh,' said one. 'Now, don't you speak in a fancy way? Just like our Jack. Only our Jack's friendly and nice—'

Matty was already out of there and walking down the street—in fact, she'd gone quite a way before she stopped to steady herself. Jack Rutherford knew nothing about antiques, but doubtless he had plenty of other skills. *Vain, witless man.*

She hurried on towards the wharf, where as usual the quayside was lined with horses and heavily laden carts and the air was filled with the banter of the teams of Irishmen building the new warehouses close by. Once on board *The Wild*

Rose, she stowed her purse in the cabin locker, then went through her list of jobs to be done.

I need to put more varnish on the tiller, she reminded herself. *And I'll take my mattress on deck to air for an hour in the sunshine...*

She began to roll her mattress in order to carry it up the steps. But as she did so, she caught sight of her reflection in the little mirror hanging on the cabin wall.

Something seemed different somehow about her eyes and her expression. And there was an unfamiliar sensation fluttering in her stomach like a light and teasing touch, making her restless and unsettled. Unfortunately she thought she knew exactly what—or rather who—had caused it. Shaking her head, she carried her rolled cotton mattress up on deck and spread it out.

Jack Rutherford was a rogue, undoubtedly. He truly hadn't a clue about the fact that the majority of his goods were worthless trash—and even worse, he didn't seem to care. But he'd also shown he could be rather formidable—his ruthlessness in tackling those villains had been quite chilling. Despite his teasing ways there was a stark maleness about him that thoroughly rattled her—and when he'd rested his hand on her shoulder, the warmth of his fingers had sent little sparks of surprise tingling all along her veins.

She thumped hard at the mattress. That man must have more dark secrets than she'd had hot dinners. Yes, his smile was light-hearted, but Jack Rutherford was made for trouble—trouble she could most certainly do without.

She went back down to her cabin. There were plenty more jobs to be getting on with, but something made her want to take out her silk purse again from her locker and examine her treasures once more.

So she did. And it was then that she realised, with a jolt of sickening shock, that the most precious of them all—the golden Roman coin—was not there.

For two years now, she'd been haunted by memories of the day her father found that coin. He'd believed it marked the site of an old Roman settlement—believed, in fact, that he was on the verge of the most exciting discovery of his career—but he'd died soon afterwards. On the day of his funeral, Matty had stood beneath the solemn yews by his grave and silently repeated the vow she'd made to her father as his life slipped away. She would pursue his dream and she would find that site herself, whatever it cost, whatever it took, to ensure that her father's name was always remembered with reverence.

But instead, she'd lost the only proof of the site's existence—the Roman coin.

For a moment Matty couldn't move. Then she went over to check her coat, just in case, but both pockets were empty. Her heart was hammering now and her throat was dry.

You fool, Matty. You absolute fool.

Chapter Four

It didn't take long for Jack to persuade the reluctant innkeeper to pay the pie girls, after which he announced to them that he had another visit to make that afternoon.

'I'm going to Mayfair,' he told them.

'Mayfair?' The women gasped a little. 'My, aren't you the fancy one?'

But if the girls imagined him arriving in Mayfair's streets in style, they were mistaken. True, Jack smartened himself up by giving his one decent coat a good brush and cleaning his boots; he'd tied on a plain cravat and he'd shaved. But the effect was rather spoiled by the fact that he hitched a ride from Paddington with the driver of a corn cart, a chatty fellow who was clearly surprised to have an apparent member of the gentry as a passenger. When Jack told him to stop at the corner of fashionable Park Lane, the driver looked even more startled. Of course, thought Jack, the people who lived hereabouts wouldn't usually arrive on a corn cart, unless it was for a drunken bet.

He tipped the driver handsomely—which again caused the man's mouth to gape—and walked on to nearby Grosvenor Square where, on reaching an imposing mansion, he struck the door so loudly that the butler opened up with a look of distinct apprehension on his face.

But the butler's caution swiftly melted away. 'Why, Master Jack! It's truly good to see you, sir!'

'Hello, Perkins,' Jack responded. 'It's good to see you, too. How are you? Keeping well, I trust?'

'Well enough,' answered Perkins darkly, 'considering the circumstances, if you understand what I mean. If you'll wait here a moment, I will see if Lady Fitzroy has come down yet from her bedchamber.'

Lady Fitzroy. Damn, would he ever get used to that? And—her bedchamber, at this hour? 'Are you saying she's been unwell?'

'She is, as you know, sir, in a delicate state of health. But I will ascertain if she's risen.'

So Jack waited, which meant he had time to

think about the events of the day so far—in particular the lad in the long coat and the hat pulled down low. The lad with the brooches and the Roman coin.

Jack had become well used over the years to summing people up. Sometimes in the army he'd had to decide in the blink of an eye whether a man was friend or foe, because it could mean life or death. That lad had loitered in the shadows, which was enough in itself to set alarm bells ringing. His long coat was scruffy, he was slightly built and that wide-brimmed hat shaded half of his face. His voice was a little gruff, which you could say was typical of a lad trying to sound older than he was.

Except he was a she. The boy was a girl.

If he—*she*—had kept the visit short, Jack might have been fooled. But in no way could the girl keep up the pretence during the fight with those bully-boys. During that brief but vicious scrap her voice had slipped back to its natural register and she'd been forced to abandon her male swagger completely as the action speeded up.

Then when that big hat of hers slipped back to let the candlelight fall on her face, he'd felt the breath hiss from his lungs—because her chestnut hair, cropped like a boy's, gave her an unusual elfin charm. Her features were refined, her skin delicate—and her clothes, drab and over-large though they were, still couldn't obscure the fact that she was slender and graceful. Before she crammed that ridiculous hat back on, he'd had a full view of her pretty green eyes and charming little nose and, most noticeable of all, he'd observed an *extremely* kissable mouth.

Only it seemed she preferred using her lips for verbal sparring than for any kind of amorous encounter.

He paced the hall as he waited for Perkins to return. The girl had a sharp tongue—and she used it. She'd been damnably rude, yet somehow he'd felt more thoroughly *alive* trading insults with her than he had for a long time. But then, there was another puzzle.

She knew about antiques. She knew about history. She couldn't be more than what, eighteen or so?—but in her scornful assessment of Jack's premises, she'd betrayed the education of a scholar. And there was yet another surprising facet to her character. Jack could have been in real trouble when those villains burst in on him, were it not for the way she neatly came to his rescue. She had courage and ingenuity, as well as learning.

A puzzle indeed.

It was at this precise point that Perkins returned. 'I am pleased to say, Mr Rutherford, that Lady Fitzroy will see you in the morning room.'

Jack declined Perkins's offer of escort and made his own way along the hall, briefly glancing at the grandiose objets d'art positioned everywhere—paintings, sculptures and onyx-topped tables.

His first thought: *I could sell all this for a tidy sum.*

His second: *I'd prefer to sling the lot in the Thames.*

Darkly relishing the notion, Jack climbed the wide staircase to the first floor, where his mother was in the morning room, reclining on a sofa. She looked extremely pretty in her gown of flowered muslin—fragile, too. Then again, thought Jack grimly, anyone would be fragile if they were married to Sir Henry Fitzroy.

'Jack,' she said as he crossed the room to bow over her hand. 'Oh, Jack, how good to see you!'

He drew a chair up close. 'How are you, Mama?'

She sighed. 'I feel that I could be well again,

if only I could return to Charlwood. If only I could live there again, in the countryside. London doesn't suit me, I fear.'

It was all too clear London didn't suit her, thought Jack. And it ought to be clear to her brute of a husband also! Suddenly he felt all kinds of emotions well up inside—regret and more—but for now he forced his feelings down and drew a slim little jewellery case from his pocket. 'Here,' he said. 'A present for you, Mama.'

He handed her the leather case and watched her open it. Inside was a bracelet he'd discovered in a cluttered drawer at the back of Mr Percival's place—a pretty little thing made of gilt and paste, hardly worth any more than the case he'd put it in. But he guessed his mother wouldn't care in the slightest.

He was right. 'Oh, Jack, darling,' she declared. 'I love it! It's so pretty!' And she fastened it round her wrist straight away.

His mother was like a child in her enjoyment of simple things. She was also like a child in her underestimation of how cunning some people could be—take his recently acquired stepfather, for instance, Sir Henry Fitzroy. Jack watched her as she stroked and admired the bracelet, thinking that, although in her late forties, his mother was still like a china doll with her blue eyes and fair hair and delicate skin. And like a china doll, she was so easily broken.

'Is he here?' Jack asked shortly. He didn't need to spell out who he meant.

His mother hesitated. 'No. Henry had an appointment with his bank and then he was going on to his club.'

'Good timing,' Jack said. His mother knew very well what he thought of her second husband. 'That means you and I can talk without being interrupted.'

His mother raised sorrowful blue eyes to his. 'What is there to talk about, Jack? Charlwood Manor is Henry's now. There's nothing to be done, so perhaps we should all try to get on together.'

Me? Get on with that arrogant bastard? Never. Fitz hated Jack and Jack hated Fitz—it was as simple as that. He drew in a deep breath. 'Anyone else,' he said in a low voice. 'If only you'd married anyone else…'

Immediately he regretted it, because his mother suddenly looked very tired again. 'You warned me about him,' she whispered. 'When you were home on leave, before you went off again to fight in Spain. But, Jack, after you'd gone, I was so lonely! And then, when you were taken by the French, Henry told me all the awful things they do to their prisoners of war—floggings, chains, starvation. Darling, I really couldn't bear it. So when Fitz showed me the letter, about having to pay a ransom for your freedom, well, I just *had* to do what he advised. And of course he helped me with everything!'

I bet he did, thought Jack grimly. *I just bet he did.*

'Your ransom was such a great deal of money,' his mother went on. 'I didn't have anything like such a sum, nor could I afford the repayments if I were to borrow it. Fitz explained he would gladly have paid it himself, but he hadn't got the money to spare. He said the only solution was for me to marry him, so the Charlwood estate would be his—then he could raise a loan on it to pay those wicked men for your freedom. So in the end I got you back safely, for which I'm so grateful. But how I miss Charlwood!' She put a hand to her forehead and closed her eyes. 'Gracious me, I feel a little faint...'

Swiftly Jack went to ring the bell and within moments a maid hurried in and took one look at Lady Fitzroy. 'Oh, m'lady. Are you feeling unwell again? Let me fetch some of the tisane the doctor ordered for you!'

On her way out she paused to whisper to Jack. 'Sir, your mother—it's so sad. We do our best for her.'

'I can see you do,' he said gently.

She curtsied and left. Thank God, he thought as he closed the door behind her, that his mother still had some of her loyal staff from the old days, though goodness knew how they put up with Fitz and his overbearing ways. Soon the maid was back to offer his mother the tisane and some soothing lavender water to dab on her brow while Jack moved away to gaze out of the window. But he wasn't seeing the street full of carriages or the grand London houses. No, he was seeing the green countryside of Buckinghamshire and an old, pretty manor house just two miles from the market town of Aylesbury. He was picturing the house's gabled roofs and mullioned windows, and the yellow-pink clusters of honeysuckle that climbed the walls.

Charlwood Manor. His childhood home.

He was remembering how his mother used to wander happily through the garden picking scented blooms for her parlour. How he, as a boy, used to climb trees or go shooting in the woods with the gamekeeper, or maybe roam for miles on his pony pretending to be a soldier, as his father had been.

Two years ago, while Jack was a prisoner of war in France, his mother had remarried. And Charlwood—the house, the gardens and the three tenanted farms—belonged by law to her new husband, Sir Henry Fitzroy, who was an old enemy from Jack's army days.

When Jack had returned from France he was still physically weak from his long captivity, but straight away he'd gone to tackle Fitz. 'Why did you lie to my mother, you bastard? There was no ransom demand!'

'You can protest all you like, dear boy,' Fitz had drawled. 'Your mother agreed to marry me because I told her I could get you home. And—one way or another—you're here.'

'No thanks to you. You're a liar and a cheat.'

Some of the colour had retreated from Fitz's cheeks at that, but he'd merely shrugged. 'You try proving your wild accusations. If I were you, though, I really wouldn't bother. During your long absence she needed someone to look after her and she chose me. Charlwood is mine now, Jack. Stop fantasising over the place—it's time to face up to a new reality, just as your mother has.'

The real irony of it was that Fitz had no taste for country living—in fact he preferred to spend most of the year in this Mayfair mansion. Indeed, Jack thought grimly, its garish opulence suited Fitz right down to the very last crystal chandelier.

The maid had left now and Jack went back to sit beside his mother.

'Oh, Jack,' she whispered. 'I'm so tired.'

'Rest, Mama. I'm here. Rest.'

Soon her eyes were closed and Jack took her hand to stroke it very softly, though inside his thoughts were ablaze. *She's been married to Fitz for less than two years. But he is destroying her.*

Yet what could he do? His mother really believed she'd saved her son's life by marrying Fitz; but what she didn't know was that Jack's freedom owed nothing at all to Fitz—for there had been a secret exchange of prisoners, carefully negotiated between the French and English governments. Fifty French officers were released from prison camps in England in return for fifty English ones, and Jack remembered anew how he and his fellow officers had been told about it one morning in their prison near Lille. Shackled and half-starved, they'd been lined up and told that they were going home.

Only Jack found out soon enough that he had no home to go to.

Suddenly he heard voices in the hall below: the sharp words of an order followed by some servant's meek reply. After checking his mother was still asleep, Jack left the room, straightened his coat and headed downstairs.

It sounded as if Fitz was back.

Sir Henry Fitzroy was fifty, twenty-four years older than Jack. He'd been with the British army in Spain for a year and had briefly been Jack's superior. He had proved himself an atrocious officer.

And now, as Jack descended the stairs, he saw that Fitz was reprimanding poor Perkins about something or other. There was no trace of the army officer about Fitz now—indeed, with his carefully coiffed pale hair and his expensive blue coat with its padded shoulders, he looked more like a city fop than a man of action.

Something must have alerted Fitz to Jack's presence, perhaps the servant's straying glance, because Fitz turned round in irritation, only to flinch slightly on seeing who it was. But he recovered quickly enough, waving his hand at Perkins in an impatient gesture of dismissal. 'Well, well,' he said, facing Jack full on. 'I only wish I could say this was a welcome surprise.'

Jack walked towards him. 'You,' he said, 'are a despicable excuse for a man. My mother is not well. She wants to return to the country. She needs fresh air and peace.'

Fitz drew out his snuff box to take a leisurely pinch. 'My God, Rutherford. Still harping on about Charlwood? The house became mine on my marriage to your mother—do I really have to keep reminding you of the fact?'

'She only married you,' Jack stated calmly, 'because you forged a ransom demand and told her you would pay it.'

Fitz laughed. 'As I said before—prove it.'

Jack clenched his fists. It just might be possible to extract some evidence of the secret prisoner exchange from the War Office, but his mother had agreed to marry Fitz because of the faked ransom letter. How could Jack prove Fitz's trickery, when Fitz would surely have destroyed the letter long since? Jack's mother was no doubt the only person who'd seen it—to force her to bear witness to her new husband's lies without physical evidence of the forged document could quite possibly destroy her.

'I will find proof,' promised Jack. His voice was harsher now. 'I swear I will. Even if I have to rattle every bone in your body to do it.'

Fitz looked a little pale again, then recovered. 'Get back to your drinking and gambling dens,' he tried to scoff. 'That's all you're good for these days—'

He broke off as Jack moved closer. 'I'm good at fighting,' Jack said. 'I'm really very good at that, Fitz. Never forget it—do you hear me? *Never.*'

Fitz was perspiring now. 'You lay one finger on me and—'

'No need to panic.' Jack took a step back. 'You'll be relieved to hear that I'm leaving. But I'm going to prove that it's *you* who's the liar and the cheat. You wait. You just wait.'

He took a cab back to Paddington, which was stupid of him because it was an unnecessary extravagance. *Should have walked, you idiot.* It was almost six o'clock by the time he unlocked the door of what was currently his home and he looked around the cluttered shop in mingled exasperation and gloom. That girl dressed as a boy had been absolutely right. He was completely hopeless at running this place.

He ran his fingers over some vases and heard her scornful voice again. *'They were most likely made last year, not in Holland but in Stoke-on-Trent.'* For heaven's sake, he'd been mad to even think he could make money from this venture—and now the place was even more of a wreck thanks to those villains who'd paid him a visit this afternoon! Pieces of broken pottery still lurked in every corner.

And so, surrounded by fakery and memories, he sat there with a large glass of cheap red wine for company and steadily drank his way through it while playing with a well-worn pair of carved wooden dice, left hand versus right. *That way*, a soldier friend once told him, *you never lose.* You could also, Jack reflected, say that you never won, either.

That particular friend had died in the French prison. Jack had survived, but he'd been wasting precious time ever since. He rubbed his hand tiredly through his wayward black hair, acknowledging that he had to pull himself together.

After returning from France, he'd taken lodgings with some old soldier friends and started playing cards for money in various disreputable gambling dens. He had an excellent memory and the card sharps avoided him because he could always detect their cheating—but by God, it was a risky way of life because if you won too often you made bad enemies. Taking on Mr Percival's small business had been an equally impetuous venture—and this afternoon's encounter with that knife-wielding gang had forced him to admit that the shop had been a stupid idea from the start.

His priority now was to claim back the Charlwood estate from Fitz, but he needed money to put any plan into action. Rifling through his pockets, he found only small change—but there was also an invitation card sent by an old army acquaintance to join him tonight at White's. A visit to the exclusive gentlemen's club might be just what Jack needed, because there would be gambling and the stakes would be high.

It was now eight o'clock and the night was yet young. He drained his second glass of wine, then rose to prepare himself. Maybe he had sunk low. But from there the only way was up—and a little more money wouldn't go amiss.

For the first couple of hours, his visit to the club in St James's Street actually went rather

well. There were quite a few former army officers present in addition to the friend who'd
invited him and, once they'd all moved to the
card tables, it wasn't long before Jack started
winning, though the sums he won weren't vast.
Being full of good intentions—*quit while you're
ahead for once*—he was about to pocket his profits and leave when someone else walked in.

Fitz.

'Ah,' said Sir Henry Fitzroy. 'The failed soldier. The card sharp—'

Jack had already risen to his feet. 'Say that
again,' he said softly, 'if you dare.'

Jack's fellow officers were already on either
side of him. 'Careful, now,' one of them murmured in Jack's ear.

Another was addressing Fitz. 'Be prudent,
sir. Rutherford tends to react rather badly to insults—'

'Especially when they're damned lies!' Jack
had shaken himself free. He said to Fitz, 'I'll tell
you what. How about a game of piquet? Shall
we set the stakes at say, five shillings a point?'

The onlookers gasped at the amount. Jack's
friends shook their heads in dismay. Sir Henry
Fitzroy said grimly, 'With the utmost pleasure.'

Within minutes the word had spread and men came in from all parts of the club to watch.

Jack won steadily at first—it was almost too easy, because he was more skilful at calculating the odds and knowing just how far to push his luck, whereas his opponent was a careless braggart. Heated and slightly flustered, Fitz kept throwing tricks away and turned far too often to his wineglass. But then Fitz started to win—slowly to begin with, then more and more steadily. Jack's expression didn't change as his own pile of chips grew smaller, though once the game drew to an end he rose to his feet.

'I hope, Rutherford,' Fitz drawled from his chair, 'that you're not thinking of leaving without paying your debts?'

'The remainder of my cash is in my coat,' Jack said calmly. 'Which I left with the porter out in the lobby. If you'll follow me there, I'll settle up with you.'

Jack led the way out of the room, but the minute they were outside and on their own he spun round and jabbed his finger at Fitz's chest. 'You were cheating. You treacherous, jumped-up apology for a man, you were cheating.'

Fitz's face was a little pale now. 'That's ridiculous! Just because you're not as good a player as you thought you were...'

'Your sleeve.' Jack bit the words out. 'You hid some cards up your right sleeve. Didn't you?' And before Fitz could move, Jack had grasped the cuff of his coat with one hand and was reaching up the sleeve with the other—to pull out half a dozen cards. Jack stepped back, splaying them scornfully in his hands. 'Oh, Fitz,' he said softly. 'You just cannot bear to lose to a better man, can you?'

Fitz was blustering. 'That's impossible. I don't see how that can have happened...'

Jack was gazing at him steadily. 'Of course, I could have challenged you in *there*.' He nodded towards the card room. 'In front of all and sundry. But it would be rather bad form since you are, by great misfortune, my stepfather—so give me back the money you won and I'll leave.'

Fitz must have seen the deadly intent in Jack's darkened eyes, because he reached into his pockets and handed the money over without a word. Jack took the coins and checked them. What a specimen. What a coward. Fitz, still perspiring, was looking around nervously as some other club members entered the lobby and hailed him by name.

Jack said with scorn, 'It's all right, Fitz. I'm going now. As a matter of fact, I find that I'm in extreme need of some fresh air.'

Chapter Five

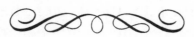

Jack walked all the way back to Paddington. It was late by now and cold yet clear—scattered stars could be glimpsed high above London's rooftops—yet he wasn't alone on the streets. True, most respectable folk were abed, but there were plenty of others for whom the night was yet young: drunken bucks who staggered along arm in arm singing bawdy songs, ladies of the night who loitered in search of customers, thieves who lurked down dark alleys. But all of them took one look at Jack's dangerous expression and gave him a wide berth indeed.

Once he was home Jack headed straight up to his attic bedroom where, after stripping off his coat and shirt, he poured cold water into a basin and used a well-soaked cloth to douse his face and shoulders. Reaching to wash his back, he winced briefly as the rough cloth skimmed the scars from the floggings he'd had in that French prison. They'd healed, but he knew he would always bear those marks, on his body and in his soul.

He'd survived because of the secret prisoner exchange. But Fitz, the wretch, had convinced Jack's mother that there had been a ransom note from the prison's governor: 'I saw the note, Jack!' his mother had told him time and time again. 'Even though it was in French, I was able to understand most of it. It said that unless your captors received five hundred guineas within two weeks, you would die in that dreadful place.'

That letter had been forged by Fitz—Jack was sure of it. He was equally sure Fitz would have destroyed it as soon as Jack's mother had married him. And he would never forget the look of outright triumph on Fitz's face when the odious man first presented himself as Jack's stepfather.

'Were you looking forward to going home to Charlwood?' Fitz had asked softly. 'What a shame. The place is mine now—and you can rest assured that you will never set foot inside there again. *Never.* You understand me?'

Jack towelled himself dry and realised he'd run out of brandy. Hell, he'd need a good dose of the stuff to help him sleep tonight. Then he remembered that the landlord of the alehouse along the road was always ready to sell a bottle to late-night customers, so after pulling his shirt and coat back on he headed downstairs out into the lamplit street, bought brandy from the alehouse and set off home again.

But suddenly his eyes were caught by something bright and shiny that peeped out from beneath some rubbish gathered in the gutter. Frowning, he bent to pick it up.

It was a gold coin. Holding it in his palm, seeing how it seemed to wink up at him, he let out a low whistle of surprise. Because it was a very *old* gold coin.

Roman, if he wasn't mistaken.

The next day Matty stood outside Mr Percival's antiques shop, rapping at the door. It was midday and the public house down the road was filled with lunchtime drinkers who spilled out into the street. She knocked again. She'd already called last night and twice this morning, but each time the shop was closed. People were everywhere— but it looked as if Jack Rutherford had vanished into thin air.

She tried to peer through the window. 'Mr Rutherford? Are you in there?'

One of the lunchtime drinkers came wandering over. 'You'll be lucky, young 'un. That Mr Percy's not opened up at all this morning—he's most likely done a runner for not paying his rent.'

And Matty's fears gathered.

Yesterday, after her visit here, she'd lost her gold coin. She'd searched the lanes between the wharf and here, but she was growing more and more convinced that she'd mislaid it in this shop and Jack's absence only served to confirm her suspicion. The man knew not a thing about antiques, but he would have known her coin was valuable because she, like a fool, had told him so.

She suddenly found herself remembering the warmth of his strong hand on her shoulder. *'You and me together, youngster. What a team!'* But the memory made her shiver now. If Jack Rutherford had found it, he probably couldn't believe his luck.

It was starting to rain and most of the drinkers had retreated inside the alehouse. She knocked one last time and was about to depart when something caught her eye. She'd already noticed that a few cheap posters had been pasted to the nearby wall advertising all sorts of services, most of them rather dubious. But one of the posters particularly drew her attention, because it said *An Auction Of Historic Artefacts and Heirlooms.*

She examined it more carefully. The auction was to be held at a sale room in Oxford Street in two days' time. She peeled the poster off the wall and folded it so it fitted in her pocket. And an idea bloomed.

The scent of delicate perfume hit Jack's senses from the minute he entered the luxurious room around midday two days later. 'Why, Jack, my dear!' came a sultry female voice. 'What a delightful surprise!'

This was a far warmer welcome, Jack reflected, than the one he'd received from Sir Henry Fitzroy in Grosvenor Square the other day, though this was in an equally imposing mansion. Lady Vanessa Lambert didn't rise from her *chaise longue,* but her eyes were dancing with merriment as Jack strolled over to raise her fingers to his lips.

'Now, what brings *you* here, Jack?' She was dressed in an exquisite and rather low-cut day gown of blue silk. 'Some errand of pleasurable intent, I hope?'

'How,' responded Jack gallantly, 'can a visit to you be anything other than a pleasure, Vanessa?'

She laughed. 'Scoundrel. Sit down, do, and tell me what you've been up to.'

Lady Vanessa had become an extremely wealthy widow a few years ago at the age of thirty-two and was eager to enjoy the various pleasures of her new-found independence. She had other admirers, of course, but Jack was a firm favourite. Now she pointed to a chair by the window and Jack settled himself there, reflecting that to tell Vanessa what he'd been up to recently might puzzle her rather—because Jack had been searching the lanes and alleys of Paddington without success, looking for a girl dressed as a boy who happened to have left something rather valuable by his shop. In the end he'd reluctantly given up. He'd also given up the shop as a dead loss, which meant it was time to make fresh plans.

He leaned back in the chair, adjusted his carefully tied cravat and looked straight at Lady Vanessa. 'I need your help,' he said.

She looked amused. 'So what can I do for you this time, Jack? What mischief are you plotting?'

Jack couldn't help but notice how she'd allowed her blue silk gown to slip even farther from her shoulders to reveal an expanse of creamy skin. 'Vanessa,' he said, 'you make me sound like some rogue adventurer.'

She leaned closer. 'But you *are* a rogue adventurer! Which is one—just *one*—of the many reasons why I'm rather partial to you. Now come along, confess—you have some naughty plan in mind. Don't you?'

Just then a footman entered with champagne and two glasses; Jack waited while the champagne was poured and once the footman had gone he raised his glass and said, 'Your health, Vanessa. You're right, I do have a plan in mind. Now tell me—am I right in thinking your late husband visited the auction houses quite regularly? Did you ever go with him?'

She sipped her champagne and eyed him over her glass. 'As rarely as I could. I have always preferred to spend my time more enjoyably.'

'Very wise of you. But what exactly happens at these sales? I gather there are catalogues to study and then you make your bid. Does a good deal of money change hands?'

She laughed aloud. 'Whatever is this, Jack? You're not taking that peculiar little shop of yours too seriously, are you, my dear?'

'Oh, I'm bored with it.' Jack made a dismissive gesture. 'But perhaps it's made me realise there could be some other way to make money in the antiques business.'

'Plenty of money to be lost, too,' she answered, rising from her *chaise longue*. 'But I'll find you some of my husband's boring old catalogues, shall I?'

She left and Jack realised that almost without knowing it, he'd reached inside his pocket for that gold coin. It brought back an immediate picture of the young woman who'd shown it to him—and unfortunately he could imagine all too well how she must have felt when she found that she'd lost it.

'I could not,' Jack muttered to himself, 'have done any more to find her.'

He'd tramped the streets of the neighbourhood asking about her, but she was difficult to describe because to the casual eye she just looked like all the other lads who hung around the area. The words *needle* and *haystack* kept springing to mind—in other words, he'd got precisely nowhere, just received odd looks, some of them hostile. In the end he gave up, but he still remembered her melodious, cultured voice. He also remembered the appealing tilt to her nose and her clear green eyes; then there was her hair, cut very short but in a way that made you want to run your fingers through its cropped softness...

'Jack!' Vanessa was back in the room. 'I've

found these old catalogues in my husband's study.'

He took them. 'May I borrow them?'

'My goodness, you can keep the lot and welcome. They're only gathering dust. But you're not leaving already, are you? You've only just arrived!'

He was draining his glass and standing up. 'Vanessa, you are a true friend. But I have several plans to set in motion.'

She sighed. 'I rather thought you might. What are these mysterious plans? Are you going to stop being a tease and tell me?'

'Well,' he began, 'there's this auction in Oxford Street this afternoon—'

'Goodness!' she broke in. 'You really *are* taking this antiques business seriously, aren't you?'

He grinned. 'You know me. I'm always open to new experiences.'

She laughed in reply. 'Oh, I do know it. And I like to share these experiences with you, Jack.'

He suddenly leaned close. 'Then share this one with me. Will you accompany me to this auction today?'

Chapter Six

Oxford Street—that afternoon

Matty realised the minute she entered the vast auction room that all eyes were upon her. *Big mistake, Matty. You're the wrong age. You're wearing the wrong clothes.*

She had walked breezily in past the porters at the door, but once inside she found herself in the presence of dozens of well-dressed gentlemen and dealers, most of whom turned to stare hard at her. One of them even came up close to peer at her through his *pince-nez.* 'You a delivery boy, youngster?'

'That's right.' She touched her hat as a gesture of respect. 'I've been doing deliveries, sir. I'm just taking a peek before I go.'

Quickly she'd glided back into the shadows and after that she was ignored, much to her relief, because it was almost three o'clock and time for the sale items to be brought on to the stage by the auction-house porters. Time, too, for the auctioneer to climb to his podium and spread out his papers, but Matty wasn't watching him. She'd managed to pick up a catalogue in the entrance hall and was scanning it for what her father used to call *Cinderella pieces.*

'If you're lucky,' her father once said, 'there'll be at least one in every auction. Something that may be neglected, unnoticed—but it could turn out to be the best of the bunch!'

Her father had found the Roman coin close by the canal at Aylesbury some fifty miles northwest of London. The coin was gone, thanks to Matty's unforgivable carelessness—and if she was to reach her father's lost treasure site and make amends for losing the coin, she would need money to travel there. She'd thought fleetingly of finding a buyer for her Celtic brooches, but dismissed the thought. *I will not be parted from any more of my father's treasures.* So she'd sold a pair of copper cooking pots she never used to Bess, who'd always admired them, and she had Bess's coins in her pocket now. She was praying there would be a Cinderella piece for her today, so she could make enough money for her journey. She needed some luck—she really did.

It was then that she realised two latecomers were being ushered in, much to the annoyance of those who had to move out of their way. And Matty's pulse suddenly raced, because, my goodness, there was no mistaking the first of the latecomers, with his dark, unruly hair and his casual arrogance.

Jack Rutherford. Even now, as if completely unaware of the disruption his arrival had caused, he was chatting to his companion, an elegant woman in a green gown and matching pelisse, who was laughing merrily at whatever he was saying while resting her gloved hand on his arm.

So his shop might be closed, but he still took a lively interest in the antiques trade—even though he didn't know the difference between ancient Chinese pottery and earthenware made in Stoke! Matty frowned. He looked considerably smarter than when she'd seen him last, for he was wearing a dark coat, a starched cravat and polished boots. But there was still something about him—perhaps it was those angular cheekbones and the hint of blue-black shadow already darkening his jaw—that caused the other men in here to gaze at him with some suspicion.

Matty, too, couldn't tear her eyes from him. *My coin*, she was thinking. *Did he find my coin?*

She wanted to make her way over and tackle him right now, but she would have to wait, because the auctioneer was banging his gavel for attention and the sale was about to begin. A hush fell over the room.

'For our first item, ladies and gentlemen,' called the auctioneer from the stage, 'we have some very fine English silverware! Seventeenth century and of *exceptional* quality!'

Normally Matty was fascinated by antiques, but today she couldn't concentrate and it was, of course, because of that man—she could see him from the corner of her eye, exchanging whispered comments with the woman in green as one item after another went under the hammer. Her mind wandered, especially since there was nothing here she could afford—all the items for sale, from eighteenth-century watercolours to alabaster statuettes, were far too expensive for her. Then, suddenly, she caught her breath.

Because the auctioneer was holding up something small but gleaming bright. 'Here we have a rarity indeed, ladies and gentlemen!' he was calling out. 'This is a last-minute but welcome addition to our sale today. A rather fine Roman coin...'

It was hers. She knew it was hers. She found

her eyes flying to Jack Rutherford and saw that his gaze, too, was fixed on that coin. The woman at his side had tightened her hand on his arm and was watching also.

The auctioneer was describing the coin with relish. 'Now, this golden coin is in almost perfect condition, except for a slight dent on one edge. And in a few moments, I shall be inviting you to make your bids—'

He broke off, because one of the clerks had come on stage to have a word in his ear.

Matty's heart was thumping against her ribs. That dent on the edge proved it was hers beyond all doubt. *'How interesting,'* she remembered her father murmuring as he examined the coin. *'This jagged mark here, Matty—do you see it? It must have been hit with a sword, or maybe an axe. This coin might have seen battle!'*

And it had been put in the auction by Jack Rutherford—she had no doubt of that now. Even as she watched, she saw how he had detached himself from his female companion and was moving through the crowd to get closer to the podium, no doubt eager for the bidding to start— but his face was a picture when Matty pushed her way through and tapped him on the shoulder. 'You're a thief, Jack Rutherford,' she said. 'That coin is mine, and you know it.'

People were turning to stare. Jack's first expression was one of surprise, but very quickly recognition dawned. 'You,' he said. And by then the lady in green had come to join them, looking puzzled.

'Jack, who is this young fellow? What on earth is going on?'

Jack turned to her swiftly. 'There's been a slight misunderstanding,' he said. 'I'll explain to you later, Vanessa—'

A slight misunderstanding? Matty was incensed. She put her fists on her hips. 'You'd better explain to me first, if you please!'

More people were listening in, wide-eyed, and Jack muttered to Matty, 'Look. Not here. We can talk later—'

'Hush!' The auctioneer's strident tones rang out across the room and once more he banged his gavel. 'The sale of this rare Roman coin is about to commence!'

The bidding began at one guinea, but the offers came in swiftly and Matty's heart sank lower as the price rose. 'Five guineas,' she heard the auctioneer declare. 'Ten? Yes, we have ten. And now—now, I'm offered fifteen guineas, ladies and gentlemen...'

That was when Matty realised that Jack Rutherford's elegant female companion was raising her gloved hand to catch the auctioneer's eye. 'Twenty guineas,' she called.

Matty felt her breath catch. *What?* Jack's lady friend was bidding for the coin?

'Any more bids?' called the auctioneer. 'Twenty guineas I'm bid, by the lady in green. Twenty-five guineas, anyone?'

For a moment silence reigned, but then an elderly man at the back raised his hand.

'Twenty-five,' called the auctioneer. 'Twenty-five guineas, to the gentleman at the far end of the room in the black coat. Have we any more bids?'

This time the silence remained unbroken. Jack's companion—*Vanessa*, he'd called her—smiled at Jack. Then, with a rustle of silks and a hint of very expensive perfume, she slipped away.

And Matty realised the woman had been there to push up the bidding. She was his accomplice.

Matty turned on Jack, feeling dizzy with loss. 'You must have known that coin was mine! How could you do such a thing?'

'Look,' he began, 'let me explain. I found it a few hours after you visited me. It was lying in the road. You must have dropped it. And *of course* I realised it was yours.'

'Then didn't it occur to you to try to return it to me?'

He was looking exasperated now. 'Yes, it most certainly did! I've been up and down just about every street in the area, knocking on doors, calling at shops, but I got nowhere, because I couldn't even give them your *name*...'

'It's Matty,' she said abruptly. 'My name is Matty. And I don't live in a house, I live in a boat on the canal.'

'The canal?' He clasped his hand to his forehead. 'Of course. I should have guessed...'

'Quiet!' The auctioneer was banging his gavel again. 'Silence, please, ladies and gentlemen! Now, for our next item...'

Matty felt chilled to her core with disappointment. It was her fault for being so careless with the coin in the first place and now it had gone for good. She looked directly into Jack Rutherford's blue and rather sombre eyes. 'I shall never forgive myself for losing it,' she said steadily. 'And I won't be able to forgive *you*, either. I went to your shop again and again, but you were never there. As far as I could tell, you'd vanished.'

'I had to close up, because I had certain matters to attend to. And about the coin—yes, I'd given up hope of finding you, but it's not what you think—'

She waved her hand dismissively. 'Ming,' she scoffed. 'Delftware. My goodness, what a complete fraud you are. I've no proof at all that the coin was mine, so there's nothing I can do except to say that I hope you're proud of yourself.'

And with that, she vanished into the crowd.

'Matty!' he called. 'Listen to me. *Please!*'

But by the time he'd fought his way to the door, she'd gone.

'Damn it,' Jack muttered softly to himself. *'Damn it.'*

He strode over to the desk at the back of the room where the elderly man in the black coat was handing over his twenty-five guineas for the coin. Jack slammed his hand down on the desk, making the clerk there jump. 'Keep your money,' he said to the elderly man.

'What on earth...?'

'I said, keep your money. Look, it was me who put the coin in the auction, but unfortunately,

I've just been informed that it's a very clever fake. I'm sorry to disappoint you.'

'I'm not at all sure that it *is* a fake, young fellow. I know a fair bit about these things!'

'It's a fake,' Jack declared, 'believe me.' He picked up the coin and, as the man spluttered with indignation, he headed for the door. Once outside Jack stood and cursed again under his breath.

What a mess.

That girl Matty. He really had tried his hardest to track her down. There'd been no sign at all—and now he knew why. She lived on the canal. And he knew it was common for the young women on those working boats to dress in men's clothes, which were far more suitable for working life than dainty frocks.

The problem was, she wasn't a typical canal girl. She was well spoken and intelligent—and hadn't she told him her father was a historian? She'd intrigued Jack from the moment she walked into his shop and he'd relished both her knowledge of history and her smart tactics in helping him foil those bully-boys. Her outright courage had made him smile.

Women were usually just a pleasant distraction in Jack's life. But this one! She was independent, she was brave and when she'd spoken to him just now—*what a complete fraud you are*—her green eyes had blazed with passion. They were rather stunning eyes, he reflected, with those long dark lashes, and her anger gave a charming pink tinge to her cheeks that stirred up thoughts he really shouldn't be having…

Like wondering what else might make her blush so charmingly.

Stop it, you fool. Because it must appear to her that he had let her down horribly.

By now it was late afternoon and he decided to walk the four miles back to Paddington. The distance was nothing compared to the marches he and his fellow soldiers had had to make across Spain, and soon enough he was leaving behind the shops and houses to be surrounded instead by the warehouses and brickfields to the west of the city. Here every street was busy with tradespeople going about their business and he attracted hardly a second glance—when suddenly he saw five men coming purposefully towards him.

'Jack Rutherford,' the first one said.

At first he wondered if they were part of the same gang who'd demanded money for protection, but it was unlikely since this lot knew his name. Jack braced himself. 'Gentlemen. To what, I wonder, do I owe the pleasure of your company?'

They looked taken aback by his mocking tone, but quickly gathered closer. 'We have a message for you, Rutherford,' their leader growled. 'Get out of London right now. Or you'll find yourself in Newgate.'

'Newgate? Whatever for?' Again Jack spoke lightly, although his brain was working like mad.

'For thievery, that's what. Fancy a nice long spell in gaol, do you?'

Surely they weren't talking about the Roman coin? He found himself reaching to touch the outline of the coin that sat deep in his pocket. 'What, precisely, am I supposed to have stolen?'

For answer, the man handed him a note and Jack glanced at the scrawled initials at the end. *HF.* Sir Henry Fitzroy. Damnation! Quickly he scanned the rest of the writing.

You recently gave your mother a bracelet, made of gold, diamonds and sapphires...

What? He read it again in disbelief. This was absolute nonsense! The bracelet he'd given his mother was a pretty trinket, that was all! There were no gems. No gold. The ridiculous note went on.

I can prove that this bracelet was stolen and denounce you to the authorities. Unless, that is, you disappear tonight and never show your face in London again.

Jack would have laughed, except it wasn't really funny. So Fitz must have substituted his bracelet with one containing true gemstones and most likely Jack's foolish mother wouldn't even have noticed. 'This is a heap of lies,' he said, 'concocted by the idiot who presumably paid you to deliver this—'

Thwack! One of the scoundrels had produced a club from out of nowhere and had taken a swing at his chin. Jack staggered back to prop himself against a nearby wall. By the time he could see straight again, those men were disappearing into the shadows.

So Fitz was determined to drive him out of town. Jack rubbed his bruised chin, considering his options. His first impulse was to confront Fitz again and attempt to prove that he had *not* given his mother a stolen bracelet, but his mother would be a shaky witness and Fitz was a wily opponent. Besides, Jack had far more important business to settle with Fitz, so perhaps the time had come for him to make a strategic if temporary retreat.

But where should he go?

Once back at Mr Percival's he unlocked the door of the cluttered shop to be met by a cloud of spiders' webs and the sound of mice scuttling into corners. Good God, what a wreck. He didn't think he could spend another night here.

Suddenly he found himself thinking of Charlwood Manor, his home. Now, *that* was a place he'd like to see again, but if Fitz suspected he was heading there, he might take even more drastic action against him. So how best to reach Charlwood without alerting Fitz?

Jack rubbed his bruised jaw again. And suddenly—right out of the blue—he came up with a rather startling answer.

Chapter Seven

The next morning Matty was hard at work on the deck of her boat, scrubbing and cleaning. White clouds drifted overhead in a blue sky and all the canal boats moored around her glittered in the sunshine. She'd discarded her hat and coat and was polishing the brass work, pausing only briefly to make herself a pot of tea before pouring yet more linseed oil on her cloth in order to burnish the nameplate—*The Wild Rose*.

Her father had once told her how her mother had loved the roses that grew in the hedgerows along the canals and the memory made her suddenly yearn for the countryside. Made her long to sail her father's boat north to find that lost treasure he'd been so close to discovering.

A fine job you've made of realising your father's dream so far, Matty. All you've done is lose his precious coin.

She sighed and was just rolling up her shirt-sleeves ready to start work again when a man's voice from behind made her jump.

'The Wild Rose,' the voice said. 'I like the name, Master Matty.'

Oh, no. She would recognise that languid, upper-class drawl anywhere. It was Jack Rutherford. She swung round, bumping her arm painfully against the tiller.

Scorn for him filled her heart, but nevertheless she felt a little breathless as she rubbed her bruised arm. He stood casually on the wharf with his arms folded, looking ridiculously at ease in a loose, rather scruffy leather waistcoat and breeches, with his dark hair ruffled by the light breeze. And Matty wished that she hadn't taken off her coat; because though he was smiling, something about the look in his blue eyes was rather disturbing. Nevertheless she met his gaze full on and said, after a moment, 'Was it some lady's husband who gave you that bruise on your chin?'

'What?' Clearly her comment had startled him, but then he touched his jaw and grinned. 'No, it wasn't anything to do with ladies. I had what you might call an unfortunate encounter with a bunch of ruffians.'

'They do seem to pick on you, Mr Rutherford. Don't they?' She'd turned her back on him and began polishing the stern rail. *Just ignore him. You've already said goodbye to your coin. With a bit of luck, he'll go away soon.*

But he didn't. 'There were five of them this time,' he told her helpfully.

She stopped and looked at him. 'Clearly you attract trouble everywhere you go. Don't expect any sympathy from me.' She went back to her polishing, adding calmly, 'Your face won't look too good when you finally get round to opening your shop.'

Silence. Then he said, a little more hesitantly, 'The truth is, you see, that I won't be opening it up again. Ever.'

Matty found her breathing was coming rather fast. *He's a thief and a liar. Thanks to him, my father's coin is lost for good.* Why was he here anyway? To apologise? Did he actually expect her to take him seriously? This time she faced him squarely. 'I can't imagine you were making much money from that place anyway, except by trickery or downright thievery.'

Once more she returned to her polishing, but he wasn't put off. 'Listen, Master Matty,' he said from behind her. 'About your coin...'

Her breathing hitched again.

'Just as I tried to tell you at the auction house,' he went on, 'I found your coin lying in the gutter close to my shop on the evening of the day you visited me. I searched for you for days, looking everywhere for you—at least, I *thought* I had. But I had no idea you actually lived on a boat, of all things. Not until you told me yesterday.'

'Oh, yes,' she said. She'd abandoned her polishing and planted her hands on her hips. 'Yesterday. The auction room—what an enlightening experience that was. Do you know, I'm not ever likely to forget how you were so eager to return my coin to me that you sold it off to the highest bidder. But you made a mistake there. You could have asked a far higher price for it, if you'd gone about it in the right way. As it happened, your attempt to make money out of my father's coin was every bit as pathetic as your efforts to make money from your fraudulent antiques shop. Now, is there anything else?' Her voice was icy. 'Otherwise, perhaps you'll allow me to get on with my jobs.'

'There is something else,' he said. And he held out his closed fist.

Very reluctantly, Matty drew nearer. She'd met plenty of villains in her time, but this man alarmed her more than any of them. He didn't seem to take life seriously, but Jack Rutherford's easy smile sent a tiny shiver of warning from her head to her toes. *Be very careful. He's a rogue and a trickster...*

Then he opened his hand. She saw something gleaming there and her self-control vanished. She gasped aloud. 'My coin!'

He nodded. 'It's yours.' He handed it over.

Her fingers fastened round it as if to convince herself of its reality. 'But that man at the auction. The elderly man in the black coat. He bought it...'

'No. I told him there'd been a mistake and it wasn't for sale after all.'

She was still holding it very tightly. 'My thanks,' she said rather stiffly. 'Now, is that all? If you don't mind, I have rather a lot of things to see to here.'

But to Matty's astonishment Jack seemed reluctant to go. He'd thrust his hands in his pockets and was calmly examining *The Wild Rose*. 'It's a nice boat you have here, Master Matty.' He started walking up and down the wharf beside it, bending over to examine certain details while whistling softly to himself. He paused when he saw the teapot and said, 'I don't suppose you could offer me some tea?'

Once more Matty was lost for words, but finally she managed. 'Why on earth *should* I?'

He put his head thoughtfully on one side. 'Perhaps because there are one or two things I'd like to discuss with you. Maybe I could come on board, even if I don't get any tea?' He gestured around. 'You can probably see that we're attracting quite a lot of attention here.'

She'd certainly noticed. She'd also noticed that it was Jack Rutherford who was attracting the attention, not her. 'You could always just leave if you want to avoid their stares,' she suggested with a shrug.

'I *could*. But I'd be disappointed because, you see, I've always fancied taking a look round one of these canal boats.' He gave her what he no doubt thought was a winning smile. 'Besides—' he stepped a little closer '—I have a proposition for you.'

'Let me guess. You think you've found a genuine antique? Or maybe you're trying to hide from yet another gang of ruffians?'

She thought she saw a brief shadow pass across his face, but he laughed and said, 'Look, young Matty. I can't blame you for not trusting me, but I really want you to listen to this proposal of mine. You might regret it if you don't.'

'I doubt that very much,' she answered. 'But since you were prepared to bring my coin back— I can spare you ten minutes.'

'And a cup of tea?'

She sighed. 'You might as well come aboard.'

'My thanks, Master Matty.' Lithely he stepped over the rail on to the deck and promptly sat down on one of the two stools there. Rather fiercely, Matty poured tea from her pot into a second mug and thrust it towards him.

He's just a petty crook. And there are plenty of your friends around should you need any help.

But he made her uncomfortable. And a lot of that was to do with the way he spoke—his voice was as smooth as silk, yet with a kind of steely edge beneath every word. And then there were his blue eyes, which were crinkled in a smile now—but she could imagine them narrowed and cold and more than a little disturbing.

Instinctively she shifted her stool back. Surely he'd guessed she was a woman? But even if he had, why should he care? She shook herself into some sense. Whatever he'd come here for, it certainly wasn't for female company. That woman he was with at the auction room was much more his type. No, he'd come here simply to return her coin and for that she was forced to be grateful. But his next words dismayed her.

'I've been talking to some of your friends,' Jack pronounced. 'And they've told me, young Matty, that life's been rather tricky for you since your father died.'

Talking to her *friends*? How dare he? She faced him coolly. 'Then they've no business to tell you so.'

'Don't misunderstand me—your friends are very loyal.' He sipped his tea thoughtfully. 'But I was interested in what they told me, because I owe you quite a big favour for helping me fight off those ruffians who came calling at my shop the other day. Now listen.' He leaned forward. 'I gather that running a boat like this on your own is rather a challenge, in more ways than one.'

She replied witheringly, 'Excuse me? What, exactly, has that got to do with you?'

She realised he'd pulled a couple of old wooden dice from his pocket and was turning them slowly over and over in one hand. 'I also picked up a few stories,' he said, 'regarding what you plan to do next. And I heard some tale about how you intend to head north to look for buried treasure.' He stopped playing with the dice and assessed her coolly. 'To put it plainly, Master Matty—I've never heard anything so ridiculous in my life.'

And at last, Jack got the response he wanted.

He had taken a risk coming here. He guessed he was still in danger from Fitz's men—he also guessed that if he put a foot wrong now, he was likely to be in just as much danger from this girl's friends. At this very minute Jack was keeping a wary eye on some hefty bargemen who'd paused nearby to give him a none-too-friendly once-over and, if young Matty chose to denounce him as an enemy, he'd probably find himself tipped headlong into the water. She might even push him in herself.

Once again, he found himself rather admiring this slim girl who took care of her boat and her horse all on her own. But his dismissive comment about her search for treasure had clearly disturbed her, which was his intention; because for the first time she dropped her air of cool contempt and rose to her feet to pace to one end of the narrow deck, then back again.

And then she faced him, with her hands on her hips. In her thin shirt. And men's trousers...

My God, thought Jack suddenly. *She has a*

quite delectable figure. Her waist was tiny. Her pert breasts were pressed against the shirt's fabric, while those trousers did nothing whatsoever to disguise the firm roundness of her bottom. He was also rather fascinated by those faint freckles dotted over her nose and by the way her hair was ruffled by the breeze. As for her large green eyes framed by thick dark lashes, and that extremely kissable mouth...

But now young Matty was speaking her mind to him, loud and clear. 'You need to check your facts, Mr Rutherford,' she was saying witheringly. 'So you think my search for treasure is ridiculous? I told you, didn't I, that my father was a historian? Shortly before he died, he believed he'd found an important historic site—and that was where he discovered the Roman coin. He was convinced there was more to be found there. Much more.'

Jack was aware that he'd tensed, but he smiled condescendingly at her. 'Roman treasure. How very intriguing! But has it occurred to you, young Matty, that this coin might simply have been dropped by some traveller long ago and your father's notion of a treasure hoard was mere wishful thinking?'

That pretty mouth of hers was curling slightly

in scorn. 'My father specialised in Roman history at Oxford University. He wasn't fooled by anyone. He was *sure* there had been a Roman settlement nearby.'

'And this site—was it close to London?'

'Not at all.' She spoke curtly. 'It was, in fact, near to the town of Aylesbury.'

He felt his pulse racing faster. *Steady, Jack.* 'Ah,' he said. 'So to reach it, you and your father must have travelled north-west on the Grand Junction Canal?'

She didn't answer straight away because she'd risen to tighten a mooring rope. Slight as she was, he saw how she retied the bulky knot as deftly as he'd seen other women handling their embroidery silks.

She only turned back to him when she was completely satisfied with what she'd done. 'That's right—the Grand Junction Canal. My father had been invited to give a lecture to an antiquarian society in Aylesbury. He knew there had always been rumours of Roman remains in that area and so, the morning after his lecture, we went to explore. That was when he found that coin, in an area of rough pasture close to a stand of pine trees.'

This time Jack's heart thudded so hard that it

was an effort to keep his voice steady. He turned the dice thoughtfully between his fingers. 'Then why,' he asked—smoothly, provokingly—'didn't he stay there and explore the site fully?'

'Because he always wanted to do things correctly! Legally!'

She was quite passionate now, Jack saw, in her father's defence. 'What do you mean,' he said, 'legally?'

'I mean that anybody less honest than my father would have dug on—but my father refused to carry out any further investigation without the landowner's permission. So we went to the owner's house, the two of us.'

'And what was it like, this house?' Jack asked the question softly, but his senses were stretched taut. In truth, he expected her at any minute to tell him to mind his own business—but to his surprise, she didn't.

'It was quite beautiful.' Her voice was suddenly as quiet as his. 'It was Jacobean, my father thought, with wonderful gardens. It wasn't a vast place and it was all a little neglected, but my father was enthralled by it.'

And Jack realised it was as if she'd forgotten who he was. Forgotten that she didn't trust him, lost as she was in her world of memories. His hand had tightened round his dice. 'Go on.' He spoke very softly, very carefully, afraid of breaking the spell.

'When we knocked at the front door,' she said, 'it was answered by an elderly servant. My father explained that he was interested in some lost Roman ruins that might lie nearby and the servant took us straight away into the library—which was treasure in itself to my father. Much of the material there must have lain untouched for a century or more. And among it all, my father discovered an old map—on which the Roman settlement was actually marked.'

'Did you see this map, Matty?' He was reluctant to break into her reverie in case her hostility reared its head once more, but she nodded her head slowly.

'I did. My father made notes, then asked the servant if he could come back again very soon. He wanted, you see, to check for the name of the mapmaker in his history books, since he'd never heard of him. He went to the house again the following day—but this time, the owner arrived.' Her voice had changed. 'And he had him thrown out.'

Jack caught his breath. 'The *owner* arrived? Two years ago? Are you sure?'

She was looking at him directly now, her chin showing stubbornness. 'Don't you believe me?'

'Yes. *Yes.*' Jack chose his next words carefully. 'But do you know this man's name?'

'No, and I have no wish to.' Her voice was bitter now.

'This second time, I gather you weren't at the house with your father?'

'No. That second time, I didn't go with him.' And he saw that her eyes were haunted by something very like grief.

It unsettled him in a way he hadn't expected. 'So you've now decided to try to find the treasure by yourself, Master Matty?'

Fire sparked in her green eyes, quite vanquishing that hint of vulnerability. 'I'm absolutely determined to find it. For my father's sake.'

Jack allowed the corner of his mouth to curl. 'So you intend to trespass, do you?'

She tilted her chin. 'If necessary, yes. And do you really think you're in a position to criticise me?'

He smiled. 'Now, you're not trying to tell me I'm dishonest, are you?'

She didn't deign to reply, which was an answer in itself. So he rubbed the bruise on his jaw rather thoughtfully and said to her, 'Sometimes, you know, a thief and a ruffian can prove quite useful.'

She was facing him squarely. 'I've no idea what you're plotting now, Mr Rutherford, and to be quite honest I've no desire to know. My thanks for returning my coin. But I've things I need to be getting on with.'

And that was it. The spell was broken; clearly she was regretting telling him so much and it was quite obvious she couldn't wait for him to leave. He put his hand on the boat's rail as if about to step off on to the wharf, but then suddenly he turned back to her.

'Listen, Master Matty. Here's a thought.'

'Really?' she enquired politely. 'An intelligent one? An *honest* one?'

He laughed, but pressed on. 'It's my understanding that these boats take at least two to manage them, don't they? One to lead the horse and the other to handle the tiller. Now you've been talking as if you're prepared to sail up to this treasure field near Aylesbury by yourself, but it'll take days. And surely you'd never do it all on your own?'

She was squaring her shoulders now, obviously not realising that the action strained her shirt even further over those rather pert, rather delightful breasts just beneath. He fixed his eyes firmly on her face to wait for her answer, which came promptly and predictably.

'It's been two years,' she declared, 'since my father died. And I can assure you, I've managed very well! Hercules is strong and well trained—'

'But you've not made such a long journey on your own before,' he cut in pointedly. 'Have you? Your friends told me so. Aylesbury is at least fifty miles away, isn't it?'

She all but tossed her head. 'Your concern for me is remarkably touching. But I shall manage perfectly well, thank you! I also know that if there's any difficulty, the canal folk will help me. So in conclusion, Mr Rutherford, I'm going to set off as soon as I can. And at the moment, you're in my way, so I'd be grateful if you'd move yourself.'

'Don't,' Jack said. 'I mean, please don't go by yourself.'

'What?' She looked incredulous.

'Listen to me. I've not a great deal to do at the moment. And,' he went on before she could interrupt, 'I wouldn't mind trying something a bit different—an adventure, if you like. So here's my suggestion. Why don't I come with you on this journey of yours?'

She was shaking her head in disbelief. 'Why on *earth* would you want to do that?'

He rested one hand casually against the boat rail. 'I told you. I've really nothing much on, now that I'm no longer an antiques dealer.'

She gave a snort. 'You think you ever were?'

'Perhaps not,' he admitted ruefully. 'But maybe I'd rather enjoy a canal trip—you know, learning different skills, catching new sights.' He leaned forward. 'You have my word that I'll do exactly what you tell me. And I have a little money to spare, which would help out, surely? My motives are quite straightforward. I just happen to rather fancy a little jaunt on the waterways.' He grinned. 'I could be your first mate. Your number one assistant. How about it—*Captain* Matty?'

Chapter Eight

He'd drawn even closer while he spoke. And this time, though his voice was as calm as ever, Matty felt there was suddenly something rather dangerous in those strong features of his. 'Listen, Master Matty,' he went on. 'You've had your griefs and troubles, for which I'm heartily sorry. But I've been in the midst of scenes that I wouldn't want to begin to describe to you and sometimes it seems to me that the only way to get through life is to treat it as a light-hearted adventure—yes, a jaunt, if you like. Otherwise you would never smile again. You'd never *sleep* again.'

He moved back, giving her space—which she most definitely needed, because his words had chilled her to the bone. She shivered. She also burned, because he'd been so close. What was *wrong* with her?

Suddenly she was aware that amidst all the usual clamour of the wharf, there was a different sound—the sound of men singing. Men who'd been in the alehouse, she guessed, her alarm system working full tilt as they came closer. There were about a dozen of them and they were striding—no, staggering—along the wharf arm in arm and bellowing out their song.

Some talk of Alexander,
And some of Hercules
Of Hector and Lysander
And such great names as these...

She guessed they must be old soldiers. Many of them lived in the poorer districts like this, drinking away what money they had and reliving past battles with their fists after the alehouses had closed. Already quite a few of the men from the nearby barges were keeping a wary eye on them, because the ex-soldiers were suddenly veering in the direction of the boats—Matty's in particular.

They were pointing. They were coming ever nearer and Matty's heart began to hammer. Then she saw Jack leap lightly over the boat rail on to the wharf so he was facing them—and he had a big grin on his face. *What on earth...?*

'Well, I'll be damned,' Jack Rutherford was saying. 'If it isn't that bunch of ale-swilling rogues from the Grenadier Guards!'

Within moments all the men had surrounded him, slapping him on the back and taking turns to grip his hand. 'It's Major Jack, lads,' they were exclaiming. 'Major Jack, the hero of Salamanca! What on earth are you doing here, sir? Not taken to living on a barge, have you?' They didn't wait for his answer, just roared with laughter at the notion. 'We're off to the George and Dragon up the road, Major Jack. Come with us, why don't you? Surely you won't say no to a pint with the lads for old times' sake?'

Jack hesitated slightly. One of the men pointed to Matty, who by now had tugged on her coat. 'You can bring the lad with you if you like. Any friend of yours is a friend of ours.'

Matty shook her head. 'Thanks,' she said in a gruff voice, 'but I've jobs to do.'

'Suit yourself.' The man turned back to Jack. 'You coming, Major?'

'I'll join you for a pint shortly, lads. You can be sure of it.'

He watched them go. Then he stepped back

on to the boat and looked at Matty. 'They were some old friends of mine,' he said.

'So you were in the army?'

'Yes,' he said. 'Once.'

She should have guessed straight away, from the way he'd fought those men who'd charged into his shop that day and from the look that sometimes darkened his blue eyes—it was the darkness that belonged to a man who'd seen too much not just of life, but of death. *I've been in the midst of scenes that I wouldn't want to begin to describe to you.*

She said in a low voice at last, 'Why on earth didn't you tell me?'

'Perhaps it didn't seem relevant at the time.' Jack drew a little closer. 'Listen, Matty. I'm going to join those men for a drink. It would seem rude not to.'

'Of course,' she said witheringly.

'But in the meantime, I hope you'll think hard about the offer I've made—'

'I don't need to think hard about it at all,' she cut in. 'My answer's a no.'

'Now that's a pity,' he said softly.

Just for a moment, that slightly mocking tone had gone from his voice and she felt a slight tremor beginning somewhere deep inside. His eyes never shifted from her face, but she felt he was assessing just about all of her from her head to her toes, seeing *everything.* She found herself fighting back a dismaying surge of heat.

But the very next minute he was gone, to catch up with his soldier friends. As she heaved in steadying breaths—*Calm yourself, why are you letting the man distract you so?*—she watched the men heading towards the alehouse laughing and talking, with Jack in their midst.

It was just as well he had gone. She needed time to cool down.

So she knew now that Jack Rutherford had once been an army officer, but he'd not told her an awful lot of other things and she feared he hid much darker secrets. He'd been in trouble, that *had* to be so, or he would never be running that hopeless shop and getting into brawls with wearying regularity.

And whatever his past, the question remained—why on earth would someone like him want to travel on her boat? He'd given her no proper explanation. He'd said that he'd fancied an adventure, which was such a flimsy reason that she'd laughed aloud. For a man like him, the slow pace of canal travel would be boring beyond belief.

It was impossible for another reason as well,

that disturbed her as much as his roguish character. They would be together, just the two of
them, for day after day. And he was so very...
male. She shivered a little again. That gleam
in his mischievous eyes just now. The way he
quirked the corners of his mouth and looked at
her from under his black eyebrows almost in
stark challenge—a challenge that set something
odd fluttering through her body...

Ridiculous, Matty. He was trying to cajole
her into letting him travel on her boat. But once
again—why?

She began to repair a frayed rope and did her
best to push the scoundrel Jack Rutherford out
of her head. Why on earth had she told him so
much about her father and his treasure quest?
It was because he'd goaded her into it, that was
why. Lucky for her that his army friends had
turned up when they did—in their company he
would quickly forget all about her and the canal
jaunt he'd fastened on. With luck, she would
never see him again.

But she didn't feel the sense of relief she ought
to. Which made her even more cross with herself.

'Forget him,' she muttered as she pressed on
with her tasks. *For heaven's sake, you've quite*

enough to do without taking on board a rogue like him.

She found it was a relief to go and visit Hercules in the nearby stables, where she leaned her cheek against his warm neck. 'I really don't know what to do, Hercules,' she whispered. 'There's this man called Jack Rutherford, who says he'd like to help me find my father's treasure. And finding it is what I want more than anything, you know? But I don't think I can trust him. So I can't possibly take him with me. Can I?'

But Hercules wasn't listening—because he'd heard footsteps coming up behind them. Just as she had.

'Talking to your horse now?' a man's voice said. 'Is he offering you good advice?' She whirled around. It was Jack Rutherford, of course, with his coat slung carelessly over one shoulder.

'Better advice than you'd give me,' she replied calmly, her hand still on Hercules's neck. 'And I thought you'd still be at the alehouse with your soldier friends.'

He shrugged. 'I didn't want to leave *you* for too long, young Master Matty. Even though you do have some rather odd habits. Talking to your horse, for example.'

He'd put one hand in his pocket and Matty watched as Jack—whistling 'The British Grenadiers' under his breath—drew out a carrot.

'He doesn't like carrots,' she stated.

'Are you sure?'

And Matty watched in disbelief as Hercules gobbled the offering down. *Hercules. You traitor!* 'I've told you, Jack,' she said flatly. 'You're not coming with me on my journey.'

He turned with a smile to Matty. *White teeth,* she thought a little dazedly, *lovely white teeth, what a smile…* 'Yes,' he said, 'but look how much your horse likes me! Everyone likes me except you, Master Matty.'

She didn't grace him with a reply. Instead she asked, 'How did you find me here?'

'I spoke to your friends, Bess and Daniel. They pointed the way to the stables. Oh, and they told me there's going to be a party on the wharf tonight. Did you know?'

She found that she'd backed up against the wall of the stable—this place seemed too small with his all-too-masculine figure in it, as well. 'Of course I know there's a party tonight,' she said irritably. 'Two of the boat people are getting married. I've been invited.'

'So have I now.'

'You?'

'Yes.' He'd started stroking Hercules's mane. That simple action—his long lean fingers so dextrously caressing the silky strands—suddenly for some reason made her throat go dry. He turned his dancing blue eyes on her. 'Sounds like fun,' he added. 'Well, I'll be off for now. But I'll see you later, Master Matty. At the party, yes?'

Unable to think up a suitable retort, Matty merely frowned; and frowned even more when she saw, to her incredible annoyance, how before he left he rubbed Hercules's nose one last time and her foolish horse closed his eyes almost in ecstasy.

'Ridiculous, vain man,' she muttered to herself.

But there was a strange, almost aching feeling low down in her chest which made her fear that at the touch of those cunning fingers she could almost become a traitor herself.

Never. And she wanted no further involvement with him, no, not if he were the last man on earth!

* * *

Matty was determined not to let Jack Rutherford's announcement that he was coming spoil the party for her, because she had been looking forward to it for days.

It was a fine, warm night. The nearby alehouse had supplied several large trestle tables and barrels of ale, and the pie shop sent over a quantity of pies hot from its ovens. The Irish labourers who'd been invited to join the celebrations brought along a troupe of musicians who played fiddles and penny whistles, and they were already setting the evening air alight with their rousing tunes as Matty arrived.

It should have been a perfect scene, but Matty's spirits were low.

Jack Rutherford troubled her excessively. Yet, as the party got into full swing and there was still no sign of him, she felt a curious sense of emptiness. No doubt he'd found some other way to spend his evening—maybe his army friends had hauled him off to another Paddington alehouse, or perhaps his Vanessa had decided to claim him for the night.

Matty felt rather hot all of a sudden at the thought of Jack with Vanessa.

She was sitting at one of the outdoor trestle

tables with Bess and Daniel. Matty was clad in her usual attire of coat and breeches, though her friends had gone to some trouble: Daniel wore his best waistcoat and Bess had decked herself in a flowered frock and hooped gold earrings. They were just settling down when Jack Rutherford arrived, balancing four tankards on a tin tray. To Matty's consternation he sat on the bench beside her, nodded to Daniel and Bess, and deposited the tankards on the table.

'A pint of ale for you,' he said to Daniel, 'and lemonade for you, madam.' He placed one of the smaller tankards in front of Bess. 'Some ale for me and a half-pint for you, young Matty, but go easy on it, won't you?' Then he began complimenting Bess. 'Why, you look as lovely as the bride, Bess! I'll wager your Daniel had to fight off plenty of suitors when he started courting *you*.'

'And I'm thinking,' chuckled Bess, 'that you're a cheeky young whippersnapper with spoonfuls of honey oozing from that tongue of yours. Get away with you, do!'

But she was blushing like a sixteen-year-old and Matty looked on with growing amazement and exasperation. 'How on earth,' she said to Jack when Bess and Daniel were engaged in chatter with the group at the next table, 'do you know my friends?'

'How? Well, I saw that Daniel there was struggling a bit earlier to get a barrel of water on to his barge, so I gave him a hand. You see, I can actually be quite useful.'

Matty pursed her lips.

At least, she noted, he had eased up on the charm for a while when the groom made his speech and kissed the bride. Jack was silent also when the Irish fiddlers launched into a wild jig and the groom whirled his bride round and round while everyone clapped and cheered.

But after that, there was no stopping the man. Especially since he was proving to be extremely popular—not only with the boatmen, who'd somehow learned he had been in the army and clamoured for battle talk, but also with the ladies.

The women from the canal boats had dressed themselves up in all their finery for the wedding party. Like Bess, they had brought out treasured items like gold earrings and lace shawls. And they were all enjoying themselves even more than usual—because of Jack.

Did he flirt? To be perfectly fair to him, acknowledged Matty reluctantly, he didn't need to.

He was completely surrounded by willing partners once the dancing started up and—typical of the man—he was good at it. Matty remained seated during the dancing and tried not to look too often, but there was still no escaping his presence.

Jack Rutherford is trouble, she was thinking. *He draws attention wherever he goes. I was quite right to refuse his offer to come with me...*

Just moments later Jack himself came to flop down next to her. 'Phew,' he said. 'I'm not sure I can keep up this pace. You haven't danced yet, young Matty. Haven't you seen a girl who takes your fancy?'

Matty was incredulous. Surely he'd seen through her disguise by now? *Surely* he'd learnt from the others that she only dressed as a boy and kept her hair short for the sake of convenience?

Apparently not. Matty took a hearty swig of her ale, nearly choked and put it down. 'I rather think,' she said tartly, 'that the girls here only have eyes for you.'

'Ha!' He'd turned to face her again and grinned, amused. 'I'm a novelty. That's all.'

No, thought Matty to herself. *That's not all.* Unfortunately for her own peace of mind.

Jack looked utterly relaxed, but all through her mind and body danger signals were being set off. He appeared quite unconscious of his own masculine appeal, but that loose-fitting leather waistcoat was unbuttoned and his shirt was undone at the top so Matty could see close up his tanned throat and the beginnings of a scattering of dark hair on his muscular chest. And as he leaned closer she felt a strange kind of heat that made her grow warm in all kinds of places she didn't like to think about. Her first instinct was to retreat and to shield herself from his hard, bright gaze.

But she knew—she was *certain*—that she had no time in her life for men like him, with their trickery and falsehoods. She kept an expression of scarcely veiled scepticism on her face as he drank more of his ale and then turned to her again.

'Now, young Matty, I'm enjoying this party very much. But what I'm really interested in is this story of yours, about the treasure field your father thought he'd found. What exactly are you planning to do when you get there again? Start digging the place over by yourself?'

She gave him a withering look. 'You really know nothing about archaeology, do you? You speak of the whole affair as if it were like…like planting potatoes!'

He grinned. 'Isn't it?'

'No! Of course it's not!' How this man *annoyed* her. 'It's vital, first of all, that you pinpoint your site as accurately as possible, then you must mark out your ground and search one small section at a time, examining every single inch.'

'Isn't there a quicker way? Like ploughing up the field?'

'Do you honestly think you could risk damaging valuable finds by taking a horse and plough to the land?'

Mischief still sparkled in his blue eyes as he shrugged. 'Search me. Potatoes, ploughing, Roman villas—it's all a mystery as far as I'm concerned.'

Matty said with icy politeness, 'Then you'd better stick with dancing Irish jigs, Mr Rutherford.'

'Perhaps you're right.' He gave a sigh of contentment, leaning back and putting his hands behind his head. 'Dancing in the Irish way is really great fun. As I said, you should find some willing lass to show you the moves and give you a kiss—maybe that would sweeten that temper of yours, young Matty... Stop. Stop! Where are you going?'

Matty, tested beyond endurance, had risen to go. But Jack was reaching out to grasp her wrist and was laughing. 'Very well. I know I'm being annoying. But you really should try, you know, to loosen up occasionally. To enjoy life a bit more.' He suddenly peered closer at something she was holding in her other hand. 'What's that you've got?'

She planted a sheet of handwritten paper on the table, hating the way her wrist was still tingling from his touch. *Insufferable man.* 'While you were enjoying yourself, I've been talking to someone who's recently sailed up to Aylesbury. I was making notes about the channels and the locks, so that I know what to expect on the way.'

'Hmm. Let me see.' Before she could stop him, he had picked up her sheet and was reading aloud. 'Paddington to Bull's Bridge—thirteen miles. Bull's Bridge to Marsworth Junction—thirty-three miles. Marsworth Junction to Aylesbury Wharf—six miles.' He put the paper down and looked at her. 'I make that a total of fifty-two miles. How long do you think it will take you?'

She shrugged and took her sheet back. 'Possibly three days, maybe four. A young horse can tow an unladen boat a distance of around twenty miles a day, but Hercules needs to take the journey more slowly and the canal's often very busy. I might have to wait a while to get through some of the locks and tunnels.'

He gave a whistle of interest. 'There are tunnels?'

She gave him a rather scathing look. 'Of course. Some of them are almost a mile long.'

'A *mile*? Now, that sounds fun.' He leaned a little closer. 'I don't suppose you've changed your mind about letting me come?'

'No,' Matty said decisively. 'Not a chance.' Nearby, a woman was taking orders for ale and pies; Jack hailed her and soon—despite Matty's protests—two substantial platefuls of meat pie plus a couple of brimming tankards of beer were placed in front of them.

'Well,' said Jack, raising his tankard. 'Cheers, young Matty—and eat up, or you'll never grow into a big strong lad who charms the lasses. Now, I get the message. I know you and I will be parting company soon since you'll be going your way and I'll be going mine. But I really am rather intrigued by your tale of ancient treasure. And I think you said your father went twice to the house, to ask permission to search this field—but you went once only?'

She answered flatly, 'That's right.'

'And you formed the impression that the house seemed unoccupied by its owner?'

Why on *earth* was he asking all this? 'No! I didn't say that at all. In fact, I'd seen some evidence that the owner had been there only recently, because someone had been composing a letter.'

Jack raised his eyebrows. 'So you and your father went rifling through the household's correspondence, did you?'

She felt the colour rise in her cheeks. 'No! We were looking for historical documents in the drawers and this letter had been put in there with them by mistake, I assumed. I didn't read it all, but it caught my attention because it was written in French.'

'Ha! The language of poets. Someone's attempt at a love letter, perhaps?'

'Not at all! It was in very poor French, actually, and it was only in note form—it said something about a chateau near Lille. And I noticed that it was dated just two weeks prior to our visit.'

The wedding party was still in full swing and

the Irish fiddlers were playing as wildly as ever. But for Jack, with those few words, everything— *everything*—changed.

Chapter Nine

Jack wondered if she had any idea what impact her words had had on him. So far his insolence had provoked her out of her usual caution, but he guessed that any minute those pretty lips of hers would clamp shut again. A chateau. Near Lille... *Steady, Jack. Be careful.*

He drank a little of his ale and put the tankard down again. 'How do you know some French?'

She met his gaze steadily. 'My father taught me.'

'Of course. The scholar. So you were able to read it all?'

'Only enough to realise it was about some place called Chateau Esperance, but then I lost interest—because it was clearly of no relevance to my father's search. Or, for that matter, to you.'

If only she knew. He managed to say, 'Of

course. Nevertheless you seem to remember it quite clearly.'

'You think so?' Her reply was crisp. 'In fact, I'd forgotten it completely until you asked me if the house had appeared unoccupied.' She paused, looking with a frown at her plate of untouched food. 'Look. I'm afraid I really can't eat all this.'

'Of course,' Jack said quickly. 'Forget the pie—it was silly of me to order it. And please, go on. You said your father went again to the house, by himself?'

She hesitated. 'The next day he returned there without me.' She looked up at him suddenly and this time her face was haunted by grief. 'As I said, the owner of the house arrived and ordered his servants to throw my father out. That night, my father died—and I shall always, *always* believe that was the cause of it.'

The owner of the house. That man, thought Jack grimly, must have been Fitz—who most definitely wasn't the owner, not two years ago, but clearly he was already at work on it. That piece of paper Matty had seen proved it. And what if, by the slimmest of chances, it was still there?

'I'm sorry about your father,' he said to her. 'So sorry—'

And then he had to break off, because all of a sudden he found himself surrounded by a group of eager men from the party. 'We hear you were at Salamanca, Major! Did the battle really last as long as they say? Did you know Lord Wellington himself?'

Jack had risen to his feet, smiling, but at the same time he was groaning inwardly. *Please. Not now.* 'Let's talk all about it another time, eh, lads?'

But they wouldn't be put off, hard as he tried. He glanced back at Matty.

Damn. She'll be wishing she'd not said a word of what she's just told me. She'll be wishing she'd bitten her tongue off first.

Meanwhile his admirers, who'd formed a solid ring round him, were still firing their questions—and to be perfectly honest, he wished them anywhere but here.

Matty watched Jack Rutherford deal with yet more enthusiastic admirers, noting how he answered their questions patiently and was polite and modest about his war experiences. There was none of that hateful boastfulness she had seen so many former soldiers indulge in.

But he troubled her, deeply. It was as if those blue eyes of his cast a spell that coaxed out her deepest secrets—she'd even told him about her father's death, which it still hurt even to *think* about. She guessed he was hiding a great deal behind that light-hearted mask, a great deal she didn't understand. For instance, why was he so insistent about wanting to travel with her? And why was she mad enough to feel tempted by his offer?

She looked up at him brightly as he finally returned to her side. 'Your fame is certainly spreading, Major Rutherford. You're quite the celebrity of the evening.'

Looking suddenly weary, he raised his hand in dismissal of her comment and sat down next to her again. 'They're deluded,' he said flatly. 'They've no idea of the realities of war and its aftermath.'

She frowned. 'Am I to take it that your military career didn't exactly come to a glorious end?'

His face was still shadowed. 'No,' he said quietly. 'It didn't.'

Matty's heart sank even further. But then he was on his feet again, clearly preparing to go, and suddenly she felt something tugging hard at her—a sense of acute regret, because she'd actually started to wonder if here, perhaps, was someone she could have trusted...

Stupid. Don't be so stupid, Matty.

He picked up his tankard of ale and drained the last dregs. 'Well,' he said as he put it down, 'it's been interesting meeting you, young Master Matty, and I'm truly sorry this hasn't worked out. You know, I really quite fancied a canal journey.'

He gave her a slight smile. *Oh, that smile.* The lingering sadness behind the mask. Shocked by her own reaction, she began to say, 'I'm glad you realise it's a ridiculous idea. I think we might get on each other's nerves rather swiftly—'

And then she broke off and was jumping to her feet. Jack swung round to see where she was looking and he let out an exclamation—because charging into the midst of the party were a dozen men armed with clubs, who began laying about them left, right and centre.

Jack was already running towards the heat of the action, noting with some relief how swiftly the canal folk organised themselves. He saw that a couple of the older men were already herding the women and children back towards the boats, out of harm's way; saw, too, that the Irish had joined in to help the canal folk defend themselves and it was just as well, because these attackers, with black scarves half-masking their faces, clearly meant business.

Jack's army training came to the fore as he shouted orders to the men nearest him. 'Stick together. Grab their weapons if you can. Use your fists, your boots—fight dirty, lads, because that's what they're doing!' With those words he threw himself at the enemy, and the boatmen and the Irish were right behind him, yelling out their own battle cries.

The fighting was dirty all right, but their attackers were clearly surprised by the unity and ferocity of their intended victims. It wasn't long before the enemy started to fall back, though Jack urged his men to keep up the pressure.

'This is a nasty attack,' one of the boatmen gasped to him. 'We've not had anything as bad as this before.'

No, thought Jack. *No, I imagine you haven't.* And he had a cold, sick feeling in his stomach as he fought on.

By now most of their opponents were turning to flee. Just a few of them persisted, but before long the canal folk were chasing the last of them down the street, while Jack stood there and heaved air into his lungs. The others were buoyed by the victory, but there was darkness in his heart.

'You looking for young Matty?' one of the men asked him. Jack nodded.

'Matty helped to get the women and children back to the boats. And will doubtless be there still, down at the wharf.'

Jack hesitated, but even as he did so he caught sight of a slim figure in a long coat and big hat. The man had been wrong; she was no longer at the wharf, but was running towards the stables. And then he realised exactly why she was running: it was because a plume of smoke was rising from those stables where all the canal horses were kept.

Dear God. Those villains must have set the stables ablaze before they left.

By the time he got there Matty was already plunging a bucket into one of the big rain barrels nearby so she could hurl water on to the flames.

Jack quickly seized another bucket and joined in, though Matty scarcely glanced at him, so frantically was she working—out of desperation, since the fire was spreading and the horses were whinnying in terror, tossing their heads and stamping in their stalls.

Jack yelled out to anyone within hearing, 'Help. We need help over here!'

Within moments people arrived. 'Tell us what to do, sir.'

'Some of you men get the horses out. And the rest of you—do you see the buckets over there? We have to make a human chain right to the canal's edge, so we can get a constant supply of water back here. Understand?'

Their replies came back in chorus. 'Aye, sir.'

The next ten minutes passed in a haze of smoke and fumes, but the terrified horses were successfully led away and soon a steady supply of water was coming by bucket from the canal. Most of the structure had been saved, but the stink of scorched straw and timber remained. Jack stepped back and drew his hand across his brow, feeling that old blackness gathering in his heart. That soul-destroying weariness.

He turned swiftly as he realised several of the boatmen were coming towards him—led by Daniel, who was reaching out to shake his hand. 'Thank you.' Daniel was clearly their spokesman. 'We were mighty lucky to have you around just now. There are some nasty types in this part of London, but we were a match for them, weren't we?'

'A match for them indeed,' said Jack.

One by one they took his hand so it was some time before Jack could see Matty again, but he spotted her at last. He'd realised that the rescued horses had been safely tethered close by the wharf and she was with them, soothing the still-terrified creatures, stroking them and murmuring to them. He had a sudden vision of her looking at him with that same tenderness and for one heart-searing moment he couldn't get the vision out of his head.

Slowly he walked over to the wharf to join her, though she had her back to him and didn't see him at first. He noticed how her coat was all smeared with soot, but he guessed she hadn't even realised—and most likely wouldn't care if she had.

'How is Hercules?' Jack asked her. 'I hope he wasn't harmed?'

Her expression was guarded as she turned round to him. 'He has no injuries,' she answered. 'But he's had a bad fright.'

As have we all, thought Jack. She had moved on down the line to where Hercules stood and just for a moment Jack thought he saw a single tear streaking the smoke marks on her face. But he had to be mistaken, surely—because she was as tough as they came. And now she suddenly faced him and said, 'You saved the day, Jack. How does it feel to be a hero?'

He felt a renewed jolt at that, but gathering himself together he said, 'You were the brave one, Matty. You were the first to spot the fire and take action.'

She was shaking her head. 'That's because I have a bad feeling that all this—the attack tonight and the fire—might be because of me.'

That sense of shock again. 'Why on *earth*—?'

She looked up at him with those clear green eyes of hers. 'A year before he died, my father led a campaign to bring down the high mooring fees charged by the owners of this wharf and was successful. But six months ago the owners suddenly raised the fees again, so I did what my father would have done—I opposed them. I dealt with all the paperwork and we won. At least, I *thought* we'd won. But now I think I'm probably responsible for all this. I think the wharf owners are getting their revenge.'

She was looking again at the smoke-blackened

stables and he saw how her shoulders slumped in sudden weariness.

As he watched her, in that long coat and the boots that were slightly too big and with her hat slightly crooked over her soot-speckled face, he felt another sudden tug in the region where his heart ought to be, because she showed not a trace of self-pity. She was young and alone in the world, yet she was as brave as anyone he'd met, man or woman. He felt a surprising surge of something unexpected—sympathy, yes. But there was admiration, too.

And contempt, for himself.

He said slowly, 'Are you still thinking that it might be time for you to get out of here? I've already told you that maybe I can help you with that.'

Her eyes widened. 'I've explained to you, haven't I? There are so many reasons why I can't take you with me! You know nothing about boats, you'd be nothing but a hindrance...'

He jumped in on her hesitation. 'But it could be the only answer, don't you see? You can't make such a long journey on your own, you've said so—and if you had anyone else to call on, I imagine you'd have done so.'

She looked around as if for some miraculous

outside intervention that just didn't come. She rubbed her palm across her forehead, unknowingly spreading those soot-stains on her nose, and somehow those smudges made her even more endearing. He found himself trying to imagine Vanessa saving those horses the way this girl had. *Impossible.*

She said at last, 'The problem is, I don't think we'd make good partners.'

'You did make your feelings clear,' he said drily.

'I usually do,' she shot back. Then her expression softened slightly. 'But on the other hand, if I really am the cause of tonight's attack, there might be more trouble while I'm around. Unfortunately, I know I can't make the journey to Aylesbury without a companion. And so I'm beginning to think that I have no option but to accept your offer.' She looked up at him. 'You must understand that I cannot afford to pay you anything at all.'

Jack shrugged. 'No need for payment,' he said. 'After all, as you pointed out, I'm not qualified in any way. Besides, I never expected any money— I just fancied the trip. So we're agreed? You'll be captain and I'll be first mate?' He was holding his breath.

At last she said, in a voice that almost burned him with its intensity, 'Do you promise—really *promise*—that I can trust you?'

Feeling like the biggest rogue in Christendom, he answered, 'I swear.'

She nodded then, lifting that defiant little chin of hers. *What a lovely profile she has*, he thought suddenly. Why didn't she have any admirers? Were all the men around here blind?

He thought that she sighed a little. 'Then we'll set off,' she said, 'at first light tomorrow.'

Jack's breath hitched slightly. *No. That would be too late.* 'Not earlier?' he said as casually as he could. 'Like—now?'

'Now?' She looked startled. 'Not many barges travel by night, because it's difficult for the horses to negotiate the towpaths in the dark.'

'But now you'll have me. I can lead Hercules.'

'That's true.' She frowned. 'But do you really think we need to leave here so very quickly?'

'That was a pretty ferocious attack, Matty, and if their target really is you, then they might be back soon. Tonight, even.'

Good God, man, he rebuked himself, *since when did you become such an accomplished liar?*

'So, yes,' he went on aloud, 'I think it might

be an extremely good idea to set off as soon as we can.'

'I see.' She still looked shaken. 'I suppose we can travel part of the way by night, certainly—though some of the locks are shut after dark.'

That was a blow. 'You mean we can't get through them?'

She appeared to be considering hard. 'Let me think. Most of the locks we can deal with ourselves, but we'll have to stop at Willesden, since that's manned only by day. Though it's at least four miles away, and that's as much as we'd manage anyway in one night.'

'I see.' He felt relief well up. 'I didn't realise.'

'I imagine there's quite a lot you don't realise.' She gave him a tight smile. 'I can see you have a great deal to learn—Jack.'

'I can see that I do, Captain Matty,' he answered. 'And I realise you're not exactly delighted to be taking me along with you on this journey of yours, but look at it this way. The sooner we set off, the sooner you'll reach your goal and the sooner you'll be rid of me.'

To which she had no reply whatsoever.

Chapter Ten

'*The sooner you'll be rid of me,*' he'd told her. Clearly she was taking him at his word, because as soon as they reached *The Wild Rose*, she brought up some maps of the canal system from the cabin while Jack lit a lamp on deck. Spreading them out, she carefully began to explain the journey and Jack listened, trying to understand as much as he could of a world about which he knew so little.

What an amazing young woman she is, he thought. *So calm. So knowledgeable.*

Though when she came to the end, something of her vulnerability showed at last as she lifted her green eyes to his and said, 'Jack. If those men were after me—and I think they were—then what if they try to find me again?'

This time it took a moment to answer. But then he said lightly, 'Don't worry, Master Matty, I'll protect you—although from what I've seen of you so far, you seem pretty much able to look after yourself.' He stood up. 'Before we set off, though, I have to go back to the shop to pick up a few things.'

'Really?' Her voice was businesslike again. 'I hope you won't be bringing much, because there's very little storage space. Let me show you the cabin.'

All the time, Matty kept telling herself that she had no choice. She had to trust this man, but she still couldn't believe she was actually doing this. Was she crazy, setting off into the night with a stranger? Already, on finding herself down in the confined space of the cabin with him, she felt his presence as something dangerous, something that set the air around her simmering with un-known tensions—whereas he, as she might have guessed, was looking around as if he hadn't a care in the world.

'This is neat,' he said. 'Tidy. I've never been on one of these boats before, but really, you've got everything you could want down here, haven't you?'

'Just about.' She flung open a small locker and

added a little tightly, 'This is all the space I can spare for your things.'

'Suits me. I'm used to travelling light.'

And she thought, *Of course*. He was a soldier. Then she realised he wasn't even looking at the locker—he was looking at her bed. *Bed—oh, my*. She hadn't properly thought about *that*. Her heart began to thud.

There was only one bed, which her father always used while Matty slept on a thin cotton mattress which could be rolled up and stowed away by day. Her father had also rigged up a makeshift curtain to afford them each some night-time privacy, which was fine for a father and his young daughter. But to share this small space at night with Jack Rutherford?

Matty felt a headache coming on. *He'll have to sleep on deck*, she thought rather wildly. He can rig up some sort of shelter from any rain…

She suddenly realised he was about to leave. 'Right,' he was saying, 'I'm going to get my things now. But I'll be back very soon, Captain Matty.'

He grinned, patted her shoulder in a friendly way and disappeared from her view. She sank back a little dizzily on the bed.

If only he wouldn't keep teasing her. Touching her. She *hated* being touched by a man, which was partly why she dressed as she did— it stopped men pawing and leering. But it was somehow different with Jack Rutherford. His touch burned her. It made her feel all sorts of sensations she wasn't used to. Worst of all, she didn't hate the effect he had on her—and that was the trouble. She was going crazy—and she was certainly mad to allow him to share this journey with her.

Oh, no. What on earth have I done?

Ten minutes later she was harnessing Hercules up to the boat. It was unusual for anyone to be setting off at this time of night, but she'd clung to the faint hope that her actions might pass unnoticed. Unfortunately it wasn't long before she saw Daniel approaching, carrying a lantern.

'Now, then, Matty.' He looked mystified. 'You're harnessing up old Hercules. What on earth for, lass?'

'Jack Rutherford and I,' she said, 'have decided we're heading north.'

Matty knew the reaction she would get. 'Together?' Daniel exclaimed. 'And at this hour of night?'

'That's right. We're setting off very soon.'

From the look on Daniel's face, this was just as severe a shock as the fire breaking out at the stables—and now Bess had come bustling up, just in time to catch the tail end of the conversation. 'Matty,' she exclaimed. 'You're not really setting off with that young fellow-me-lad you've only just met?'

Matty was in a quandary. Should she tell them that the terrifying attack tonight was most likely aimed at her and was thus all her fault? But if she did that, they might never wish to let her out of their sight! Besides, she'd always intended to make this journey. *Always.*

'Bess,' she said, 'shortly before my father died, I made a promise to him to visit a place that meant a great deal to him.' She saw Bess's face soften slightly. 'And I've decided it's time I fulfilled my promise. I've always known it would be difficult on my own, but Jack has offered to help me. The decision is mine and mine alone.'

Bess and Daniel were still exchanging worried glances. 'Oh, lass,' said Bess at last. 'We would have helped you with this journey of yours, if only you'd asked us first!'

'You've always been the best of friends, but how can you possibly turn your back on your trade, your livelihood? I would never have dreamed of asking you!'

Their silence spoke of continuing unease, but at last Daniel said slowly, 'Aye, well, lass, it's your decision after all. But we're here if you need us.'

'I know, Daniel. And I thank you for it.'

With that, Daniel left but Bess lingered. 'Now look,' Bess said, 'I know your mother would have wanted me to have a chat about you setting off along the canal with that fellow who's latched on to you. It's just not fitting. Not proper. Surely he knows that?'

Matty met her gaze steadily. 'Actually, Bess, I'm not sure that he realises I'm a girl.'

Bess looked even more aghast. 'So what on earth are you going to do when he finds out?'

'I really don't think he cares, one way or the other.'

Bess shook her head darkly. 'Listen. I saw with my own eyes the way he danced with girl after girl at the wedding party. Men like him, they believe lasses are theirs for the taking. What makes you sure you can trust him?'

'I shall keep him at arm's length, Bess, don't worry. After all, I've been looking after myself for two years now—remember?'

Bess sighed. 'I also remember you've never done anything as scatterbrained as this, lass, ever. Another thing. I don't know if you've even thought about it—but where on earth's that scamp of a man going to sleep?'

Matty had been thinking about it all right, ever since she'd shown him her tiny cabin. But she answered airily, 'He'll sleep on deck, of course. He's already said he likes being out in the open air—he's used to it from his soldiering days.'

Bess was looking at her ominously and was clearly about to deliver a parting shot when they both heard the sound of footsteps and Jack himself came into view. He had a military-style bulky canvas satchel slung over one shoulder and was whistling an Irish jig as he strode along the quay towards the boat. The wharfside lanterns gleamed on his tousled dark hair and his muscular physique.

He halted on seeing Bess, who faced him squarely, her hands on her hips. 'Now, then. I understand you're going on a journey with our Matty. So what do you know, my lad, about barges? And horses?'

Jack put down his heavy satchel. 'As it happens, I know quite a bit about horses in general, ma'am,' he replied pleasantly. 'But I know very little about canal travel and I've a good deal to learn about boats, too. Though I think that in young Matty here, I'll have an excellent teacher.'

Bess frowned again. 'You take good care of our Matty, otherwise you'll have all us folk up and down the waterways to answer to. D'you understand?'

'I understand, ma'am,' Jack said almost meekly.

And Bess marched off.

Jack climbed on board with Matty and said cheerfully, 'Well. She doesn't like me very much, does she?'

Matty was already starting to coil up a length of mooring rope, but she paused to give Jack a steady look. 'She means it, you know. If you cause me the slightest bit of trouble, then Bess, Daniel and their friends won't forget or forgive.' Her tone changed suddenly. 'And Jack, don't— *don't* lean on the tiller like that, or it will whip round and—'

Jack gave a startled exclamation and leapt to one side as the swinging tiller almost knocked him off his feet. 'Damn,' he muttered, rubbing what must be a painfully bruised rib. 'Damn, that hurt.'

'Count yourself lucky,' Matty pointed out calmly. 'I've seen men have their arms broken if they're careless with tillers. Now, I'm going to the wash-house to clean myself up before we set off. It's at the far end of the wharf.'

'Anything I can do?'

'Yes—you can fill up Hercules's feed-box with oats.'

Jack looked around. 'How do I do that, exactly?'

'There's a sack over there on the wharf.' She pointed. 'I've paid for it. Bring it over and fill the feed-box, then take back the empty sack. You know, you're such a greenling.'

'A greenling?' Jack asked it carefully. 'What's a greenling?'

'Someone like you,' she answered, picking up her towel and soap, 'who knows nothing about canal life.' She was starting to walk off, but briefly looked back. 'Oh, and you might consider visiting the wash-house yourself. It could be a day or two before we next get the chance of hot water.'

'Right,' he said. 'Right.'

But first, he went down to the cabin to unpack his satchel. Into the locker Matty had shown him he put his one decent coat, carefully folded, followed by spare shirts, undergarments, even a cravat or two. And right at the back of the locker, he hid an oilskin pouch that contained a small pistol.

The wash-house was in a barn of a building, with a noisy laundry right next to it. But inside the wash-house anyone could pay for a private cubicle, a tin hipbath and several jugs full of hot water and Matty loved it. Once she'd bolted the door to her cubicle she stripped off her clothes and sank into the deliciously hot water, although it did occur to her that maybe she should have poured a bucket of icy water over her head at precisely the moment she began to think that ex-major Jack Rutherford might be a suitable travelling companion.

Was she mad? He was a *capable* rogue, but he was still a rogue, just as Bess had warned her. He was also a mystery, because she couldn't for the life of her work out why he wanted to come on this journey.

He'd said that he fancied an adventure; but if so, why would he choose to travel in a fashion that most men of his kind would consider not only uncomfortable, but utterly boring and even demeaning? Clearly he'd fallen on hard times, but she guessed he came from a moneyed back-

ground. He must have other friends, other re-
sources, so surely, if he wished for adventure,
he could find it in rather more exotic ways?

He was trouble. She guessed he'd not even
begun to tell her the real story of his life. Though
what about *her*? Wasn't she deceiving him, too,
by stubbornly pretending still to be a boy? Pouring the last jugful of water over her shoulders,
she let it trickle slowly down her arms and her
body.

It was no wonder that she found it easy to dress
in male attire. Her breasts were small, her hips
slender. She must be at least half a foot shorter
than Jack—who, if he'd decided to take a bath,
too, could be very close by even now. Might have
filled up his bath and stripped off his clothes…

A sudden image of him flashed through her
brain, an image that was a bit too vivid for her
peace of mind. He, too, would be soaping himself and relishing the hot water, she guessed;
maybe chuckling a little as he recalled the events
of the day. And she was going to be sharing her
boat with him for days and nights on end, all the
way to Aylesbury?

If only he'd stop *touching* her; but he did it so
carelessly, patting her arm or shoulder without a
thought. Yet somehow the warmth of his hands

lingered—and she felt that heat everywhere like an intimate caress, which she'd never wanted from any man, let alone him. But how could she stop him? Bess would tell her to slap his face, yet that would let him know just how much his touch troubled her...

She scoffed at herself. *Stop worrying, you idiot. Even if he's guessed you're a girl, it's quite obvious he couldn't care less.* She was worried, though. She was worried about how she would cope with having a handsome blue-eyed stranger in such close proximity.

Taking a deep breath, she began to soap her short hair, rubbing so fiercely that her scalp protested. After ducking her head underwater to rinse it, she stepped out of the bath and began to towel herself dry, telling herself she had no need at all to be concerned. She guessed that even if Jack Rutherford were to walk in right now and see her naked, his reaction would be complete and utter indifference.

He wasn't there when she returned to *The Wild Rose* and once more her thoughts spun almost out of control. What if he'd changed his mind and decided he wasn't going to come with her on her journey after all? She felt slightly sick with tension and when he eventually arrived she wasn't in the least bit calmed to realise that he'd visited the wash-house just as she'd suggested. He looked so different. He was freshly shaved, his black hair was all slick and gleaming, and his shirt gaped just enough to reveal that tanned chest with its smattering of silky dark hairs.

'You were right,' he said, casually draping his towel over the boat rail. 'The wash-house was a treat—though I didn't see you in there, young Matty.'

She felt hot all over. Of course—most of the men used a communal room that was much cheaper. 'I was very quick,' she said. 'In and out. You know?'

He chuckled. 'Good for you. Though I sense a note of rebuke—I took a little too long, did I? I can see you're going to run a tight ship, Captain Matty.'

She pressed her lips together. 'It was you who insisted we set off straight away,' she pointed out. 'So let's get on with it, shall we? You can make a start by studying those maps of the canal that I've left out for you.'

He glanced over to the small table on which she'd spread them out. 'Excellent,' he said, bow-ing his head over them. 'Is the house you and your father visited marked anywhere?'

'Here. You see?' She pointed. 'Charlwood Manor.'

'Charlwood Manor.' He repeated it and just for a moment she was aware of some strange tension in the air. But then he was smiling again and saying, 'Right. Map reading is one skill I do have, you'll be pleased to hear.'

'I am indeed,' she told him. Then she went to check on the boat's supplies of water and basic foodstuffs, even though she'd checked them twice already. Next she went to readjust Hercules's harness, but couldn't resist glancing back to confirm that Jack was still on deck, apparently absorbed in her father's maps and charts.

Her heart missed a beat again, because in the flickering light of the oil lamp he was no longer the careless, joking owner of Mr Percival's antiques shop. Instead there was an expression on his face that she'd noted when he'd led the charge on those men who'd attacked the party—an expression that was intent and deadly serious. She understood it then, but why now, when he was contemplating nothing more than a light-hearted canal journey? *Oh, Matty. He's dangerous.*

With an effort, she forced herself to look on the

positive side. If they set off right now, it would mean getting to her father's treasure field all the sooner—and it also meant spending the least time necessary with her new and rather disturbing companion.

They'd agreed that Jack would lead Hercules along the towpath while Matty stayed by the tiller. 'Remember that this first mile will be the most difficult,' she told Jack, 'since you'll have to watch out for the mooring ropes of all the boats that have stopped for the night.'

'Aye aye, Captain.'

Matty watched in exasperation as he jauntily approached the waiting Hercules. 'Take care!' she warned. 'He can be a bit tricky when he realises he's not going to spend the rest of the night in a warm stable!'

He raised one hand to acknowledge that he'd heard and true enough, as he drew close, Hercules snorted and shied away. Jack stroked his mane. 'Come on, old boy, and try to behave yourself for Captain Matty's new number one assistant. You're a friendly soul, really, aren't you?'

And Matty saw Jack reach in his pocket to

pull out a handful of oats. She frowned. 'That's downright bribery!'

He nodded. 'I know. Like the carrot. Bribery and corruption—there's nothing like it.'

She said reluctantly, 'You're good with horses.'

'Had a fair amount of practice.' He was stroking Hercules's neck again. 'I had to do quite a bit of riding in the army.'

'Ah, yes. The army.' She added softly, 'You've not really told me much about that yet, have you, Jack?'

He shrugged, still with that half-smile on his face. And he said—nothing.

Maybe he'd seduced another officer's wife, thought Matty darkly. Or *several* officers' wives.

She shook her head in annoyance at herself. *For heaven's sake. You're going to be spending days with the man, so get rid of these stupid and distracting thoughts right this minute.*

'I'll be ready to cast off soon,' she called to him as she checked the tiller. 'And that's when you must lead Hercules forward—though once we're moving, you'll find that he knows exactly what to do. Just keep a hand on his halter and watch for any obstacles on the towpath, because there are always unexpected hazards at night.'

'Aye aye, Captain. I'll be as watchful as a hawk for unexpected hazards, I promise.'

Absurd, annoying man!

Matty struggled for a parting shot. 'And don't feed Hercules any more oats, will you?' She was already starting to unfasten the mooring ropes. 'He'll expect them every time he sees you. He'll grow fat and lazy.'

'Little chance of that, I suspect,' murmured Jack, 'with you in charge.'

Teeth gritted, she hauled in the ropes. 'Right. We're off!' she called, taking the tiller.

Jack nodded, patting Hercules on the neck. 'Time to get going, old boy.'

And slowly, slowly the boat began to move away from the lights of west London into the darkness—with Matty fully aware that now she had no one but the mysterious ex-major Jack Rutherford to depend on. She stared ahead into the unknown. Had she completely taken leave of her senses?

Chapter Eleven

Jack had expected to feel frustrated by the slow progress they were bound to make and had reconciled himself to long stretches of boredom. But he quickly realised he was in for a surprise, because there was something deeply satisfying about the way the gleaming canal pointed the way ahead while the old horse plodded steadily at his side.

Even the night-time stillness proved deceptive, for evidence of the natural world became more abundant as his senses grew accustomed to the dark. His attention was caught by the bright eyes of water voles peering up at him from waterside verges or by bats darting past, and once he even spied a long-legged heron standing still as a statue among the reeds. But otherwise Jack had time to reflect—too much time, in fact. Because he was thinking, *I am a cheat and a liar.*

He had lied outrageously when he'd agreed with Matty that those ruffians were after her. For the men who'd attacked the wedding party were enemies of *his*. It was he, Jack, who needed to escape from the city and fast. He'd recognised the men straight away, because they were the very ones who'd delivered that message about the stolen bracelet and told him to get the hell out of London.

They were Fitz's men.

He'd antagonised Fitz badly and unfortunately his stepfather had friends in powerful places. Tempting though it was to stay and deal with him, Jack knew he needed to lay a foolproof plan to outwit his enemy. Most of all, he needed to leave London before Fitz had him slung in gaol for the supposed theft of that bracelet.

But just while he'd been pondering his next step, Matty had arrived on the scene. It was bad luck indeed for her, but for himself he couldn't have wished for better timing; because the minute she'd mentioned that treasure field and the country house she and her father had visited, his heart rate had speeded up. He'd realised that she was talking about his home. And what she'd said next was even more incredible, for she'd told him what she'd found in the library.

Once Jack had realised Fitz had married his mother and taken over the Charlwood estate, he'd consulted lawyers, but they'd all come up with the same conclusion. 'It's no good,' they'd told him. 'Your mother married Sir Henry, so all of her property is his. That's the law.'

'She only married him because he told her lies!'

'Can you specify these lies? Have you actual written proof of Sir Henry's fraud, Major Rutherford?'

Jack didn't. Yes, he'd always been quite certain that Fitz had faked the ransom letter his mother had seen, but had no proof of its existence other than his mother's testimony—his fragile mother, who would surely crumble under any rigorous questioning.

But now he'd met Matty. And this enterprising and rather unusual girl had presented him with a glimmer of hope. She had been inside Charlwood's library two years ago, shortly before Fitz married Jack's mother. Matty had told Jack she'd seen actual evidence that someone had been preparing a letter in French—she'd not had time to more than glance at it, but she did remember that it spoke of a place near Lille called Chateau Esperance—the Castle of Hope—which was wholly inappropriate, since it was the name of the grim fortress near Lille where Jack and other British prisoners of war had been chained for two long years.

Quite a few of his comrades hadn't survived captivity, but Jack was made of steel. When the news came of the official prisoner exchange, he'd done his utmost to rally his fellow inmates. *'We're on our way home,'* he'd urged them. *'Do you understand, lads? We're going home!'*

Several of the weaker ones had died on the journey; but for Jack there was a different kind of darkness, because he'd arrived in London to discover that his mother had married Fitz.

He remembered how that fresh blow had come close to achieving what the years in prison had failed to do. He would never forget the gloating look in Fitz's eyes as he put his arm round his wife and said to Jack, 'Aren't you going to offer congratulations to your new stepfather, Major Rutherford? Oh, I nearly forgot—you're not in the army now, are you? Two years a prisoner of the French. Not exactly a glorious end to your military career, was it?'

Jack had only just refrained from punching Fitz's teeth right down his throat.

And now, as he trudged along the towpath

through the night, something about his emotions must have conveyed itself to Hercules, because the horse turned his head and gave Jack a soft whicker that might even have been an expression of sympathy. Jack reached out to pat the horse's neck. 'You're a good old creature, Hercules, aren't you? And loyal to your mistress, too, I'll be bound.'

Hercules, Jack reckoned, wouldn't be nearly so friendly if he understood what Jack was really up to. In fact, he would probably use those big hooves of his to kick Jack straight into the canal; because Jack was using Matty to reach Charlwood and show him where she'd seen the draft of the ransom letter Fitz had been working on. There was only a slim chance it would still be there—but it was worth the risk.

'Have you actual written proof of Sir Henry's fraud, Major Rutherford?' those lawyers had asked him.

Not yet. Not yet. But with luck he would have, very soon.

He glanced back and saw Matty standing in the boat's stern with her hand steady on the tiller. 'I'll be aiming to keep us pretty much mid-channel,' she'd told Jack as they set off. 'We can count on deeper water there. And we're unlikely to meet anyone else at this time of night, but call to me if you spot an oncoming boat. You should see its lights before I do.'

She'd taken off her hat so that the moon shone full on her alert face, on those large dark-lashed green eyes and her cropped chestnut hair. She could, he thought suddenly, be really *very* pretty if she discarded her boyish clothes...

'There's a bridge coming up, Jack!' she called out just at that moment. 'And Hercules is nervous of going under them, so hold him steady. And remember to duck your head!'

Hmm. Maybe she was a bit too fond of giving orders for his tastes. He raised his hand to acknowledge her instructions. 'Aye aye, Captain,' he called.

But she had a lovely trim waist! And he was fascinated by the way those trousers clung to her very pert, very feminine behind... He clamped down on the sudden all-too-male tingle of interest surging in his loins, while at the same time Bess's warning words came back to him. 'You take good care of our Matty... D'you understand?'

And Jack, leading Hercules by the halter beneath the bridge, thought, *Bess was right not to trust me. She knew I wasn't telling her—or any-body—the truth.*

Jack's time in that French prison had altered him. His opinion of humankind had sunk low and, when he got out, freedom did little to change his mind—because it seemed that his old soldier comrades had been cast on the scrapheap. Yes, the public praised their victorious battles, but they wished to see as little as possible of the often damaged and maimed men who'd actually won them.

Fitz had the right idea. He'd scuttled out of the army, then found himself a cosy job in the War Office, where he could display his campaign medals and talk military tactics at his London club whenever he felt like it, safely away from the actual conflict. There were too many men like Fitz.

There were also, thank goodness, people like Matty's friends, the barge folk, who were hard-working and loyal to one another. And there was Matty herself. She was only nineteen, but she had not a hint of either self-pity or feminine guile. She was tough. She was a survivor. She would be *fine*.

And then he thought, Yes, she would be fine—

just as long as some scoundrel didn't wriggle under her defences. He clamped down hard on his wayward imaginings. *Just make sure the scoundrel who seduces her isn't you*, he told himself sternly. Besides, any false move on his part and her canal friends would probably arrive in full force to inflict a rather nasty punishment.

They'd passed through the tunnel by now and the moonlit path was becoming wider again; Hercules snorted in relief and Jack patted his neck. Somewhere in the wood bordering the canal an owl was hooting. It was all quite simple really. With young Matty's help he was going to get inside Charlwood Manor, where he'd do his damnedest to see if that draft of the cursed ransom letter still lurked. Yes, simple. And utterly treacherous of him, to use her so.

I hope you're proud of yourself, a little voice said.

No. He wasn't proud of himself in the slightest. Matty deserved far better. But the desire for vengeance burned inside him like the stars he could see blazing overhead in the night sky.

And so, his jaw set in fresh determination, Jack fixed his eyes firmly on the towpath ahead and marched onwards.

* * *

They travelled through the night past quiet fields and sleeping villages, disturbing nothing more than the occasional heron that would rise like a ghost from the canal with its great wings slowly flapping. At around two in the morning Jack had his first experience of a lock and he listened carefully as Matty gave him precise instructions.

'Take Hercules to the far side of the lock gates and tie him to that post over there—you see?' She held the lantern up to point it out to him. 'After that, he knows to just stand and wait.'

Then she told Jack how to open the heavy gates with a windlass and rope up the boat within the lock's confinement. Told him how to ensure the vessel remained steady while the incoming water entered the compartment and lifted them to the next level, also warning him that only then would it be safe to open the second set of gates so *The Wild Rose* would be free to float out along the next reach of the moonlit canal.

'Marvellous,' Jack said. 'Whoever invented the first lock was an engineering genius. Who was it? James Brindley?'

Matty showed amusement, and he noticed for the first time that she had a rather fascinating dimple at the corner of her mouth when she smiled. 'You've got your dates slightly wrong. It was the ancient Greeks.'

'Really?' He was genuinely astonished. 'As long ago as that?'

'As long ago as that.' She'd begun coiling the ropes she'd used to hold the boat while the water level changed. 'My father used to say that many of our so-called revolutionary ideas were in fact rediscoveries of old methods that were lost along the way.'

'Like the Romans, with their skill in road building?'

'Exactly.' Jack was glad to note she was actually showing some pleasure in their conversation. 'My father knew all about such things.'

'He was an Oxford scholar, I think you said?'

'Indeed.' Her voice was softer now. 'He was offered a permanent teaching post at the university, but he didn't want to be confined to any one place—though he was very fond of Oxford.'

Briefly she described the town to him, with its colleges and churches, but by then it was time to move on through the second set of gates. Matty took up her place by the tiller while Jack harnessed Hercules to the boat—and on they went. If Matty was tired, she gave no sign of it. As for Jack, he was startled to find himself feeling something of the unexpected peace he used to experience during the night marches in Spain, in those long hours when time seemed infinite. When he and his fellow soldiers tramped over rocky tracks while humming the old songs in unison.

Some talk of Alexander, and some of Hercules...

He patted Hercules's neck. 'You've got the name of a hero, my friend. Did you know that?' The horse nodded in response, as if he understood.

And the stars rode high above in the night sky, just as they had in Spain.

Chapter Twelve

They came to a halt when the sun was rising to the east in a shimmer of red and gold. Jack, looking at his pocket watch, realised it was six o'clock. He also saw that ahead of them were several moored boats that he guessed must have spent the night there.

'This is a popular spot,' he commented.

Matty had already jumped on to the bank and was busy securing the ropes to a mooring post. 'That's because the lock here is manned and doesn't open till half past six. We couldn't go any farther even if we wanted to.' She was scanning their surroundings from beneath the big brim of her hat. 'I'm going to get us some food from that farm over there.'

'What can I do?'

'There's an inn with stables down the lane. Do you see?' She pointed. 'Will you go there and buy some oats for Hercules? But be as quick as you can, in case they open the lock early and the queue starts to move.'

'Aye, Captain Matty.' He resisted the urge to salute.

After returning from the inn with the oats, he found Matty frying eggs and some bread on a little stove out on deck. 'That smells rather wonderful,' he said.

She eyed him narrowly. 'I imagine it's hardly what you're used to.'

'Then you imagine correctly.' He was settling himself on the little wooden stool she'd pulled out for him. 'It looks infinitely better.'

She slapped a couple of the cooked eggs between two pieces of fried bread, put them on a tin plate and thrust the meal at him. 'Stop trying to soft-soap me,' she said calmly. 'I'm not stupid. I know you must have led a comfortable life before your army adventures, but somehow things went rather wrong for you.' She dished out her own food and faced him steadily. 'And I think—don't you?—that it's about time you trusted me with a little more detail about how you ended up with what appears to be precisely nothing.'

Jack chewed on his mouthful of food for a few moments. 'It's tricky to sum up,' he said at last. 'I'm afraid I've always been...shall we say, a little careless with money? Easy come, easy go, that's me.'

She was sitting on the other stool with one booted foot casually resting on the boat's rail and was eating from her own plate. 'Not enough information, Jack. Not *nearly* enough. Let's start at the beginning, shall we? For a start, you could tell me about your family.'

'Nothing much to tell, I'm afraid. My father died when I was young. My mother remarried two years ago while I was...' he hesitated slightly '...away with the army. My new stepfather and I—well, let's just say that we don't get on.'

'You've fallen out with him?'

He finished another appreciative mouthful before replying. 'It didn't take much effort on my part, believe me. Yes, I've fallen out with him.'

'And why was that, Jack?'

He really longed to tell her.

Because he's a despicable coward who used to see his soldiers as cannon fodder. Because he's made my mother's life a misery. Because he's stolen my family home...

Instead he lifted his shoulders in a shrug. 'Let's call it a strong feeling of mutual dislike, shall we?'

'Are you running from someone, Jack?'

He felt the breath catch in his throat, but merely shrugged again. 'Perhaps I'm running from boredom,' he said lightly. 'I like adventure. And maybe I'm looking for my own kind of fortune.'

'Then most certainly you won't find it here.' She was watching him with narrowed eyes. 'On the canals.'

'Perhaps not.' He smiled at her. 'But I can certainly have fun trying.'

She frowned slightly, leading him to wonder just how many more lies he was going to have to damn himself with. But he was spared further questions, because she was putting down her plate and was on her feet, gazing ahead. 'It looks,' she said, 'as if the lock's being opened up. Which means that it's time to get moving. Will you be all right to carry on without a night's sleep?'

Jack swallowed the last of his tea and stood up

also. 'I'm quite happy to be on the move again. Lead on, Captain Matty.'

Once through the lock, Jack took up his usual role of walking with Hercules along the towpath while Matty stayed on board by the tiller. But her eyes kept straying to him too often for her own comfort. *He's a rogue*, she reminded herself. *A rogue with secrets.*

And as for her, she was a fool, because something about him made her feel the way she'd never, ever thought she would feel. Which was absolutely stupid of her.

What you need, my girl, is to keep your eyes on the way ahead.

And to stop watching him as he strolled along the path, whistling softly as usual. Goodness, through his linen shirt she could almost *feel* the strength of those shoulder muscles! Suddenly it struck her rather forcefully that she'd never before realised how beautiful a man's body could be, with that sweep of his lean waist down into his slim hips and those long, strong thighs...

Bucket-of-water time again, Matty. You decided some while ago to stay well away from men. Remember?

Her thoughts had darkened again. Of course

she remembered. How could she forget? Pulling herself sternly together, she called more instructions. 'Jack! Soon you'll find the path passes very close to the canal, so you'll need to hold Hercules's halter firmly. Do you understand?'

Without turning, he raised his hand in mock salute. 'Aye aye, Captain.'

And he kept on walking. *Maddening, infuriating man.*

They reached one of the longest tunnels on the canal at around eleven. 'It's over half a mile long,' she informed him as they approached its entrance.

'Really? Half a mile?'

'That's correct. And Hercules doesn't like it in the slightest, especially if there are rats. So this time you must lead him over the top—do you see the path leading up there?—and tether him at the far side. Then come back here. I'll need you.'

'That's quite an admission, coming from you, Master Matty.'

His sudden grin made her pulse beat a little unsteadily. She didn't smile back. 'And you won't hear me saying it often,' she assured him.

They had to pole their way through, which meant they each had to stand in the darkness on opposite sides of the deck and use a long pole to push at the sides of the brick tunnel. 'Thanks,' she muttered once they reached daylight at the other end.

He propped his pole casually against the cabin and gave it a pat. 'Handy things, these Egyptian oars. And no need to thank me—it was my pleasure.'

He is so smug, she thought, using her coat sleeve to wipe a slight sheen of perspiration from her brow. *He is absolutely insufferable.*

They stopped for lunch at a canalside inn, where they sat outside in the sun. 'This is my treat,' Jack announced, 'in repayment for your tuition skills, young Matty.'

He purchased ham rolls for them, with a tankard of cider for Matty and ale for himself. He joked and chatted. But though he appeared light-hearted, she noticed how he was watching the people around them all the time; indeed, the sound of someone dropping a plate made him half-rise to his feet and for a few seconds she saw his whole body tense before he relaxed again.

It probably comes from his years in the army, she told herself. He'd been a fighter. A killer. So why on earth had she been fool enough to bring him with her? The answer was simple—it was because she'd needed to get out of London swiftly. It was *her* fault those men attacked the wedding party. Though Jack Rutherford was a danger in different ways. That smile of his. The way she found her eyes wandering exactly when they shouldn't to his slim but athletic figure...

Stop it, Matty. She gulped down her cider so hastily she almost choked.

Once they got back to the boat she spoke crisply. 'Hercules is still tired after walking through the night, so I've decided that he needs a couple of hours' more rest.'

'Perhaps you do, too,' Jack replied. 'You look rather weary.' He'd been checking on the mooring ropes, then began coiling up one of the loose ones.

'Weary?' Matty retorted. 'Me? Nonsense. There are far too many things to do.'

He put the coiled rope down. 'Such as?'

She surveyed the boat and its surroundings. 'For a start, Hercules needs a new strap for his head collar—the buckle's worked loose. Didn't you notice? There's a blacksmith in Parley village, half a mile down that lane. I'm sure he can fix it, but it will probably take him a while. I also need to examine the maps and charts. The canal gets narrower farther on and I've heard there's been some silting in places, so we'll have to be careful how we go.'

'Then you study your charts,' he said, 'while I take the harness to the blacksmith.'

And before she could argue—not that she was going to—he'd slung on his leather waistcoat and was on his way, whistling as usual.

As soon as he'd gone, she went down into her cabin and sat on the edge of the narrow bed. She meant to spend the time Jack was away studying their route, she really did, but it was warm and comfortable in the cabin and she suddenly felt very sleepy.

I shouldn't have had that cider. Maybe if I lean back against the pillows, I'll be able to read the charts more easily...

Some time later she woke up in alarm. Oh, no. How long had she been asleep? Her eyes flew to the clock ticking away on the mantel. She'd slept for a whole hour.

And now there was a shadow across her bed and she saw that Jack was standing in the doorway looking down at her. Her heart thumped as she struggled to get up and straighten her clothes. She was only in her shirt and breeches— and some unreadable expression in his hooded eyes had her pulse thudding almost painfully.

'So,' he said. She saw that he was turning those wooden dice of his over and over in one hand. 'Far too many things for you to do, are there, Captain Matty?'

'I'm sorry,' she answered curtly. 'I shouldn't have fallen asleep.'

And you shouldn't have crept into my cabin without knocking.

She was gathering up her maps, angry and flustered.

He had pocketed his dice and folded his arms across his chest. He was still blocking the door-way. 'You probably need the extra rest,' he said, 'a growing lad like you. I've got that strap fixed at the blacksmith's and it's all sorted.' He pretended to fan himself a little. 'Let me tell you, it's really warm out there—the sun's going to be shining all day, I should think. It's too hot to be wearing *this.*'

Then—suddenly—he was casting aside his waistcoat. And before she could do a thing, he was unfastening several of the buttons on his white linen shirt and rolling up his sleeves. *Muscle. Tanned skin. Sinewy strength.*

Oh, my. Matty felt her heart hammer against her ribs. Surely by now he must realise she was a woman? Then why, oh, why did he persist in deliberately provoking her with such actions?

Most likely, she realised, because he couldn't have cared less. But he was watching her carefully, although his voice, when it came, was cheerful enough. 'So, Captain. What else is there for me to do?'

'You can—you can fill the water tank.' Her words came out as little more than a croak. Absolutely furious with herself, she reached for her coat and hat. 'There's a pump,' she went on, 'just by the wharf.'

'Aye aye, Captain.' He pointed to her coat and hat. 'It's getting hot outside—you quite sure you need all that on?'

'Absolutely sure, thank you!'

He nodded. 'So what are you going to do next?'

'I've plenty to keep me busy, don't you worry.' Impatiently she pulled on her boots and brushed past him to climb the ladder to the deck.

He followed without another word, picked up the empty bucket that sat on deck, then set off to the nearby pump. Matty meanwhile hauled the heavy tiller out of its socket, secured it with a rope and lowered it over the side into the canal. After that she sat on deck to study her charts—which were still spread out in front of her when Jack finally returned.

She heard him filling up the boat's water tank at the stern, then he strolled up to her and stood with his hands in his pockets. 'Why is the tiller dangling in the canal?'

She looked up at him calmly. 'I've been soaking it.'

'Why?'

'Because the wood dries out in hot weather and the tiller becomes loose in its socket. And when it's loose it can swing round and hit you hard. I've seen people get their ribs and arms broken. You've already had a taste of it.' She rose to her feet, folding away her charts, then went to start hauling in the rope. 'Now I need to lift it back into place.'

She said it calmly, but in reality the tiller was so heavy that it wasn't an easy job. In fact, she'd never done it by herself before. She clenched her jaw. Trust Jack Rutherford to arrive when she was just about to betray her weakness.

His dancing blue eyes were on her as she attempted to haul up the dripping tiller. 'Looks tricky,' he said. 'Let me help.'

'No! I can manage!'

He sighed a little. 'Look, young Matty. I thought we agreed we were partners? You supply the brains, I supply the brawn.'

'Very well,' she said. 'We can do it together—'

'No need.' He'd started steadily hauling up the dripping tiller. 'I'll manage by myself. What next?'

She pointed reluctantly to the stern of the boat. 'The tiller has to be lowered into its socket. You lift one end, I'll lift the other...'

He raised his hand to silence her. He'd already lifted the thing in his arms as if it were a child's toy—and Matty looked on without another word as he eased the tiller into its socket. Still without a word, she handed him the big wooden mallet and saw him begin to hammer it in.

She had to admit that as he stood there with his back to her, swinging the mallet in steady rhythm, it was difficult to tear her eyes away from him. Difficult to fight her fascination with the way the muscles of his shoulders bunched then relaxed in time to his swings.

I'm watching him to make sure he's doing it

right, she told herself. But another tiny voice whispered, *Liar.*

Jack worked on with an easy strength that was almost graceful. And because he'd rolled up the sleeves of his shirt, Matty could see the tendons and sinews of his powerful, sun-bronzed arms and the suppleness of his body as he swung the mallet. But her pulse, already uncomfortably fast, raced even harder when just moments later the bottom edge of his shirt billowed up in the strong breeze and she had a brief glimpse of a long, pale mark across his lower back. A mark that looked like a ridge of healed tissue.

Like...a whip scar.

This time she almost reeled in shock. Why? *How?* Had he been flogged? Perhaps as punishment when he was in the army? But he was an officer—and officers weren't flogged, surely! Maybe he'd been in some kind of accident?

Stop it. You're letting your imagination run away with you. But Matty's mouth was still dry.

She forced herself into a semblance of calm and a moment later Jack lowered the mallet, then turned to her with a satisfied expression on his face. 'That wasn't a bad effort with the tiller, wouldn't you say, Captain Matty? For a greenling?'

His blue eyes were twinkling. But all Matty could say was, 'You've a good deal more to learn, so there's no need to look so pleased with yourself.' She went to test the tiller and nodded. 'That'll do. Now it's time to be on our way again.'

Chapter Thirteen

More locks, more tunnels, more stretches of woodland in between meadows dotted with grazing cattle and fields full of ripening wheat. The familiar scenery should have calmed Matty, but her mind was still in turmoil. She'd run a huge risk taking on this man with his unknown past, but the real trouble was that she would miss him if he left now. She would miss his merry laugh—miss even his teasing. Which was the most worrying thing of all.

When the sun was setting in a pearly grey and pink sky, Matty gave the order to stop. 'We're nearly at Kings Langley,' she told him. 'We'll spend the night here.'

'How do you know we're nearly at Kings Langley?' He was looking around, puzzled.

How best to explain? Every experienced canal traveller knew where they were on the waterways. You knew by the sweep of the canal and by the hills on the horizon. You knew by the angle of the sun and by the stars and moon at night. And here, there happened to be a good landmark. She replied, 'I know we're a mile from Kings Langley because of *that*.' She pointed to an old black-and-white timbered building on the edge of a hamlet full of thatched cottages. 'It's an inn—do you see it? They always make the canal folk welcome and they have stabling for Hercules, so I suggest we moor up and have an early night. We've made good progress today.'

Jack scanned the horizon as if reluctant to stop. 'How much farther do we have to go before we reach Aylesbury?'

'At this rate we should be there within a couple of days—if the weather stays fair. I'm doing no more night marches.'

He nodded. 'Very well. I'll take Hercules to the inn. Are we going to eat there?'

He looked hopeful, but Matty hesitated. 'I don't know. I've got some bread and cheese, as well as some apples...'

'Come on,' he coaxed her. 'Something hot will do you good, young Matty. Build up those muscles of yours. And it'll be my treat. Right?'

Oh, my. Jack Rutherford really did trouble her

sorely. That he was strong and capable was obvious; indeed, she would never have got this far without him. But he was such a distraction! She found herself overtaken by yet more unwanted thoughts as she watched him stroll off towards the village with Hercules. Somehow, the man had managed to have a most unwelcome impact on both her brain and her traitorous body.

Eating at the inn turned out to be not the best of ideas, either, because Jack attracted attention the minute they entered—chiefly from the landlady and her two daughters, who rushed to serve him.

Needless to say, they hardly gave Matty a single glance. Jack patted her on the shoulder as they ate their meal. 'Never mind, Captain Matty,' he said consolingly. 'Give yourself a year or so to grow a few inches and build some muscle, then you'll be fighting the girls off.'

She almost choked on her food and solicitously he patted her on the back. 'There now. Did that mouthful go down the wrong way? Drink up your cider. Although,' he went on as he handed her the glass and she gulped it down, 'you really ought to develop a taste for a more manly tipple. Ale, or whisky, even—now whisky's a proper

man's drink. Have you finished with your food?
Can't eat any more? Very well, then—shall I pay
the bill?'

Still speechless, she nodded and dabbed her
streaming eyes with her handkerchief while the
landlady dealt with Jack's payment. 'Thank you,
good sir,' Matty heard her saying. The woman
was actually blushing, for goodness' sake. 'Now,
we couldn't help but wonder,' she went on, 'are
you and your young companion on one of them
canal boats?'

'We are.' Jack smiled back at her. 'We travel
where we please, you know? There's nothing
better than waking up in the morning and hearing the sound of water lapping all around. You
look ahead and there's the canal stretching off
into the distance—and you never know what the
day will have in store. Wonderful! The world is
just waiting to be explored.'

'Well,' the landlady said. 'You *are* a poet,
aren't you? I love a bit of poetry, I do. So you're
fond of your boat, sir—but, you know, if you've
a fancy for a more comfortable berth tonight, I
can always find accommodation for you here.
And I've a fine home-brewed ale I keep for my
special guests...'

Matty didn't stay to hear the rest. She was

heading for the door by the time Jack bade farewell to the landlady and caught her up. 'Hey,' he was calling indignantly. 'Hey, Matty! Wait for me.'

She swung round to face him, her hands on her hips. 'Are you quite sure you don't want a—"a more comfortable berth", Jack?'

He laughed. 'No, thanks.' He leaned closer and lowered his voice. 'Any more of that ale of hers and I don't think I'd have a clear enough head for hammering in the tiller or turning a windlass. Or, come to think of it, for whatever other tasks you've got in store for me, Captain Matty.' He clapped her on the back in a friendly fashion. 'Besides, we're partners, aren't we? The boat's my home and that's where I'll sleep. Everywhere you go, I go.'

Which very words came back to her rather unnervingly, very soon.

Jack stepped on board the boat first and stood on the deck, yawning and stretching as the first stars peeped out of a darkening sky. And he thought to himself, *Now for a bit of mischief. Sorry, young Matty, but I'm afraid I just cannot resist it.*

'So, Captain,' he announced to her. 'We need

to start off at the crack of dawn, you say? As far as I'm concerned, it's been a long day, so I don't think I'll have the slightest trouble getting to sleep. Now I think I spotted a spare mattress rolled up in that cabin of yours below, so I suggest I spread it out next to your bed. I assume you'll have no problem with that?'

He noticed her colour heighten slightly. He knew it was really quite wicked of him, but she looked utterly delightful when she went pink.

'Well,' she said, 'well, I—' She thought for a minute, then said defiantly, 'I snore.'

'Listen, young Matty. In Spain we soldiers sometimes slept twelve to a tent, packed top to tail like sardines in a barrel. If snoring is the worst you get up to, I'll count myself extremely lucky, believe me. So let's just squash in together down there and, I assure you, I'll be asleep in no time. Like I said, it's been a long day. You go first.'

Oh, my. Matty's pulse was hammering as she glanced at the hatch leading down to the cabin. 'No,' she burst out. 'No. You mustn't...'

'Mustn't what?' He asked the question with complete innocence.

She swallowed on her rather dry throat. 'I've already warned you that I snore.'

'In that case I'll give you a poke in the ribs,' he offered. 'That'll soon cure you.'

'Don't you dare!' She braced herself. 'Anyway—there's worse than that.'

'Worse? Really?'

'I—I have nightmares!' she declared rather wildly. 'I walk in my sleep. Who knows, I might even lash out and hit you!'

'Now *that*,' he said solemnly, 'truly does sound terrifying.'

She stepped back a little. 'Terrifying?'

'Yes. And so, Captain, I surrender. I'll make myself comfortable up here on the deck.' He looked around. 'Fortunately it looks like being a fine night.'

She sat rather suddenly on one of the deck stools and heaved in a deep breath. 'Look, Jack. This whole trip was probably a very bad idea.' She shook her head. 'I was quite wrong to allow you to come with me. I should have travelled by myself.'

He pulled up a stool to sit opposite her before saying in a quiet voice, 'Now, let's both of us think for a minute, shall we? Have I let you down yet, young Matty?'

'No. No, you haven't. But...'

'Listen,' he went on in the same surprisingly

gentle voice. 'I've told you that I'm only too happy to help you and I mean it, since I've not exactly got a lot of pressing business at the moment. My shop was a dead loss, as you know—hardly surprising, as I haven't a clue about antiques. And as it happens, I'm actually rather enjoying this boating adventure. So why not try to explain yourself a bit more?'

He saw her flinch again. 'Explain what, exactly?'

'Explain to me,' he said, 'why this whole trip is so important to you.'

She hesitated. To her dismay, she was finding she liked Jack Rutherford more and more. She was having to admit that his jokes and his teasing lifted her spirits. Also—which was most ridiculous of all—she actually felt *safer* when he was around.

Safer? Oh, Matty. With a man like him?

'I'm waiting,' he prompted quietly. 'But take your time.'

'I want,' she began, 'more than anything, to find the Roman site I spoke of near Aylesbury. Not for the money, Jack, but for my father's sake. Do you understand?'

'I do.'

'I want to find out everything I can about the

settlement he believed existed there,' she went on, 'and tell my father's colleagues about it, so they can continue the work that he would have done.' She looked straight at Jack. 'As my father lay dying, I promised him I would do this.'

She fought down the sudden stab of heartache that came with those dark memories. Jack was silent a moment before he said, 'And I imagine you're the kind of person who always keeps your promises.'

'I like to think so. And I hope that you keep your promises, too.' She lifted her eyes to his in direct challenge. 'Do you?'

'I do,' he said gravely.

She looked at him a little longer then said, 'Very well. But we'd better be up early tomorrow, since we need to leave by six.'

He grinned suddenly. 'Aye aye, Captain Matty. And, as I said, I'm happy to sleep on deck.' He was already looking around the boat. 'I see you've a sheet of tarpaulin over there. I was thinking that I could rope it up between the cabin roof and the stern rail, so it will give me shelter if it rains. And I'll take that spare mattress from below, if that's all right with you.'

Though she'd hesitated at first, he now saw her

give an almost inaudible sigh of relief. 'Yes,' she said. 'Yes, what an excellent idea. But—'

'No "buts". From what you told me, anything's better than the sound of your snoring and your nightmares.'

She looked a little embarrassed. 'At least it's a warm night.'

'You think I care if it's hot or cold? Listen,' Jack declared, 'I've camped on mountainsides in Spain where the snow was eight inches deep!'

'Boasting again,' she said lightly and he realised how glad he was to see that familiar gleam of amusement in her eyes. 'Next you'll be telling me you fought off mountain wolves single-handed.'

'Well,' he said, 'as a matter of fact...'

'Enough!' She held up her hands now and she was almost—*almost* laughing. 'I know you and I declared a truce. But I warn you, I could change my mind.'

He hung his head, feigning penitence. 'Aye aye, Captain.'

'I can do without the "Captain" bit, as well,' she replied crisply. 'Will you bring up the mattress, or shall I?'

'I'll get it. And perhaps you can spare me a blanket or two?'

It didn't take him long to get everything neatly rigged. After Matty had brought up the mattress she glanced at the tarpaulin awning, hesitated a moment, then said, 'Right. I'll leave you to it. Goodnight—Jack.'

'Goodnight, young Matty. Sleep well.'

Jack began softly whistling to himself as he spread out the mattress. But he stopped once she'd gone down the wooden steps to her cabin again and he thought, She was young—but by God, she was brave. All in all, he reckoned she had twice the courage of many of the men he'd fought alongside in battle.

He made a few adjustments to the tarpaulin shelter, then pulled off his boots and settled down on the mattress, his hands clasped behind his head.

Yes, he admired Matty. And he felt she was beginning to have a grudging respect for him, though he guessed she'd be very angry indeed once she realised he'd known all along that she was a woman. He'd already noted the way she stared at him almost in disbelief whenever he pushed her too far with the 'Captain Matty' business. Surely soon she would challenge him outright—and then she would be absolutely furious with him for his deception!

But not quite as mad as she would be if she knew his other secret. If she ever found out that he'd only teamed up with her because she was heading for his home.

Jack wanted Charlwood back for good. That was his one and only goal in life. Without a doubt, he could have made the journey to Charlwood more quickly and more easily some other way. Indeed, canal travel was trickier than he'd thought—he could still feel that bruise on his ribs where the tiller had whacked him that first night. But if he'd travelled by road, he reckoned he might well have had Fitz's men to contend with. Fitz wanted Jack ruined and the trickery with the bracelet was probably just the start. It was quite likely he might have paid men to watch the toll roads and posting houses to see if Jack passed through—but surely Fitz would never, ever think of looking on the canals.

And of course there was that other, even more important reason why Jack had decided to travel with Matty.

She had been inside Charlwood itself. She had glimpsed evidence that two years ago Fitz had been composing the fake ransom letter there, to force Jack's mother into marriage. If—and it was a big 'if'—the document was still lying forgotten somewhere in Charlwood's library, Jack might have exactly what he needed to confront Fitz directly and force the man to confess his vicious scheming.

Jack turned again on the mattress. Normally he fell asleep almost immediately—it was a soldier's gift, they said, to grab sleep where you could, because you never knew when or if you'd get the chance again. But he kept being disturbed by tantalising thoughts of Matty. Wondering if maybe she was wearing that flimsy little nightshirt he'd glimpsed folded neatly by her pillow...

She'd told him she sleepwalked. With just a bit of luck, she might sleepwalk up here and snuggle up next to him under the blanket. He grinned to himself. He wouldn't mind if she snored, he really wouldn't.

His arousal disturbed him. He fought down his surging thoughts. *Hands off her, right?*

And, sighing only a little, Jack fell asleep at last.

Matty had indeed put on her nightshirt and climbed into her narrow bed down below, but she kept the lamp burning for quite a while and listened to Jack Rutherford tramping about overhead, tripping on a rope and cursing under his breath. All was quiet now, which meant that hopefully he was asleep—but awake or asleep, he worried her more and more. Because she still couldn't understand why he'd been so eager to come along with her.

Perhaps he needed to get out of London in a hurry because of debts, or maybe some of his fake antiques had landed him in hot water. Nothing about him would surprise her, yet she had blindly put her trust in him.

Oh, Matty. You fool.

And she was a fool in more ways than one, because whenever Jack Rutherford merely raised his eyebrows at her in that teasing way of his, she felt her common sense vanishing into thin air.

She'd always been caught between two worlds—she knew that. She didn't truly fit into the lives of the canal folk, or the genteel society of the Oxford scholars her father had once known. So far it hadn't mattered in the slightest, because marriage was the last thing on her mind—indeed, men in general were the last thing on her mind. She shivered a little as the dark memories she thought she'd swept aside threatened to resurface.

But there was something about Jack Rutherford that unsettled her badly. And it wasn't just that he was handsome, it wasn't just the way he teased her. Strangely enough, she felt there was something vulnerable about him—indeed, sometimes those merry blue eyes of his looked almost haunted, as if he, too, was remembering things he'd much prefer to forget.

Something inside her was hurting a little, for *him*. Slowly she rose from her bed to extinguish the lamp, telling herself she was being completely ridiculous—he wouldn't want her sympathy, and most certainly he wouldn't want anything else from her.

Suddenly she found herself recalling that woman—Vanessa—who'd been at his side at the London auction. Now, *she* was much more his type—beautiful, worldly, sophisticated. Matty was the very last kind of female Jack would be attracted to. And anyway, how could he even feel any liking for her, when all she had done—most of the time anyway—was to order him around?

'Aye aye, Captain,' he liked to say with a grin.

At least she offered him some amusement, she thought rather tightly to herself. And in return, he was helping her to fulfil her promise to her father.

'I'm so sorry I let you down, Papa,' she whispered. 'I'm sorry I was so weak. So stupid.'

Forcing back the bitter self-rebuke, she climbed back into her bed and tried to concentrate on sleep, for she had a long day ahead of her tomorrow. But still she lay awake—chiefly because she was all too aware of that scoundrel of a man on the deck above. She was pretty sure that *he* wouldn't be having any difficulty at all in slumbering soundly. Muttering under her breath, Matty pulled the blanket over her head and slipped at last into restless dreams.

Chapter Fourteen

The next morning Jack woke with a start and wondered where on earth he was. In an army tent? There was a tarpaulin sheet stretched out a few feet above him, which really did remind him of the old campaign days—but why were there ducks quacking nearby, for God's sake?

Gradually the fog began to clear from his brain. Of course. The canal. *The Wild Rose*—and young Matty, who was no doubt still sleeping rather sweetly below deck in her cabin.

He fumbled for his boots, then looked at his watch and saw it was already six o'clock. Realised, too, as he gazed around, that Matty was by no means asleep but was on the bank, immediately recognisable in her long coat and that big-brimmed hat.

Beside her stood Hercules. So she'd already fetched him from the inn's stables, he thought rather guiltily. Quickly he began taking down the tarpaulin and folding it up, then he pulled on his waistcoat, by which time he could see that Matty was trying to ease on Hercules's harness, but the old fellow was showing his stubborn streak.

Jack, nodding a silent thanks to the ducks who'd woken him, paid a quick visit to the food locker, then hopped nimbly over the stern rail on to the bank.

She had her back to him. She looked diminutive next to that enormous horse. 'Hercules,' he heard her saying, 'come along, *please*. I'm only trying to put your harness on, you awkward, awkward beast!'

Jack arrived to stand next to her. 'Let me put it on him,' he offered. She didn't look thrilled, but she stood aside, her lips pressed together.

He smiled at her, then turned to Hercules and held out his right hand palm upward. In it was an apple and Hercules perked up instantly. 'Bribery and corruption,' Jack said to Matty. 'You know, there's really nothing like it.'

He could have sworn that she sniffed a little as she thrust the harness towards him. 'In that case, you'd better see to Hercules while I get us into the queue.'

'What queue?'

She pointed along the canal and for the first time he saw the line of stationary boats. 'There's often a wait here,' she told him, 'to use the lock. But with luck everything will get moving soon. So be as quick as you can, won't you?'

Without waiting for his answer she went to step on board *The Wild Rose*, took up a heavy wooden pole and used it to manoeuvre her boat towards the line of barges.

That was some weight she was shifting, thought Jack with admiration. He looked again at the queue waiting for the lock and shook his head in wonder as he realised they must all have arrived overnight. Matty was right in saying that unless she joined the line soon, they might be held up here for quite some time.

For a moment longer he stood admiring the way she so skilfully guided her big boat. Despite her diminutive size, she was a female to be reckoned with—and also a female who might actually be rather delicious to kiss, *if* you didn't mind getting a slapped face into the bargain. He suspected that kiss might just be worth it.

It was amazing how he'd let this slip of a girl—a girl who could be as awkward as hell and who he moreover suspected of heartily disliking him—get right under his skin. While he watched her, he had almost a sense of regret, as if they shouldn't be sparring and arguing and lying to one another; because he kept being plagued by the oddest sensation that she was somehow *meant* to be at his side. He wanted to hold her and remind her that she wasn't alone, wanted to lend her his physical strength so that she would feel stronger herself...

Be honest, Jack. He wanted her in his arms. He wanted her in his bed. Which was crazy of him. He was a loner and always had been; he'd kept his feelings to himself ever since his father died. He'd vowed then to be a soldier—and even when all that went wrong, with his career and his home both lost, he'd ploughed on alone.

Yes, alone—but this girl touched him in a way no one else ever had. She was so damned brave. So lovely, too, especially when she let down her guard and he saw the clear translucence of her green eyes and those fascinating dimples that only appeared when she smiled...

He wanted to kiss those dimples. He wanted to take her luscious little waist in his hands and kiss *all* of her. Which was beyond despicable, since he was using her, pure and simple—and for God's sake, there was no need to make his crime even worse by damned well trying to *seduce* her!

Shaking his head at himself, he turned back to Hercules and started buckling on the fiddly leather straps. A few minutes later, though, he heard raised voices. With his old army instincts kicking in at any hint of trouble, he swung round to see that a bulky coal barge was heading up the canal, overtaking all the others that waited correctly in line. And right now the barge's owner was nosing its bow into the slight gap just ahead of *The Wild Rose*.

Matty had been busy coiling the ropes on her deck, but now looked up. 'Hey,' she called to the bargeman. 'What do you think you're doing? You're right in my way!'

The bargeman leaned on his long pole and stared back insolently. 'Wrong, laddie,' he said. 'As it happens, it's you who's in my way.'

Right, thought Jack. After ensuring that Hercules was securely tethered to a post, Jack patted the horse's nose. 'Now, you behave yourself while I'm away, old fellow,' he murmured, then strolled towards the canal bank.

Matty was still squared up to the bargeman and Jack was just in time to hear her say, 'You should learn the rules of the waterways. There's a queue here, in case you hadn't noticed.'

Jack heard the man laugh. 'Rules, eh? How old are you, you young imp? I'll teach you a rule or two if you're not careful—with the back of my hand. Now, get your boat out of my way, will you? Or I might just do you some damage!'

By now the man's wife, who was nearly as burly as he was, had appeared at the door of their cabin to yell encouragement. 'Aye, go on then, our Bert! Teach the young rogue a lesson, why don't you?'

It was then that Jack arrived, stepping nimbly on board *The Wild Rose* to face Matty's antagonists with a sardonic smile curling his lips. Bert looked taken aback.

'So, Bert,' said Jack. 'You'd like to teach my young friend here a lesson, would you? You and whose army, might I ask?'

Of course, Matty had known Jack was somewhere nearby. But she'd spoken to him so sharply just now that she wouldn't have blamed him in the slightest if he'd decided to wander off to the alehouse in search of more rewarding company.

But he'd come to her rescue. And Bert still looked a little shaken—though he recovered swiftly, puffing out his chest and saying to Jack, 'Clear off, will you? And learn to mind your own damned business.' With that he continued once more to edge his boat into the gap ahead of *The Wild Rose*, colliding slightly with Matty's boat as he did so and bringing his bow to within a foot of the canal bank.

Jack walked closer. 'Now, Bert, I suggest you listen to me carefully.' This time there was a hard edge to his voice. 'You move your barge out of our way—right?—and there'll be no more trouble. I also suggest you head straight back *there*—' he pointed back along the canal '—to take your proper place at the end of the queue. Where you can wait your turn, like everyone else.'

'My, haven't you a fancy way of talking?' jeered the man. He folded his big arms. 'What's the likes of you doing on the canal, Mr High-and-Mighty? Went to Eton, did you?'

'As a matter of fact—yes, I did,' said Jack.

Matty gasped. He was at *Eton*?

'I learned a little boxing there, too,' Jack added helpfully.

By now people had gathered to watch from the canal bank and Bert hesitated, clearly weighing up Jack's comment about boxing. But then his wife nudged him. 'Go on, our Bert. Show that young cockerel what you're made of.'

Bert nodded. 'Come on then, mate. Let's see how much that fancy school of yours taught you. Let's see what you can do.'

'Very well.' And before Matty could even blink, Jack had sprung lightly on to the deck of Bert's barge and hit him hard on the chin. Bert reeled, but after staggering around for a moment or two he recovered his balance and began waving his fists in Jack's direction, his pudgy face mottled with anger. 'You young—'

'Oh, Bert,' Jack taunted, patting the man's fists aside one after the other. 'Do make an effort, please. I'd really like to know whether there's any muscle underneath all that flab of yours. You've certainly got a big mouth, I'll grant you that. And so has your wife—'

The man bellowed and charged towards him but, with what appeared to be scarcely any exertion whatsoever, Jack stepped aside, grasped Bert by the waist and tipped him overboard straight into the water. As he splashed and struggled, his wife charged up to Jack. 'Hey. You can't do that!'

Jack shook his finger at her. 'Oh, but I can,

madam. Rules of the waterways, I believe. Your boat was interfering with our right of way.'

Matty called out, 'Right of *passage*, Jack.'

'Exactly. As my young colleague here says, your boat was interfering with our right of passage. And it still is, as a matter of fact.' Jack stepped on board *The Wild Rose* and said quietly to Matty, 'Hand me your barge pole, will you?'

Bert, gasping and spluttering, was being helped out of the water by a couple of rather reluctant onlookers. Jack meanwhile was using Matty's pole to shove Bert's barge out into the main channel again.

Jack gave Bert's wife a cheery wave as her boat drifted away. She and her husband would indeed have to retreat down the canal the way they'd come—to the back of the queue. The watching crowd applauded. Nobody liked boatmen who broke the rules of the waterways.

Matty gazed steadily at Jack as he laid down the pole. 'I suppose you're expecting me to congratulate you, as well?'

'No congratulations are due. I'm merely fulfilling my duties as your number one assistant— Captain Matty.' He grinned.

She regarded him coolly. 'So you went to Eton, did you? Then on to university, I presume?'

He hesitated. 'That's about right, Captain Matty. Oxford, in fact.'

She felt as if the boat was rocking under her. 'So when I described Oxford, you knew it better than me already?'

He sighed regretfully, but that smile of his was still lurking. 'I'm afraid I did.'

'Don't you think it would have been better—indeed, *kinder*—to tell me so?'

'I'm sorry.' He scratched his head. 'But of course I'd observed the town from a rather different angle from yours. I'm afraid, you see, that I wasn't exactly a model student.'

'I can imagine,' she said tightly.

He leaned closer. 'Oh, Captain Matty. I really do hope you can't imagine *everything* I got up to.'

Matty found herself backing away, even more unsteady. 'They've started to open up the lock,' she told him curtly. 'It's time to get ready to go through.'

'Aye aye.' And he left the boat to return to Hercules, while Matty just stood there. Eton and Oxford! So what on earth was he playing at, travelling like this, with her?

She experienced a fresh pang of unease—not least because of the way she'd felt when Jack, like some hero of old, had faced up to Bert and slung him in the water. She'd felt all warm inside, in a good sort of way.

Imagine what it would be like to have him at your side for more than a day or two. As a companion. A friend. Perhaps even more...

Ridiculous, Matty! She crushed the thought as swiftly as it had come. Her strength lay in her independence—and that was how it must continue.

The trouble was, there was something else that worried her exceedingly. If she could just see Jack as a useful and temporary travelling companion, that was fine. But there was more—and she was reminded of that *'more'* in a thousand tiny ways, like when he leaned towards her and said something in that intimate, teasing way of his. Sometimes he touched her, too—she knew it was in fun, in friendship, but she felt it everywhere. She felt it like the most intimate of caresses, from her tingling lips down to her most private place.

Somehow he'd changed her. She, who'd been blindly certain she had no room in her life for men. Everything had changed since Jack Rutherford's sudden arrival in her life.

And she hadn't the slightest notion what to do about it.

* * *

The lock was open now and the line of boats was beginning to move. Before long they'd passed through the gates and were on their way again, this time coming upon no more unexpected hindrances. Jack walked ahead of *The Wild Rose* with Hercules, whistling softly as usual with his hat tipped to the back of his head, but he seemed, she thought, rather quiet. And even when they stopped for lunch after tying up the boat beside a grassy meadow, Jack said very little. After consuming a hearty portion from their store of bread and cheese, he was preparing to sprawl out in the sun and have a doze when Matty said coolly, 'I'm afraid there's no time for that.' She rose to her feet and began picking up the remains of their meal. 'We need to be on our way again.'

He sat up immediately. 'Very well, Captain Matty. As ever, I'm at your beck and call. What's next on our agenda?'

Matty was brushing loose grass from her breeches. 'We're approaching the longest tunnel on our route and it's another place Hercules hates. The water tends to drip from the roof on to his head and sometimes there are bats that frighten him.'

Jack nodded. 'Would I be better leading him round the outside of the tunnel like last time?'

'I don't think so. The towpath inside is good, so he'll manage all right, but you'll have to hold him firmly. You'll have to talk to him and soothe him.'

'Soothe him, eh?' He grinned. 'I reckon I can manage that.' Then he hesitated. 'Matty...'

'Yes?' She'd already started to walk back to the canal, so he had to increase his stride to catch her up.

'Matty,' he said, 'I'm grateful to you for giving me this chance. For trusting me. This is a journey I'll not forget.'

She felt something rush through her, some intense emotion she couldn't define, but she merely shrugged. 'Believe me,' she said, 'I won't forget this journey in a hurry, either.' As they reached the boat, she pointed to the mooring post where Jack had fastened one of the ropes. 'For heaven's sake, Jack. You've tied that rope with the wrong knot—it should be a round turn and two half-hitches. Didn't I tell you? Didn't you listen?'

'You did tell me,' he said humbly. 'I'm sorry.'

But Matty saw the merriment in his blue eyes as he went off to retie the rope.

* * *

Matty guessed they were covering a good three miles an hour. The weather stayed fair, but always they faced fresh challenges. There were more locks for a start, each one presenting a different problem. She knew that if you tied up your boat too tightly, the vessel could capsize—she'd seen it happen. She did wonder if Jack might start to take offence as she spelled everything out; but he seemed to take all her instructions in his stride, giving that mock salute of his that should have irritated her madly, but instead prompted a kind of melting of her insides.

This is ridiculous, Matty. He's secretly laughing at you. No doubt he's saving up dozens of stories about this journey to chuckle over with his friends when all this is over. You must keep your distance...

Not easy on a boat, where they were of necessity almost side by side for much of the time. After they'd passed through yet another lock, he asked her if she would let him use the tiller and as he took hold of it, he was clearly concentrating hard on her instructions. But she found concentration more difficult, because even if she avoided looking straight into his eyes, she was distracted by his firm mouth and the shadow of stubble on his chin, even by the steady pulse she could detect just at the base of his throat. And she found herself possessed by the wildest imaginings.

What would it be like to put my hand on that pulse and feel it beating? What would he do?

He would look at her in the utmost astonishment most likely, then burst out laughing. But her treacherous body hoped for something different. Fight it as she might, she was starting to feel too vulnerable whenever he was near—her temperature was rising in all her most sensitive places. And she could not afford this ridiculous weakness.

She could easily guess he would see it as an excellent joke. Very well, let him laugh—soon they would be within reach of Aylesbury and she could dispense with his services, after which he was welcome to continue with his own plans, whatever they might be!

Most of the time Jack walked with Hercules and she encouraged it. *The farther away the better*, she told herself firmly. Thankfully, both the canal and its idyllic surroundings were having their usual calming effect on Matty, but every so often she found her wayward eyes straying to his figure up ahead. And each time, she was unable to stop herself feeling that funny little flip in her stomach again. There was something so free and easy about him as he strode along the towpath, singing in his clear, tuneful voice.

Tom, he was a piper's son,
He learned to play when he was young;
But the only tune that he could play
Was over the hills and far away.

He was highly educated. He'd been an officer in the British army, had been admired by his men. What on earth had happened to his life? In her experience, men who'd been soldiers never stopped boasting about their glory days, but Jack was the exact opposite.

Surely he'd not been upset by the bloodshed and the harshness of the campaigns? Far from it, to judge by his willingness for a fight. Maybe— and this, she feared, was much more likely—it was because he'd got himself into trouble. Bad trouble, if indeed he'd been flogged. Maybe he'd been convicted of theft, or desertion, or worse.

She felt utterly confused by the image he presented of carelessness and frivolity. She knew anyone with any sense would be extremely careful of Jack Rutherford—and yet she was trusting him? With her boat, her horse and herself? 'But I have to,' she kept muttering under her breath. 'For my father. I promised him that I would find his treasure field.'

And she had to keep that promise. Because it was her fault that her father had died.

It was just then that Jack's cheery voice rang out. 'I see another lock ahead, Captain Matty!'

She clasped the tiller and looked to where he was pointing. 'It's Gatesby Gap. This one's un-manned. Right, Jack, you know what to do, don't you?'

'I'm learning,' he called back. 'Oh, I'm learning.'

In fact Jack felt oddly light-hearted. He knew the feeling couldn't last—no chance of that—but for the moment all that seemed to matter was the slow, steady rhythm of Hercules's hooves plodding along the towpath and the smooth expanse of the canal ahead. Indeed, the peace of the waterway was disturbed by nothing more threatening than the occasional bobbing of a black-and-white dipper or the jewel-like flash of a kingfisher darting by.

Whenever they came to a lock or a tunnel, Matty called fresh instructions—and he never ceased to be amazed by her competence. She knew what to do just as thoroughly as any of the older canal folk; indeed, sometimes he found himself forgetting just how young she was.

But he never forgot she was a woman.

She certainly fooled everyone else they met on their way, with her loose clothes that disguised her slender frame and her hat pulled firmly over her cropped chestnut hair. She used a curt, almost gruff voice whenever she spoke to the innkeepers or the gatemen at the locks. She walked everywhere with confidence and stood on the deck of her beloved boat with her booted legs apart, her hand on the tiller and her chin tilted in defiance.

No doubt she'd acted that way for so long that she didn't even think about it any more. But her masculine garb did very little, in Jack's opinion, to diminish her female charms. In fact, to him her attempt at disguise somehow made her all the more appealing, because he couldn't help but notice even more strongly the things that made her so deliciously feminine.

Her small but full mouth. Her amazingly long lashes. Those tiny freckles scattered across the bridge of her delicately upturned nose…

Stop it, you wretch. Mentally he chided himself. He knew full well she hadn't wanted to bring him with her on her boat. The trouble was, he suspected that she was reluctantly starting to *trust* him.

So how was she going to feel if she ever discovered his own secret motives for undertaking this journey?

Of course, his intention was that she wouldn't find out. But she was far from stupid and it wasn't beyond the realms of possibility that his plotting might be exposed; in which case, her slowly growing belief in him would be shattered.

Did it really matter? Tiredly, he rubbed his hand through his hair while gazing ahead at the approaching lock. *Yes.* It did matter to him. But what else could he do? It was absolutely essential for him to get into Charlwood to see if Fitz's draft ransom letter was still there—because it might represent his only hope of regaining his lost home.

Chapter Fifteen

That afternoon another strap on Hercules's harness broke, which meant they had to come to an early halt miles from any habitation. 'To be quite honest, I should have had a completely new harness made up,' Matty told Jack. She looked worried. 'In the meantime we need a saddler to mend it—but we're a long way from any that I know of.'

Jack knew by now that the ever-efficient Matty had the names of good tradesmen pencilled in on her map, which they now studied together. And she was quite right. There wasn't a saddler until the next lock four miles away.

'I'll walk there,' Jack said decisively. 'Along the towpath. Will you be all right on your own, Matty?'

'Of course I will! But it will take you some time…'

'Maybe two to three hours there and back. I'll just fetch some cash from my locker in the cabin.'

'No! I will pay!'

'You won't. I insist on paying—and don't argue, because the sooner I get started, the sooner I'll return. Agreed?'

'Very well,' she answered slowly. 'You'd best be on your way.'

Jack fetched money from his locker and that small pistol, too. He slipped it into a pocket inside his loose-fitting waistcoat, slung the harness over his shoulder and set off along the towpath. He didn't like leaving Matty on her own, especially since he felt that uncanny warning of danger he used to feel before the start of battle—or when Fitz was around, for that matter. Nevertheless he made swift progress and reached the next lock in just over an hour. It was a busy spot, with an alehouse where men were drinking outside, and when he asked a passer-by the way to the saddler's several of the men turned to stare at him.

Again he felt the prickle of danger, though the man he'd asked about the saddler's seemed good-hearted enough as he glanced at the harness Jack carried. 'You and your horse come to grief somewhere, have you?'

'You could say that,' Jack answered. 'I was out in my gig for a drive. But my horse tripped on a rabbit hole—and next thing I knew, this piece of harness had snapped.'

The man peered closer at Jack. 'I'm thinking you're not from round here.'

'I'm visiting,' Jack said quickly. 'Staying with friends.'

The man nodded, pointing along the street. 'You'll find a saddler who'll fix your harness over there. Just past the church.'

'My thanks.' Jack set off again, raising his hand in acknowledgement.

He felt a strong sense of relief when the saddler told him he'd be able to get the job done swiftly. He'd noticed at the alehouse that they served food and was briefly tempted, but something was telling him he ought to be out of here and heading back to Matty. As soon as the saddler had neatly tied up the repaired harness with a piece of rope, Jack paid him and slung it over his shoulder. Then he set off again.

After a mile or so of open fields there was a stretch of woodland which grew close up to the towpath, engulfing it in shade. Jack quickened his pace, because he'd thought he'd heard something. Some*one*. Maybe more than one...

He carried on walking, but his every sense was fine-tuned now, his every muscle taut. Within moments there were footsteps pounding up behind him and he swung round to see two men charging straight for him. Without a moment's hesitation he hurled the heavy bundle of harness at the first, knocking him backwards, then felled the second man with a punch to the gut.

Two of them. If that's all, I can manage this...

The first man was after him again, but Jack grappled with him and this time succeeded in throwing the villain to the ground. But then he felt a sudden, sharp pain in the back of his upper arm and, springing round, he saw the second man holding a knife that was stained with blood. Jack's blood.

Jack leapt on him, grasping for the wrist that held the knife and twisting it until the man dropped his weapon and sank groaning to his knees.

I've probably broken several of his wrist bones, Jack thought grimly. *Serve the bastard right.*

He kicked the knife away and this time pulled out his pistol—wished he'd had it in his hand at the start, damn it. At the sight of the gun, both men cowered on the ground, pleading, 'Don't shoot. Please don't shoot!'

His right arm, the one that had been stabbed, was still usable, thank God, but it was starting to hurt. 'Go and sit with your backs to that tree,' Jack growled to his attackers. He gestured with his gun. 'You can do your snivelling next to each other. And then you can tell me who sent you after me. Quickly. I've not got all day.'

'It was a rich gent who gave us our orders,' the first one babbled in fear. 'Don't know his name. He must have been fifty or so—had light-coloured hair and fine clothes and a fancy way of speaking. Kept taking snuff as he talked. Treated us like we smelled bad.'

Fitz. Just as Jack had thought. He gritted his teeth. 'Go on. Tell me the rest.'

'He knew you were making your way along the canal—someone told him, he said. Someone he talked to by Paddington Wharf…'

Damn, thought Jack ferociously. He'd already guessed that Fitz might not be satisfied merely by Jack's departure from London. But Jack had thought he was safe on the canal and he didn't think Matty's friends would blab to strangers about her new travelling companion.

Unfortunately, though, there were plenty

of other people who had seen him around the wharf—the folk who'd served food and ale at the canalside wedding party, for instance, and the Irish labourers. All Fitz probably needed to do was to flash a few coins around.

Oh, yes, someone would say. *You're looking for a dark-haired young fellow who used to be a soldier? He's set off north on a canal boat, of all things!*

Jack gazed at the two miserable specimens of manhood huddled on the ground by the tree. 'So you two were paid to watch for me. Is there anyone else on my trail?' They glanced at one another and Jack pointed his pistol anew. 'Want a little encouragement?' he added softly.

'No. Wait!' the first man pleaded. 'You're right—we're not the only ones looking for you. That man in the fancy clothes, he knew you were on the canal, but he didn't know how far you'd got. So he's set a couple of men at every lock north of here and offered a reward for anyone bringing you to him. Seems to want to find out what you're up to... Don't kill us! Please, we beg you, don't kill us!'

'You know, I'd really quite like to. But you talked about a reward. How much is this man offering for my capture?'

'Ten guineas, mister.'

Jack cursed under his breath again. Still pointing his pistol, he used his other hand to free the rope that wrapped the harness, then tossed it to the man who'd done the talking.

'Use one end to tie your friend by the wrists,' he ordered. 'Don't either of you move away from that tree, or I'll shoot. Understand?'

The man did exactly as he bade and Jack moved closer, picking up the other end of the rope so he could tie it round the second man's wrists before using the last of the rope to lash both men to the tree trunk. Finally he stood back in some satisfaction.

'If you're lucky,' he said, putting his pistol away, 'someone might pass by and free you. If you're not lucky, you could be spending the night here together. I wish you sweet dreams.'

And he was off. *Back to the canal. Back to Matty.* His arm was bleeding and his mind was whirling. So Fitz, damn him, wasn't content to have driven Jack out of London. Clearly he was regretting not having instantly had Jack clapped in gaol on that trumped-up charge of theft.

It wasn't long before Jack came upon a stream beneath some beech trees, where he stopped to strip off his waistcoat and shirt to wash the blood from the sleeve. His wound wasn't deep, so after tearing a strip from the lower edge of the shirt he bound it around his arm, squeezed as much water out of his shirt as he could and put his clothes back on again. After that, he picked up the harness and set off once more.

Fitz was on his trail, damn it. Most likely because he had guessed Jack was planning some kind of counter-attack—but Fitz surely couldn't know what Matty had glimpsed in Charlwood's library all of two years ago?

It was still essential for Jack to get to Charlwood. But maybe it was time for a fresh plan.

Matty had been keeping herself as busy as possible. After grooming Hercules, she'd cleaned the already spotless cabin, then scrubbed the deck for the fourth time in two days. After that, she couldn't think of a single other thing to do—but she had to find something, to stop her growing more and more anxious about Jack.

He should have been back by now. But what if he didn't return? What if he'd decided he'd had enough of this so-called adventure and had taken the opportunity to disappear? Here she was, miles from anywhere—and he'd vanished, along with Hercules's harness! Soon she would have to admit that he had left her in the lurch—and then she would need to swallow her stupid pride and ask the next passing barge for help.

She felt quite ill at the thought, though it wasn't her fear of being alone—she was used to that. It was because if he didn't return, she would feel she'd made one of the stupidest mistakes in her life.

For she'd actually begun to think she could trust him.

The mischievous, maddening man—she'd begun to believe he was on her side. That maybe he even *liked* her. Probably it was just as well he'd disappeared, she thought bitterly. Before she made even more of a fool of herself, one way or another.

And then—when she was about to give up—Jack appeared at last, emerging from the thicket of woods alongside the canal. Such were her emotions on seeing him, relief mingled with anger at his lateness, that her voice was unnaturally tight as she greeted him. 'You took your time—' she started to say, but then broke off.

He had the harness over one shoulder and he saluted her in his usual nonchalant manner, but by then she'd realised that much of his shirt—at least what she could see of it under his leather waistcoat—was wet through. She caught her breath. 'What on earth has happened to you? Surely you didn't fall in the canal?'

He'd stepped carefully on board. 'It was hot, young Matty,' he answered. 'So I decided to take a swim.'

Suddenly Matty's pent-up emotions over-whelmed her. She'd been so *worried*! 'Fine!' she declared. 'A swim! Another time, though, just let me know, will you, if you're going to indulge in a spot of leisure? Didn't you even *think* of me waiting here? Worrying about you?'

His face remained surprisingly expressionless, which made her all the more angry. 'I'm sorry,' he said at last. 'Actually, I met with a slight delay. But I got your harness mended. Here it is.' He laid it carefully on the deck then looked at her steadily. 'And at this point, young Matty, it really is time for me to say…' He hesitated.

Matty clamped her fists to her hips. 'To say what?'

'That it's best if, from now on, you continue your journey without me.'

Matty let her hands fall back to her sides. She felt slightly faint, as if the air had suddenly been punched from her lungs. She said at last, 'Would you care to repeat that?'

His burning blue eyes never left her. 'I've decided you and I ought to part company.' He shrugged a little. 'It's rather slow going, this canal business, isn't it? I've got places to reach. People to see. I'll hire myself a horse and continue my journey by road.'

Each word hit her like a hammer blow, yet still she didn't let her voice rise—she felt proud of that. 'I thought that we shook hands on our bargain,' she replied at last. 'And I certainly didn't realise that the bargain included you accompanying me only part of the way, then running off and leaving me in the middle of nowhere.'

Suddenly he looked weary. 'I'm sorry, truly I am—but in fairness, you did tell me that most of the time you can manage Hercules and the boat perfectly well on your own. And you also explained that you could get plenty of help if you needed it—'

'Stop.' She stepped closer. '*Stop*. Just tell me. Why did you take so long getting the harness fixed? Why is your shirt wet through? Surely you took it off before you went for your swim? What exactly has happened to make you break your promise to me?'

He hesitated a little too long. 'As a matter of fact, I got caught up in a bit of an argument.'

'And that's scared you, has it?' Her disappointment made her scornful. 'I've seen you hold your own against a dozen men without an ounce of fear, and yet now you're running away because of a—a minor *brawl*? Please, have the decency to at least tell me the truth. Somebody's after you, aren't they? And now you've been spotted—so you've decided to abandon me. Thanks a lot, Jack.'

'Look, Matty. I'm truly sorry—'

She cut him off impatiently. 'Do you think your enemies will have tracked you here, to my boat?'

A faint hesitation. Then a half-smile, which she didn't understand. 'No,' he said. 'No, I guess they'll be out of action for a while at least.'

'But there might be more men waiting for you ahead?'

'It's quite possible, yes.'

'Will these men be looking for me, as well?'

He shook his head firmly. 'It's me they're after, not you. As I keep telling you, you'll be fine— just as long as you travel on without me.'

She was breathing rather fast. 'Very well, then. Go and pack your things. I shall stop here for the night.' And try to plan what on *earth* she would do next. How could she possibly manage the rest of the journey on her own? Because despite what she'd said to him, it was going to be more than difficult.

He turned towards the steps down into the cabin, then hesitated. 'Is there anything I can help you with before I go? It looks as though it's going to rain. Do you want that tarpaulin rigging up again?'

Indeed, dark clouds were gathering fast and the first drops were beginning to fall. Matty shook her head decisively. 'I don't want you to do anything except leave. Because the sooner you're gone, Jack Rutherford, the sooner I can stop wasting my time on you.'

He nodded and went below.

Matty stared into the rain and gathering darkness. What a fool she'd been to trust him. She felt shaky, but there were jobs to be done, so, after turning up her coat collar against the rain, she stepped on to the bank to check that the two mooring stakes she'd earlier hammered into the ground were secure enough to hold the boat's ropes for the night. Then she went to see to Hercules, who stood patiently waiting for her. As for tomorrow...

She glanced back at the *The Wild Rose*, but

there was no sign at all of Jack. If he was hoping
to loiter in the cabin for an hour or so to shelter
from the rain, she'd soon inform him otherwise.
Hadn't she guessed from the start he was trouble? Yes—but that had given way to something
else, something she didn't like to dwell on. In
fact, she still felt the most enormous and surprising surge of betrayal that he'd let her down; besides which she felt fear, that her usually sound
judgement had been so very, very wrong.

She looked around, observing that close by
the canal was a barn—it was half-ruined, but
at least it would give Hercules some shelter for
the night. She went back on board. 'Jack,' she
called impatiently. 'Jack, whatever are you doing
down there?'

There was no reply, so she raised her voice.
'Jack, there's a barn close by where I think I can
stable Hercules for the night. And if you've gone
from here by the time I get back, well—I wish
I could say it's been nice knowing you. But it
hasn't exactly worked out very well for either of
us, has it?' There was still no answer. 'Jack?' she
called out, really annoyed now. 'Did you hear a
word I've been saying?'

What on earth was he playing at? Quickly she
descended the ladder to the cabin and saw he'd

lit the lantern. He was standing with his back to her and his left hand was pressed flat against the wall of the cabin while his head was bowed. She saw, too, that his right arm hung limply by his side—and his shirtsleeve was covered in blood. She moved quickly towards him, her heart thudding sickly. 'Jack. What on *earth*...? What in God's name has happened to you?'

Still he rested his hand against the wall, as if he might fall without its support. But at the sound of her voice he slowly turned. 'There was an accident,' he said to her very quietly.

Chapter Sixteen

She had already seen that the fabric of his sleeve had been sliced through, exactly where most of the blood was. He must have been attacked with a knife. *Dear God.* 'An accident?' Her sarcastic tone did nothing to hide her alarm. 'Do you take me for a complete fool?'

That brought a brief smile to his face. 'Believe me, I wouldn't dare.'

She was still struggling to calm herself. 'Sit down,' she ordered. 'However this happened, that wound needs attending to.'

Rather to her surprise, he obediently sat down on the edge of her bed while she poured water into a bowl; then, with scissors, she cut away the sleeve of his shirt and removed the makeshift bandage he'd knotted around his upper arm. She saw that the cut was long but shallow and heaved an inner sigh of relief because the flow of blood had almost stopped.

Carefully she began to bathe the congealed blood away, sensing him flinch. 'Am I hurting you?'

'Not in the slightest.'

'Liar.' She was folding a wad of fresh linen and pressing it to the cut. 'Can you hold that while I tie it on?'

He nodded, that spark of humour glinting in his blue eyes again. 'Will I live?'

'Long enough to cause plenty more mischief, I'd guess.'

'I didn't want to bring any mischief on you, Matty,' he said, rather more quietly this time. 'I told you. I'll be on my way as soon as you've patched me up.'

She said nothing, but began wrapping a long strip of bandage around his upper arm. He was leaving her and it was just as well. Because she was becoming more and more troubled by the fact that day by day, her carefully built defences were crumbling. Every time she was close to him—every time they talked—another barrier seemed to fall away. Right now, as she wrapped the gauze bandage round his arm, she couldn't help but notice that while it was muscled as thickly as any labourer's, his tanned skin was like silk under her fingertips, causing her to feel a strange and dizzying melting in the pit of her stomach.

Bess had warned Matty often. 'Watch for men's roving hands, lass. Once they start kissing you, they can't stop—their urges get out of control. So until you meet some nice young fellow who asks you to marry him, you keep the whole lot of them at arm's length. Do you understand?'

Two years ago Matty had let Bess's words of warning fly out of the window. Two years ago, when Matty and her father were moored close to the treasure field at Aylesbury, she'd met a man she thought was clever and attractive, but he'd turned out to be a cheat and a liar. And she'd vowed never again to be misled by flattering glances and a charming smile. But then along came Jack Rutherford. And here she was, tending his wound, her pulse pounding dizzily, her own feelings racing stupidly out of control.

Not again. Never again. My father might be alive still, if it wasn't for me letting him down so badly.

She fought to suppress the sudden, sharp ache in her throat. 'There,' she said to Jack as she firmly tied a knot in the bandage. 'Unfortunately your shirt is quite ruined, so I'm going to find you another one.'

'I don't think,' he said, 'that any of your shirts would fit me.' His eyes lingered on her figure just a little too long for her comfort.

'Of course they wouldn't!' Her pent-up emotion made her voice taut. 'But I have some shirts of my father's folded away in a cupboard. Can you take yours off while I fetch you one?'

'Aye aye, Captain Matty,' he said.

But he didn't move.

He's waiting for me to go, she realised. It was as well. She didn't particularly want to be presented with the sight of Jack Rutherford's tanned and muscular chest.

She hurried to the cupboard where her father's clothes were still kept and lifted out a folded shirt. Jack was taller than her father, but this should fit him—or so she very much hoped. By the time she came back to him, Jack was sitting on the bed and was examining the bandage. With the upper half of his body quite naked, he looked even more formidable than before. His figure was lean with little spare flesh; but his shoulders and chest were packed with muscle.

And just at that moment he looked up and gave

her a smile that set her insides pounding. 'You've done a fine job of patching me up,' he said. 'The bleeding seems to have stopped completely.'

'Just as well,' Matty replied tartly. She held out her father's neatly folded shirt and he rose to take it. 'I don't want you ruining this one.'

'Of course not. My thanks.'

He sat down again, his face strangely expressionless; she guessed he was waiting for her to leave again before he put it on. 'I'll fetch you a drink,' she said quickly. 'I suspect brandy would be best.' And she headed for the cupboard where the brandy was kept—but then, she made the mistake of glancing back.

He'd raised his arms in order to slip her father's shirt on over his head—and this time he had his back to her. Which meant that she could see, quite clearly, the raised marks of many old scars cruelly criss-crossing his spine.

Her breathing stopped completely. So she *hadn't* imagined that brief glimpse of scar tissue! And now she was faced with the full horror of those multiple white, raised ridges that cut through the tanned smoothness of his skin…

At some time in his not-so-distant past, Jack Rutherford must have been flogged to within an inch of his life.

Matty felt sick. *Nothing's really changed*, she told herself shakily. *You knew from the start you were dealing with a rogue.*

Brandy. She'd promised to get him brandy. Swiftly she opened the cupboard, but her hand shook as she lifted the bottle down and pulled out the stopper.

She'd gone completely against the urging of Daniel and Bess and her own common sense in agreeing to take this man with her. What was even more dangerous, she'd grown to actually *like* him—she'd enjoyed seeing his teasing smile, she'd even started to believe that he was on her side after all. And somehow his unexpected arrival in her life had seemed like the best thing to happen to her for a long, long time.

After pouring out a generous measure of brandy, she went to hand it to him. He'd covered himself up by now—*thank goodness*—and reached for the glass as she approached.

'My thanks,' he said. 'You've done an excellent job.'

'Maybe.' She was already looking around. 'But you need some kind of support for that arm.' She picked up a folded square of white linen which she fashioned into a makeshift sling. 'Put your arm through here.'

But now—now she needed to knot the two free ends around the back of his neck.

She had to draw very close to him. He smelled of sunshine and leather—he smelled all-male and she felt a little dizzy as her fingers accidentally brushed the warm skin at the nape of his neck. As for her fingers, they had a mind of their own, because they wanted to run themselves more firmly over that surprisingly silky skin. Wanted to tangle in his dark curly hair, then move on down beneath the collar of his shirt to explore the sinews and muscles of his shoulders...

His *scarred* shoulders.

Pull yourself together. The knot was tied and she stepped back calmly, but her fingertips still tingled from where they'd touched him. 'There,' she said in her best matter-of-fact voice. 'I think that should do the trick. But you must keep the sling on for the next couple of days while your cut heals—and don't jolt your arm, whatever you do.' It was a miracle, she was thinking, how she could sound so calm.

'Thank you.' He examined the sling, then his eyes were on hers, sombre and searching.

'Think nothing of it.' She was putting away her scissors, deliberately avoiding his gaze. 'After all, that cut might have turned into yet another nasty scar if it wasn't cleaned up properly.'

There was a moment's silence, during which he'd pulled those dice from his pocket with his left hand and was slowly turning them. At last he said, 'You've seen my back, haven't you? I'm afraid I'm not a pretty sight.'

'Not particularly, no.' Her heart was thundering and her hands were shaking a little. She drew in a deep breath and faced him squarely. 'And now, I really think it's time you told me the truth, Jack. The *complete* truth. Who's after you? What, exactly, have you done?'

The time to Matty seemed endless. Did she want to know? Could she bear it? The dice clicked between his fingers again and again until at last he spoke. 'The truth is, Matty, that I'm afraid I have a rather nasty fraudster on my trail. And he wants to put me in prison for robbery.'

Each word hammered into her. 'Are you innocent?'

'Yes. Completely.'

Oh, how she wanted to believe him. 'Then why are you running?' Her voice was almost a cry of despair. 'Why not face this man outright, instead of all this hiding and deceit?'

His eyes never left hers. 'There is a slight problem. You see, this fraudster is rich and powerful. At the moment his word is far more likely to be believed than mine, because I've not exactly covered myself in glory since my army career ended.'

Her heart plummeted. She was glancing at those dice. 'You're a gambler? A trickster?'

'Let's say I have certain skills that quite a lot of crooks would envy, shall we? I certainly do *not* cheat. But I can detect other people cheating—and that's what really makes me enemies.'

She heaved in a deep breath. 'Those scars. Who was it who treated you so badly, Jack?'

'It was the French.'

'The *French*?' Something that was almost relief surged through Matty. She'd been fearing the worst for so long now—fearing that it was maybe a punishment inflicted by his own officers for desertion or disobedience. But the French...

She moistened her dry throat. 'You mean you were captured by the enemy?'

He nodded wearily. 'I was taken prisoner by the French three years ago. I was hauled off to a military jail along with other captured British officers and kept there for two years.'

In a low voice she said, 'That cannot have been easy.'

He shrugged. 'I was one of the lucky ones because I got out alive. The man who carved these dice for me was in the prison, too. He died of pneumonia, along with many others. I managed to get home—but it turned out that my worst enemy of all lives in London.'

Her emotions felt raw. 'And he's the man who's made false accusations against you? Sent his men after you?'

'Exactly.'

She wanted so much, so very much, to believe him. She said at last, 'Why is your enemy doing this, Jack? What's his aim?'

'His aim is probably to see me dead.'

She let out a gasp.

'Look, Matty,' he went on, 'I should have told you all this from the very beginning. I had no right at all asking you to take me on board your boat. And most of all, I had no right not to tell you that I knew—right from our meeting in the shop—that you were a girl.'

She sat down rather slowly on the edge of her bed. And Jack thought he had never despised himself so much in his whole life.

'So you were pretending?' she whispered. 'All the time?' She looked crushed.

'I'm afraid I was.'

Then he saw that old stubbornness firming up her delicate features; saw the anger in her lovely eyes. 'So why did you carry on treating me the way you did? Calling me *Captain* and teasing me about sharing my cabin for the night? Why, when all the time you must just have been laughing at me? Don't you feel that's rather despicable of you?'

What the hell could he say?

He could, of course, try to explain that he'd been intrigued by her from the moment he first saw her. That he'd been astounded by her courage and independence and he had enjoyed her company. That above all he'd relished the opportunity the pretence gave him to be so close to her, hour by hour, minute by minute. In short, he'd found her quite captivating.

He realised she was speaking to him again.

'So you knew I was a girl that day?'

He sighed, rubbing his free hand along the back of his neck and touching the knot of his sling. 'Yes.' *It was mostly because of your eyes*, he thought to himself. Your incredible dark-lashed green eyes. And your cropped hair, shiny as a fresh-shelled nut, that I want to run my hands through now, this minute, even though you're looking at me as though I'm something that's crawled out from under a stone. And then there's that dimple that peeps out only occasionally and those lips of yours that I've been wanting to kiss for far too long now...

He said at last, 'Look. I was completely wrong to pretend for so long, but I thought that perhaps you realised it was a pretence. I thought maybe we were both happy to keep it up, if only for safety's sake—'

She repeated, very slowly, 'For safety's sake?'

He spread out his hand in a kind of mute appeal. *Not making very good progress here, Jack.* 'Well.' He tried again. 'You're a girl and I'm a man. While we're together like this—in such close proximity—things could become a little tricky.' Dear God, he was really in deep water now. 'So keeping up the lie...' he struggled on '...was like—like putting up a kind of safety barrier between us.'

'A safety barrier? So you actually thought that I might be in danger of throwing myself at you?' Her tone was withering.

He sighed. 'No. Of course not. But it has stopped a certain amount of embarrassment. It has prevented, shall we say, any personal emotions being involved.'

Her eyes, he saw, were still sparking with anger. 'By which I assume you mean *my* emotions? My silly, frail, female emotions?'

'Well, of course I could see from the start you were better able to take care of yourself than most females—'

'Don't you dare to patronise me!'

He was finding he was almost glad of her anger. Realised he would have completely deserved it had she reached for those copper pots that hung over the stove and started throwing them at him one by one. He felt like raising his hands in surrender, but his right arm was in a sling so instead he spread out his free hand as he used to when explaining the details of some rather intricate army manoeuvre to a bunch of new recruits.

'Look, Matty. I wouldn't dream of patronising you. As I said, I guessed from the beginning that you felt happier if strangers assumed you were male, so I decided to pretend I was fooled, too. Of *course* I should have been honest with you from the very beginning, but please believe that none of my actions arose from any lack of respect. On my honour, I never for one moment intended to mock you or belittle you.'

She rose to her feet and walked slowly round the cabin before turning back to face him. 'This man. Your enemy. Presumably you don't intend to keep running from him for ever? Presumably you intend at some point to stand up to him and clear your name?'

'I do indeed,' he answered, 'but for the moment it's incredibly important that I keep one step ahead of him. As I told you, it's my intention from now on to travel by myself. More than likely my enemy will still be after me, but this time—with luck—he'll have no certainty as to where I'm heading or how. And so I say again, that the sooner I leave your boat the better—'

'No,' she said.

He screwed up his eyes, not understanding. 'What?'

'Listen to me.' Matty had been pacing to and fro again, but now she spun round to face him. 'I need you, Jack. I can't manage this journey without you—I've told you that. And surely—*surely* you realise that I'm a fraudster, too?'

He said again, more slowly, 'What?' *Oh, Jack. You're sounding like a parrot.*

She was waving one hand impatiently. 'You

know very well that I'm determined to find those Roman remains—the treasure field—for my father's sake. And this time, I won't be asking permission from that hateful man who told my father he'd have him beaten if he found him trespassing again. I aim to get inside that house to find the old map I told you about—the map which showed the site of the Roman settlement. If necessary, I'll break in—I mean it—and for that I'll need your help. Come with me and be my partner, exactly as you promised. Remember?'

'Matty, I'm a liability! There will be men all over the place, looking for me and looking for your boat, which they'll guess is carrying on up the canal—'

'Then they'll guess wrong. Listen to me, Jack. I've thought of a plan.'

He rubbed his hand tiredly through his hair. 'Oh, Matty—'

'Look.' Swiftly she laid out one of her father's canal charts on the table and pointed. 'A mile or so back, we passed Cowley Lock—do you remember? It's where another canal branches off leading to Slough. What I suggest is that we turn around and make our way back to Cowley Lock, then we set off along the canal to Slough.'

His frown increased. 'But we don't want to go to Slough, do we?'

'Of course not,' she said impatiently. 'But listen. All we need to do is travel perhaps half a mile along the Slough branch, then stop and rest for a day or so. This enemy of yours will have assumed that you're still on the same route as before, but he can't keep his men on the lookout for ever. After a while, he'll have to accept that you've given up, so we'll be safe to rejoin the Grand Junction canal and carry on up to Aylesbury.' She was folding the map briskly. 'Another point. While we're moored up, it will give your arm time to heal.'

'But your boat will still be recognised by its name!'

'I'll paint it out,' she said defiantly.

He was shaking his head. '*No*, Matty. I'm full of admiration—and appreciation. But I'm still afraid I'll bring danger on you…'

She made a sound of utter exasperation. 'You didn't stop to think about putting me in danger when you begged for a ride on my boat back in London, did you?'

'No,' he said hesitantly. 'But you don't know what these men are like. They can be pretty scary.'

'Don't worry.' She folded her arms across her chest. 'I'll protect you.'

A slow smile began to spread across his features. 'Very well, Captain Matty,' he said. 'Very well.'

Steadily they shook hands. And with his warm clasp, she felt a tremor of something all up and down her spine. *Business partners.* That was all they were, she reminded herself.

But she drew away a little too quickly and stumbled over the stool behind her. He caught her, holding her close with his sound arm— and just for a moment, the hardness of his body against her own sent the sweetest of sensations flowing through her, as though her very bones had melted. She clutched at what remained of her sanity only to find herself gazing up at his inscrutable face—his blue eyes had narrowed, his lips had thinned and she realised she was shivering inside at that expression of his.

Her world was spinning. And she didn't think it was fear that made her pulse thud so.

At last he let her go. 'What is your real name?' he asked softly.

'It's Matilda,' she whispered. 'Matilda Grey.'

He nodded, still watching her. 'Matilda,' he said. 'It's a beautiful name.'

He reached out to touch her cheek—and she did nothing. She couldn't believe her own inability to act; she should have slapped him away or laughed, but instead she just stood there. And something inside the cabin shifted then. The air. Or the light dancing around the single candle— all filled with that shimmering, hazy kind of magic she tried so hard to pretend wasn't between them always, pulling tightly on her heart and on her very soul.

Which was why she didn't move away, either, fool that she was, when he cupped her chin. Normally she'd have lashed out, but she only held that gaze of his and held her breath, too, because she felt so many sensations in that moment, wild and intense and mind-shattering, and none of them was fear, far from it. No, they were feelings of sheer longing.

He had put his left hand to her cheek again and she remembered the feel of his body against hers, strong and hard and warm. His eyes were devouring her. His mouth was firm and male, yet deliciously tempting, and as his fingers traced her lips she closed her eyes, bracing herself for the kiss that must surely follow...

He moved away. He dropped his hand from her face and stepped back. Her eyes flew open and her world was cold and grey and solitary once more.

'It's time,' he murmured, 'to move on, I think you said.'

Her cheeks were burning with shame. *If he'd kissed me, what would I have done?*

Kissed him back. That was what.

She hurt inside, aware of a sharp ache like none she'd ever known squeezing at her chest. But already she was looking around, brisk and businesslike as usual, busying herself lighting a lantern to take up on deck. 'You're right,' she replied curtly. 'We need to set off as soon as possible.'

'Then tell me what to do, Captain Matty. You're in charge.'

No, I'm not. I'm really not.

Her heart still hammering, she led the way up on to the deck where it was completely dark now except for her lantern. She was horrified at herself. Had he really meant to kiss her just then? Had he realised she was expecting it—no, *longing* for it? Did he despise her for her weakness? Surely he must.

Words from the shadows of a truly dark time rolled through her agitated mind. *'I thought you canal girls were up for anything.'*

Shame engulfed her, together with an absolute determination not to let anything like this happen between them again—ever.

Chapter Seventeen

Turning the boat was always a tricky task, but it was even more difficult in the dark and Matty had to do most of the work because of Jack's injured arm. But it was a relief to be doing something normal. Something practical. *Nothing's actually happened*, she kept telling herself over and over. *He probably never even noticed the effect he had on me.*

And if he had noticed, he'd likely forgotten it already. As she must.

They had to find a winding hole first, a small inlet made specially for reversing barges. Fortunately they came across one soon and Matty had the boat turned around so it pointed south towards the Cowley Junction. After that she strode along the towpath with Hercules while Jack manned the tiller. 'Whatever you do,' she called back to him, 'don't strain your injured arm, will you?'

'Aye aye, Captain,' was his instant response.

She lifted one eyebrow. 'Obedience at last, Jack? Now I'm *really* worried. Are you sure you're not going down with a fever?'

He laughed, but Matty wasn't laughing—in fact, her fears were pressing down on her. There were men after Jack who meant business, and the thought of them injuring him hurt her somewhere deep inside.

I am the one in danger, she told herself. *I am the one truly in danger.*

Jack sat with his left hand resting on the tiller, reminding himself sternly that of course it was entirely wrong of him to study Matty as she marched ahead of him under the moonlight. Entirely wrong of him to admire the feminine swing of her slender hips or to recall the way her tempting lips had parted when he'd been so close to her just now...

'Keep your hands to yourself,' Jack muttered under his breath. *No messing with young Matty. She deserves far better than you. You understand?*

He realised just then that Matty had guided

Hercules to a halt and was coming back to him. 'Cowley Junction is up ahead, Jack. There's a lock there and it's manned.'

'Is that good or bad news?'

'Good in that it means we can get through, but bad because we'll be seen. Let's hope the lock-keeper will be too sleepy to be curious. The ones on overnight duty often settle down for a snooze because they don't expect many travellers at this time of night. But all the same, I think that when we reach the lock, it will be best if you stay below and out of sight.'

Matty had to wake the lock man, who was indeed dozing in his hut at the side of the canal. He was startled to see her. 'Don't tell me you're travelling all on your own, lad?'

'Why not?' she answered coolly, hands in her coat pockets. 'It's much quieter.'

'That's because it's two in the morning!'

'Exactly—which means there are no queues.' She gestured towards the canal. 'Now, give me a hand opening those gates, will you?'

Soon enough *The Wild Rose* was heading west towards Slough, but after only half a mile Matty called a halt. 'This should be far enough,' she told Jack. 'We'll stop here for the rest of the night.'

She drove a couple of stakes into the bank to moor up the boat, then went on board. Jack, still at the tiller, offered his usual smile, but she saw that his face was drawn and pale.

Matty glanced at him sharply. 'You look dreadful. How's your arm?'

'It's fine,' he said. 'Just fine. And you look…'

She thought, just for a moment, that he was going to say something like *lovely.* Her heart stopped.

'Efficient,' he concluded. 'As usual.'

'That's because I am efficient. And I'd better change that dressing on your arm.'

'Now, I'm absolutely sure there's no need…'

'Listen.' Her voice was tight with tension now. 'Stop being foolish! The last thing I want is to have you going sick on me. An unclean wound can become infected and I've already got quite enough to do looking after the boat and Hercules without having an ill passenger on board.'

'So I'll have to take my shirt off?' His blue eyes glinted with amusement.

'It's necessary,' she answered flatly.

'Very well. I shall obey.' But that mischief still

lurked in his eyes as he began to peel off his shirt.

Matty stood with her arms folded. 'I don't enjoy this,' she reminded him, 'in the slightest.'

'The thought never entered my mind,' he answered meekly.

The solution, she told herself as she was confronted by that sleek, muscular body of his again, *is to keep reminding yourself that he's an arrogant, pig-headed male. You can also remind yourself that he's been accused of robbery.*

After all, she only had his word for it that he'd been framed by the man who was after him. Besides which there was the fact that he'd had a useless occupation as owner of a business in which he tried to make money out of old soldiers' possessions.

But the trouble was—she liked him. She really liked him. She just could not convince herself, try as she might, that he consisted of nothing but swagger and conceit, because often—now, for example—he looked almost ashamed, of his scars and of himself.

He echoed her very thoughts as she began to strip away the old bandage. 'I'm sorry,' he said quietly. 'I regret having to expose you to all this.'

'I'm here to bathe the cut on your arm,' she

answered in a clipped voice, 'not to make judgements on your life history.' She carefully drew away the bloodstained linen pad.

'Please,' she whispered under her breath. *Please let it be healing well.*

Was it a prayer? Not exactly—but nevertheless Matty's relief was enormous when she saw that the wound was drying cleanly and showed no signs of infection, though she was careful to give no indication of her inner palpitations. 'Your rather eventful past, Jack,' she went on calmly, 'has nothing to do with me, thank goodness. I'm rather more concerned about what happens over the next few days.'

'Of course,' he answered meekly. Too meekly—his eyes glinted with mischief again.

She bit her lip in exasperation. Why did she let the man get under her skin so? Shaking her head, she bathed the cut carefully in cold water and wrapped a fresh dressing round it. 'Now, you'd better have my bed for the rest of the night. I can sleep on the deck.'

'Oh, no, you won't.' He shook his head, pulled on his shirt and stood up. 'You keep your bed.'

'But—'

'Believe me,' he interrupted, 'it's blessed relief

to sleep in the fresh air after years in a French prison. I'll sleep like a log. Will you?'

'Me?' She shrugged. 'Of course. I always do.'

But she didn't sleep at all well. In fact, she lay awake for hours listening to the owls in the woods nearby, then once they were quiet at last she realised she was actually *afraid* of falling asleep—in case she dreamed of Jack. Dreamed of his dancing blue eyes teasing her, as he drew her close to his taut, muscular body and held her tight...

Truth to tell, she was absolutely mortified by the events of the last few hours. He'd known she was a woman all the time, though what really stung her was that he'd kept up the pretence for so long, even to the extent of offering her hints about picking up barmaids. That was mockery pure and simple—quite clearly he saw the whole thing as a joke.

He was a mischief-maker who took life lightly, at least on the surface. She'd met men like him before and coped with them, but this time was different. This time, she wasn't coping at all.

What really concerned her was the way he affected her when he dropped that mask of laughter; like last night when she'd bathed his cut and forced him to tell her about those scars and his time in the French prison. She'd seen a different side of him then, because he'd forgotten to assume his usual light-hearted facade. And what she'd seen in his face had been the utter, life-rending bleakness of some terrible memories.

As for that enemy of his in London, she'd noticed that whenever he mentioned the nameless man his blue eyes turned hard and cold, making her shiver. She wouldn't like to be in that man's shoes when Jack finally took his revenge, no, she wouldn't. For Jack Rutherford was dangerous and not only to his enemies. She had to make absolutely sure he had no effect whatsoever on her much-valued independence and most especially on her heart.

Matty had always loved the canals—the open air, the adventure of never knowing what the next day might bring—and she'd never needed anyone except her father with whom to share her life. Her father used to worry about her, though. 'Matty,' he'd once said, looking up from his books and his papers, 'I don't like to think of you being on your own if something should happen to me.'

She remembered giving him a hug. *'Nothing's going to happen to you, Papa. Not while I'm around.'* The trouble was that, as it turned out, she wasn't with him when he most needed her, on the evening that was to shatter her life.

Her father was well known among the scholars of Oxford and, by the time she was seventeen, more than a few of the younger ones were turning their eyes in Matty's direction. She found them all unspeakably earnest and dull, these scholars, but then a young man whose name was Alexander Corton turned up unannounced two years ago, when Matty and her father were moored near Aylesbury. Corton had strolled along the towpath to their boat and told them he was staying for a few days in the area.

'I'm a historian, Mr Grey,' he'd said. 'I'm doing some research at Oxford University. And, of course, I've heard all about your amazing discoveries.'

Matty's father, hospitable as ever, invited him on board and told Alexander Corton all about his hopes of finding the remains of a Roman settlement nearby. Her father had not noticed the way Corton's eyes kept straying to Matty; though Matty had noticed. And she hadn't been at all sure she liked or trusted the man.

Later, when her father had gone out to buy supplies in the village, Corton called again at

264   *Unbuttoning Miss Matilda*

the boat. 'Is your father here?' he asked. 'No? That's a pity. You see, I've found some very interesting old papers that might help him in his search for those Roman remains. They're in my room at the hotel where I'm staying.'

'I'll tell my father,' Matty promised. 'I'm sure he'll want to visit you. Perhaps tomorrow?'

'Impossible, I fear. You see, I have to leave for Oxford early in the morning.'

Matty hesitated and made her decision. 'Then may I see them, Mr Corton? And I can tell my father what you've found.'

'Of course,' he said.

She wondered if perhaps Corton's papers might be vital for her father's project, but when she arrived at his hotel Corton didn't have any documents at all. Instead he used the promise of them to lure Matty up to his bedroom and there he tried to seduce her, though he quickly regretted it because Matty rebuffed him in no uncertain manner. He was taken aback by both her ferocity and her scorn as she told him what she thought of him.

He'd said to her then, 'Your father's an old fool. He's living like a madman on that boat of his. And as for you—' his lip had curled '—I thought you canal girls were up for anything. My mistake.'

Matty said steadily, 'Your whole existence appears to be one big mistake, Corton.' And she walked straight out of his room; but afterwards she shook and shook.

All the way back to *The Wild Rose*, she hadn't been able to stop rebuking herself for being so naive. So stupid. She vowed that she would never, ever trust a man's promises again. But there had been worse to come, because when she reached the boat she found that her father had returned and he was clearly ill, pale and short of breath. 'I've been back to Charlwood Manor, Matty,' he told her. 'I heard in the village that it was occupied again, so I called. I wanted to explain to the owner about the old map of the Roman settlement in the library and to ask him if I might explore his land a little further. But he had me thrown out, by his footmen...'

And suddenly he was bending over, clutching his chest, clearly gripped by agonising pain. Matty ran to the village for help and a doctor came, but it was too late; her father had suffered a heart attack and died that very evening.

So would she trust another smooth-tongued stranger? *Never*, she'd vowed.

But somehow, fool that she was, she'd started trusting Jack Rutherford—for better or worse.

As soon as Jack was up the next morning he put on his sling, reminding himself that though he didn't really think he needed it, he mustn't annoy Captain Matty any more than he had done already. Sighing a little, he peered over the edge of the boat and saw a frog gazing at him from the bank. 'Morning,' he called out to the frog. 'It's a fine day to be alive, isn't it?'

The frog croaked and kept staring. Jack laughed, then rolled up his mattress and untied the tarpaulin shelter. The sun was already warm on his face, filling him with fresh energy; by the time Matty appeared from below he'd actually managed to light the small stove on deck and was boiling up water for a pot of tea.

He thought he saw a flash of relief cross her face that he was awake and fully dressed. 'Good morning,' he said cheerfully. 'Tea?' He pointed to the kettle.

'Good morning to you, too. And I'd love some tea.' Her eyes had flown to his injured arm. 'I trust you slept well?'

'Like a log.' He was already filling the teapot. 'You?'

'Oh, yes. I slept *extremely* well.'

But Jack rather guessed that she hadn't. He guessed that she had probably stayed awake for quite a while in that little bed of hers, fretting over her unwanted travelling companion. Well, he had several ideas as to how they could make this trip a whole lot more delightful for both of them; but most regretfully, he'd decided that he'd better keep those ideas to himself.

They shared a breakfast of buttered bread with hot, sweet tea and, after that, Jack offered to paint over the name of the boat. 'You've got some tins of paint and some brushes,' he pointed out. 'I saw them in the hold.'

'Jack. Your *arm*—'

'I can use my other one. Besides, I'm really feeling much better this morning. After all, it was only a scratch.'

'A scratch!'

She was preparing, he could tell, to wax indignant again. But he was already on his way to find that paint.

They spent the rest of the day uneventfully, allowing Hercules a full day to recover after his overnight travels. Jack watched in silent wonder as Matty went through all the tasks he'd never realised were necessary to keep a boat like this in good order, before she set off to fetch more supplies. In the meantime he painted over the boat's name—and gave it a new one.

He saw her stop in her tracks when she came back and read what he'd painted.

'Beautiful Lady,' she said. Then, 'Jack, why? That's ridiculous!'

'No, it's not,' he said. 'On the contrary, I think it's completely appropriate.'

He saw the colour leave her cheeks, then slowly return.

She spoke no more about it, but for the rest of the day she kept her distance from him. It was as well, he thought wryly, that one of them had some willpower, because, although he tried to keep busy doing all the jobs she set him, he was finding her more and more tempting, deliciously so.

And how horrified she would be to hear it, because plainly that was the very opposite of her intentions—so he kept things light. He chatted, just a little, about the pleasanter sides of army life and made her laugh with some of his tales. In return, she told him stories about the canals she'd travelled with her father, recalling his various finds and describing the respect in which he'd been held at the university in Oxford.

Only then Jack said, 'His early death was such a tragedy,' and for some reason she was silenced, utterly. This time there was no matter-of-fact response from her, no sharp put-down even. Just those wide green eyes, suddenly full of the most intense kind of grief.

And Jack wanted, almost more than he wanted anything in his life, to take her in his arms and comfort her. And, damn it, to kiss her. And make sweet love to her...

Almost more than anything. But first and foremost, he wanted Charlwood back.

Chapter Eighteen

The next morning they made a mutual decision that it would be safe to head back to the Grand Junction Canal and resume their journey to Aylesbury.

'With luck,' commented Jack, 'we'll have thrown Fitz's rather unintelligent hirelings off our trail. Besides, they'll be looking for *The Wild Rose*, not *Beautiful Lady*.'

Matty seemed at ease with that, so he resumed his usual role of leading Hercules along the towpath and guessed that Matty took a certain amount of relish in showing him exactly who was in charge.

'Jack,' she called out to him around noon, 'you need to slow Hercules down. I can see the towpath is slightly flooded up ahead.'

He grinned back at her. 'I rather enjoy the way you order me about. Keep it up.'

She pressed her lips together. But half an hour later—'Jack, stop for a moment and let the rope go slack, will you? We need to avoid those over-hanging branches farther along the way.'

'Aye aye, Captain.' He saluted.

He found much to interest him, such as when Matty explained that with her boat, they faced different problems to the working barges. 'You see,' she told him, 'this vessel is unladen and sits higher in the water. The lightness makes Hercules's job easier, but it also means we have to take extra care. Especially when going under tunnels without much headroom.'

Jack listened carefully and learned swiftly—he thought. 'This canal lark is a piece of cake,' he called back to her from the towpath. 'It's nothing, I tell you, compared to hiking across the Pyrenees at night in a snowstorm—'

Just at that moment Matty called, 'Look out, Jack! Just ahead of you I can see a swan on its nest, close to the bank. Slow Hercules down. *Now!*'

Too late. Jack pulled on Hercules's halter but the swan was already rising from the nest, stretching its great wings and extending its long neck to hiss at both man and horse.

'Back away!' Matty cried. 'That swan's angry, Jack. And it could break your arm…'

Jack moved to one side, lost his footing in the mud and toppled with his arms flailing into the canal.

Damn. He'd never expected it to be so cold! Trying his hardest not to swallow water, he floundered until his feet found the bottom, then he struggled back to the bank.

He saw Matty watching him. She said, 'Your arm.' She was looking at his sling, which was soaked, of course, and was slipping off.

'I don't really need it,' he answered her. 'And my arm's fine. Preparing to rescue me, were you?'

She wasn't smiling back—in fact, she looked a little pale. 'You didn't see that swan's nest at all, did you? You were far too busy telling me how clever you are.'

He brushed away some of the water that was still dripping down his face. 'True.' He gave the swan a wary look. 'Hercules wasn't worried, though, was he?'

'Hercules,' she said, 'is sensible. He knows to stand very still when there's a swan around.

Hercules is also rather large—no swan with any sense would go for him.'

She went to fetch him more clothes of her father's—a fresh shirt and some breeches—then turned her back as Jack got changed and laid his wet clothes on the top of the cabin to dry out in the sun.

'There we are,' he said when he'd finished. 'Ready for action, as ever. Onwards, Captain Matty.'

Matty was truly shaken by the way she'd felt for those few minutes when he'd disappeared under the water. She'd been absolutely rigid with fear.

Don't be such a fool. The canal's less than five feet deep!

But he'd lost his balance. And he had an injured arm. As he'd sunk beneath the canal's surface, her heart had thudded sickly. But then she'd seen his dark head emerging and he was shaking the water from his hair and laughing—although she averted her eyes rather quickly then, because of the way his soaked shirt and breeches clung to his extremely muscular male form.

He hadn't been worried in the slightest, she'd realised. His strength and ingenuity were huge

and for just a moment she'd found herself thinking, *How very good to have someone so strong
and so capable at my side.*

She swatted the thought away as she would a
troublesome fly. Someone to *help* her? Jack had
already proved that he brought with him a substantial amount of trouble—and even if what
he'd told her was true, that his army career had
only ended because he'd been captured by the
French, he was still a liability, for the simple reason that something about his light-hearted smile
made her heart give a little leap each time it was
aimed in her direction. He made her feel as she'd
never, ever felt before and couldn't afford to feel.

She mocked herself as they sat on the bank
later to eat their usual lunch of bread and cheese
from the boat's stores. Was she *really* worried
that he might try to seduce her? A ridiculous
idea! He'd only offered to come with her because
he wanted to escape from that enemy of his in
London. He was using her—just as he used ev-
erybody else in his life.

But all the same, she sneaked a look at him as
he lay there flat on his back in the sun with his
eyes closed. Since his dip in the canal, he'd got
rid of his sling and she could only assume the cut

on his arm was healing quickly—he certainly appeared to be using that arm freely enough.

And now he rested on the bank with a slight smile on his face, as if he hadn't a care in the world. His shirt had fallen slightly open to reveal that beautiful body—that beautiful scarred body.

Oh, my. She looked away again very quickly. *He's dangerous, Matty. He says he's committed no crime—but how can you be sure?*

Just for now, his mysterious pursuers appeared to have lost the trail, but who knew what hazards lay ahead? Hazards for her especially. Looking at him like this, seeing him almost vulnerable in sleep, set up a kind of restless yearning that made her feel shaken and utterly out of her depth.

It didn't help that he was in the habit of often lightly touching her when he helped her with one of the countless jobs—touching her in a thousand casual ways that set off pleasurable quivers all through her body. Or sometimes he would lean down and speak in her ear, and she would feel it everywhere, even in the most shockingly intimate of places. And she hadn't a single idea what to do about it. All in all it was just as well he had absolutely no idea of the effect he had on her. Just as well that he treated her as though she was nothing but a scrawny youngster.

The trouble was, she didn't want him to see her as a scrawny youngster. She wanted him to kiss her—like he so nearly had before.

They weren't far from Aylesbury when they moored up later that afternoon and Matty was all too aware that by this time tomorrow, they should at last be within sight of her father's treasure field. 'Please,' she whispered. *Please let nothing go wrong.*

She was sitting on deck, studying a small sketch map when Jack came up behind her. Earlier he'd told her he was going to take a swim in a nearby stream that Matty had pointed out to him—it pooled into a small lake just above a weir. 'People love to swim there,' she'd told him. 'If I remember rightly, the water is crystal clear.'

'I'll try it out,' he'd promised.

On his return he was in his breeches and boots, but was still bare-chested and was dragging a towel across his shoulders. He was as relaxed in her presence as if she were just one of his soldier friends, which showed just how ridiculous were her notions that he might try to kiss her again. Nevertheless, her pulse began racing a little and though she nodded at his casual greeting, she fixed her eyes on the map as if her life depended on it.

He'd come up behind her and was so close that she could smell the clean, soapy scent of his freshly washed hair and clean skin. Her heart was thudding hard now.

Eyes on the map, Matty.

'That's an interesting map you've got there,' he said. 'Where did you find it?'

She turned calmly on her stool to look up at him. 'My father sketched it two years ago.'

'Does it show where he found the coin?'

'Exactly.' Well, she'd trusted Jack with everything else, so she might as well tell it all. 'Here's the field with the pine trees. And do you see the house over here? That's Charlwood Manor. There's a village nearby and we can stable Hercules at the local inn, but I'm afraid I can't remember its name—'

He'd moved away now and was pulling on his shirt. 'The Pack Horse,' she heard him say.

Matty rose, frowning. 'Yes. The Pack Horse, that's it. But how did you know?'

For just a moment his blue eyes were hooded, but then he was smiling once more. 'I've been doing my research, too, you know, Captain Matty. I am your number one assistant, after all.'

Rather briskly she began putting her map away. 'Well, we must make plans for mooring here this evening. Hercules needs somewhere for the night and we need supper. I don't suppose you've managed to arrange *that*, have you?'

'I've arranged everything,' he said proudly.

She was taken aback. 'What do you mean— everything?' He was drawing closer and she could see the mischief sparkling in his blue eyes. *Oh, those eyes*, she thought rather desperately. Did they have the same effect on every female he came near?

'I've got us an invitation,' he announced. He was tucking the tails of his shirt into his breeches and she dragged her eyes quickly from those glimpses of tanned, intimate skin. 'I took a stroll over to the village and I discovered there's going to be a party tonight, with food and drinks and dancing. What do you think? Do you fancy going?'

'Us? Go to a party? *No*. That's ridiculous—we won't know a single soul! And besides, we have far too much to do—'

'Do we?' he said softly, drawing even nearer. 'Do we really? Listen, young Matty. You've already said that we can't travel any farther tonight, so why not relax and enjoy ourselves, hmm?'

Her mind had temporarily stopped working, because he'd put his hand on her shoulder. *Brain, behave.* She said, a little too sharply, 'In case you'd forgotten, we're supposed to be keeping ourselves out of sight, Jack. Those men could still be following you!'

He moved away a little to lean against the cabin wall, his arms folded. 'I've not forgotten. But they're unlikely to spot us among the guests at a party. Especially if you wear a gown.'

'A *gown*?'

He shrugged. 'Why not? You've got one hidden somewhere, surely? You'll remember that my pursuers believe I'm travelling with a young lad and if you dress as a girl, it will put them off the scent.'

'But they'll still recognise *you*, Jack!' she cried almost in despair. 'Those two men who attacked you!'

'I really think there's little chance that their employer's kept them on the job, since I left them trussed up like chickens. If they dared to report the encounter, I'd expect they were dismissed on the spot. So.' He was casually looking her up and down. 'About that gown?'

'How do you know I've even got one?'

He was looking at her thoughtfully. 'Because,' he said at last, 'it would be a criminal waste for you not to dress up as what you are, at least once in a while.'

Her heart stopped out of utter shock, but fortunately her mouth came to her rescue and found an appropriate response. 'Gowns aren't much use to me in the life I lead,' she said. 'And, Jack, I really do not want to go to a party!'

'There'll be food,' he reminded her. 'I absolutely refuse to eat bread and cheese again. Besides, I want to ask a few questions—find out the lie of the land, see if my enemy's still lurking hereabouts. In other words—' his expression was serious again now '—I actually think it's rather necessary that we attend this party.'

'Are you trying to tell me that I have no choice?'

'Well, I'm not going to drag you there kicking and screaming.'

'Generous of you,' Matty said bitterly.

He rubbed his hands together. 'So you're coming? Good.' He smiled his charming, wicked smile. 'And now I'm going to go and sort out some stabling for Hercules.'

So, thought Matty, her heart full of apprehension. This party. He wanted her to dress up and pretend to be—what? A friend? His *mistress*?

Oh, for heaven's sake, girl, grow up. He doesn't give a tinker's curse who you pretend to be— you could be his annoying younger sister, for all he cares! And for some reason she felt stupidly deflated again.

At least he was out of the way for now, leaving her a little time to bring back her pulse rate to a state of normality and restore her common sense into the bargain. She suddenly remembered that pool nearby and resolved that she, too, would take advantage of its clear waters herself.

It was a good plan. But unfortunately, as her plans at the moment had the habit of doing, it went a little awry—because as she washed her skin and her hair, she was suddenly aware of her body. Her soft breasts, rosy-tipped; the secret place between her legs—only she *shouldn't* be thinking like that, it was all wrong, because she'd vowed that after Alexander Corton she would never allow any man to get close to her again. Handsome men were particularly dangerous, because they sent your thoughts into a spin. They betrayed you and then laughed at you.

The sun was warm, but she felt cold because she knew she was making herself terribly, terribly vulnerable. She moved across to a deeper part of the pool to swim a little and while she swam she tried to plan her visit to Charlwood Manor, because she would be there very soon. But it was no good because as she dried herself in the sun and combed her hair, she was still thinking—inevitably—of Jack Rutherford.

He's using you, she warned herself again. *And soon he'll be out of your life.*

Which was no doubt just as well—wasn't it?

It wasn't long before she had something else to worry about, because as she walked back to the boat Matty had the unsettling feeling she was being followed. She increased her speed until the path forked at a clump of trees, then concealed herself behind them and waited.

There was a man coming along the path just fifty yards behind her. He'd stopped now and was looking around, as if he was searching for something—or someone. Matty kept very still. She couldn't see his face because his peaked cap shaded it, but she did see that his clothing was rough, like a workman's. After a moment he set off in another direction and disappeared into the woodland.

Matty was glad to return to her boat to find that Jack was safely back and was calmly doing his laundry—rather competently, as it happened. 'We often had to do our own laundering in the army,' he told her.

Of course. She spread her towel out over the boat rail to dry. 'Did you find stabling for Hercules?'

'Absolutely,' he answered. 'I left the old fellow munching oats, happy as can be. Have you found yourself a dress?'

She hesitated. 'I think so. Although it's very plain.'

He was pegging out some shirts on a line he'd rigged up. 'Doesn't matter in the least,' he answered.

He wasn't even looking at her and Matty drew a deep breath. No. Of *course* it didn't matter what she wore—they were only going to some village affair, after all. She was about to go down to her cabin, but suddenly she turned and said, 'Jack. You must have grown up with every comfort—servants, an excellent education. You must miss the life.'

'You think so?' He was pegging out the last shirt. 'Maybe I found that many of the rich folk I met were unpleasant rogues. Maybe I happen to prefer the kind of people I meet this way.' He looked at her directly. 'What colour is your dress, Matty?'

'It's green,' she said, 'just plain green, Jack.'

'Good.' He grinned as he reached in his pocket. 'Because I met a pedlar on my way to the village. And I bought these for you.'

He was handing her some green velvet ribbons and she shook her head, almost laughing. 'No. This is ridiculous! Anyway, my hair's far too short for ribbons!'

'Of course it isn't. Look, you could tie the ribbons at the top, so they flow down a little—see? It's what the fine London ladies do.'

'Ridiculous,' she repeated, but this time her voice was a little faint, because his hands were on her hair, his fingers brushed her forehead, and that sudden warmth flooded her again. *Oh, my.*

'I'll fetch your mirror,' he said.

Swiftly he descended to the cabin and came back with it in his hands. 'Here. Look at yourself.'

She did—and once more her heart beat faster. Yes, the green ribbon suited her chestnut hair wonderfully—but it was something else that worried her. She actually *looked* different. Her eyes had softened somehow, her lips looked fuller; in fact, her whole body felt so sensitive as to be almost tender, somehow laid open...

And it was because of him. This man who was standing next to her, waiting patiently as she looked in the mirror. He was so close she could hear him breathe.

And her body yearned for his touch. Her small breasts felt too heavy, her nipples pulled too tight. Inside her there was a low, almost pleasurable ache that pulsed between her legs. And he wasn't even touching her.

No. This was all wrong! She'd vowed to stay away from men, but that was before she'd met this one. Did he realise the effect he was having on her? Did he guess how vulnerable she felt?

Swiftly she tugged the ribbon from her hair, saying rather tightly, 'I must get ready.' And she swept down to her cabin.

Be careful, Matty girl, Bess would have said. *Be very careful.*

Up on the deck Jack unfolded the clothes he'd packed away in his locker at the beginning of the journey. After putting on a clean shirt and knotting an extremely plain cravat, he eased on his plain but decent coat and smoothed it down, feeling thoughtful. He'd been on his way back from stabling Hercules when something had happened.

He'd caught sight of Matty emerging from that pool.

He'd been rooted to the spot. She looked like a water nymph, he'd realised: a beautiful, extremely feminine water nymph with cropped chestnut hair, long slender legs, a deliciously rounded little bottom and small but high breasts.

He could only thank the Lord she didn't see *him*. He'd hurried quickly back to the barge feeling like a peeping Tom. God, but he wanted her. He'd realised he needed a cold dip again himself, to calm the blood surging to his loins.

He wanted revenge on Fitz. He needed justice, nothing less. The words kept pounding through his mind. But was all that so very important to him that it was worth deceiving someone as honest and brave and as beautiful as Matty?

Yes, he told himself, raking his hand through his hair. Yes, that was the trouble. To him, Charlwood was worth it. He wanted his home back— and to get it, he needed evidence of the fake ransom demand Fitz had concocted to trick his mother into marriage. There was just a chance that there was still vital proof somewhere in Charlwood's library—and surely that was worth deceiving Matty just a little. Wasn't it?

But every day—every hour—he was becoming less and less convinced.

Chapter Nineteen

A full moon lit the evening sky and the air was filled with the scent of wild roses. The beauty of the evening was beyond perfection, but Matty's heart was heavy, because Jack had misled her once more. The party he'd so casually mentioned wasn't some small village affair, but was being held in the grounds of a beautiful country mansion—which belonged to someone Jack happened to know extremely well.

In other words, he'd lied to her yet again.

Earlier Matty had felt a tingle of anticipation as she put on her green dress and carefully tied the ribbons he'd given her in her hair. Jack had encouraged her to hold his arm as they set off together from the canal and Matty, submitting just for a moment to a delicious feeling of femininity, had felt a lightness of heart as they walked.

But gradually she'd realised they weren't going

to the village. In fact they weren't going anywhere near, but instead they were entering the
grounds of a large house whose splendid gardens were lit up with strings of lanterns hung
between the trees. Out on the lawn were at least
twenty trestle tables spread with cold foods and
there were dozens of guests. Already a troupe
of musicians were playing country airs and cou-
ples were dancing merrily beneath the lanterns.

Matty had pulled up abruptly. 'What is this?
Whose house is this?'

'It belongs to a friend of mine,' Jack had said
quickly. 'His name is Lawrence Oakley—his
wife is called Susanna. I called on them earlier
this evening and Lawrence offered to stable Hercules for the night. He also invited us both here
and how could I refuse? It's a midsummer party
for all his staff and tenants.'

'Why didn't you tell me? Why didn't you *prepare* me for all this, before we arrived?'

His eyes were shadowed. 'Maybe I hoped
it would be a pleasant surprise. I thought you
might enjoy a taste of comfort, together with
some lively company—'

'You've lied to me again.' Her throat ached
with disappointment; she could barely speak.
'You must have known I wouldn't want this,

Jack, or you'd have told me the truth.' She turned around. 'I'm going back to my boat.'

But he caught her arm. 'Matty. There's food!' He tried a coaxing smile. 'Couldn't we just stay long enough to eat something here? They've got roast hams and fruit, and fresh-baked bread...'

She tugged her arm away, quite furious by now. 'And as I said before, have you forgotten you're supposed to be hiding from your enemy? How could you even think of appearing here so publicly?'

'These good people would never gossip to strangers about their master's friends.'

'You still lied to me. You stay here by yourself and eat as much as you like, but I'm going, Jack!'

She was already too late, though, because a well-dressed man about Jack's age was coming towards them with a warm smile on his face. 'Jack! I'm so glad you made it! And this must be your good friend, Matilda.' He took Matty's hand. 'We're very happy to welcome you here.'

He'd said *we* because by then a young woman had come up to join him and the man put his arm affectionately around her waist. 'May I introduce my wife, Susanna?'

And Matty realised there was no escape.

* * *

Susanna, though, was lovely. She was also six months pregnant. Swiftly she swept Matty aside as Jack and Lawrence went for drinks. 'They'll want to be with the other men,' she confided to Matty. 'So please come and keep me company! Jack told us just a little about you earlier. He said that you own a canal boat—how wonderful! He also explained that your father was a famous historian—Jack said he'd learned such a lot, travelling with you. Jack and Lawrence were very good friends in the army and they were both aides to Lord Wellington—did he tell you that?'

She broke off as a footman brought them drinks. Matty took her lemonade and said slowly, 'I knew Jack was an officer. But—an aide to Lord Wellington?'

'Oh, indeed. He and Lawrence used to ride on ahead of the troops on Wellington's instructions, scouring enemy territory—often they faced grave danger, with no one to call on for help. How strong they must have been. How courageous.' For a moment Susanna was quiet, but then she smiled again. 'Although I must confess that Lawrence sometimes let slip tales of wild exploits when he and Jack were at university—they were rather mischievous, I'm afraid.

And then they joined the army together, but poor Jack—' Susanna broke off, looking a little anxious.

'I do know that Jack was a prisoner of war.'

'You do? Oh, my dear. I think he had a terrible time, although he hates to talk of it! Afterwards, when he finally returned home to England, he felt very strongly, you know, about the plight of the soldiers who couldn't find homes or jobs. So he did his best to help them. Lawrence told me he even set up a shop to sell their war relics for them and he gave them all the proceeds.'

Matty felt her heart pounding. *The mementoes.* 'Really?' Her voice was scarcely more than a whisper. 'He gave the soldiers all the money? Are you sure?'

'Oh, absolutely sure! It's just the sort of thing Jack would do, though I gather from Lawrence that he lost money hand over fist in the venture, what with the rent of that shop and so on. Especially as he had other problems to face.' She shook her head, then put her hand on Matty's. 'But what about you, my dear? So you live on your own—and on a boat, of all things! Have you no family?'

'My mother died when I was three,' Matty said steadily. 'My father died two years ago.'

'I'm so sorry. What particular aspect of history was he interested in?'

'He searched for places of historic interest around the country, such as the sites of battles and forts and ancient monuments. He loved travelling the waterways and I loved helping him.'

Susanna nodded. 'But—forgive me, my dear—how have you managed since his death? These boats generally need two people to run them, don't they?'

'That's why I took Jack on board.'

'But what will you do when Jack moves on?'

'I'll cope. As I coped before.'

'Isn't that a little risky?'

'Life is risky for many women, I've learned.'

'You're right, of course,' Susanna said softly. 'I've been very lucky.' Her hands moved slightly over her stomach and as she glanced over to where Lawrence stood, Matty saw how her face glowed with affection. She turned back to Matty. 'When Jack called here earlier, he asked us if he might bring a special guest. Of course, I realise you've not known Jack for long. But I think, you know, that he truly meant it—that you are special to him. Oh, look, here are the men coming towards us now...'

They were indeed. Lawrence took his place at

his wife's side and Jack smiled down at Matty. 'Will you do me the very great honour, Miss Matilda, of dancing with me?'

As he drew her into the dance she tried her hardest to concentrate on the steps, but it was nigh impossible because of the usual relentless physical effect he had on her. His very strength made her feel vulnerable and more uncertain with each pounding beat of her heart.

And it was all made doubly, triply worse by what Susanna had just told her—that before he was captured Jack was a brave officer, respected by his commanders and adored by his men. He'd endured lonely and desperate journeys into enemy territory. He'd survived years in a grim prison. And in his shop—the shop she'd been so rude about—he'd been selling those war relics to raise funds for old soldiers. Why hadn't he *told* her?

But now he was penniless and on the run. And all because of the theft of a bracelet? Surely, if he was the quality of man she suspected he was, he would stand and fight his cause a thousand times rather than flee!

The music grew faster, the dancers whirled around them and the stars shone above in the clear night air. She had been to many a village festival, she'd danced with men before. But this was different.

Magic, thought Matty suddenly. *This evening is magic. I've fallen under Jack's spell.*

Ever since that evening with the treacherous Alexander Corton, she had deliberately suppressed her femininity, keeping her hair short, wearing oversized male attire. In fact, she spent most of her time ensuring that men never even glanced at her.

But with Jack, everything had changed. For the first time ever, she allowed herself to feel attractive and feminine as he swept her into the next country dance. And it was as if he knew it.

'I sense that you've let your guard down a little, Captain Matty,' he laughed, his white teeth gleaming.

She let her eyes flash a warning. 'For now. But don't push your luck.'

He had to draw her close for the next steps of the dance. 'Maybe I've already had more than my share of luck,' he whispered in her ear, 'in meeting you.'

And the way he whispered those words became part of the magic of the warm summer night. She felt a sweet melting sensation inside.

Oh, Matty. You are in so much trouble.

Her intention had been to rejoin Susanna the instant the dance ended, but Jack was still holding both her hands in his.

'Excuse me, will you?' Matty tried pulling her hands away. 'I promised I would return to Susanna. I know we agreed to be partners throughout this journey, but don't let your sense of duty carry you away, will you? I'm sure you'll find someone else to dance with very quickly.'

He was still smiling, but something in his eyes shook her to her very core because they were shadowed. Haunted, almost. 'But what,' he said quietly, 'if I only want to dance with you, Matty?' And suddenly all she could do was stare up at him, made mute and confused by all the emotions tangled up inside her. She was lost somewhere between that look on his face and the pounding of her own heart.

He stepped back and Matty felt it like a fresh loss. Then he gave a little bow and departed while she stood there, heaving deep breaths of air into her lungs. Soon—within days—her mission would be complete and he would be gone.

Just as well, she told herself shakily. But the thought was like a knife through her heart.

She found Susanna, who began to ask her all

about her travels on the waterways. Matty answered as well as she could, but after that dance she felt as if the ground had shifted under her feet.

I look different. I feel different, she thought. *Is it because of Jack? But he's not even kissed me yet...*

'I wish he would,' she murmured to herself suddenly. 'Oh, I wish he would.' *What will you do*, Susanna had asked, *when Jack moves on?*

Miss him. That was what. She would miss him.

Soon it was time to sit down at the trestle tables to dine and Matty found herself seated between Susanna and Jack. The food was delicious, the conversation lively, and mostly Matty was content to watch and listen, though Jack turned often to offer her food or wine, or to ask in that surprisingly tender voice of his that sent all her common sense flying, 'Are you enjoying yourself, Matty?'

'Yes,' she answered honestly, because she *was* enjoying herself. The evening was delightful, enchanting even. After the food came the speeches; there was a humorous but heartfelt summary of the estate's fortunes over the last year from Jack's friend Lawrence, who completed his speech by proposing a toast to all his estate workers and servants. Then the music and dancing began again and Jack once more asked Matty to dance, but she shook her head.

Of course, she saw that as he made his way towards the dancers, he immediately had his pick of the prettiest girls. *What else did you expect?* But she still felt the bitter sting of jealousy, so when a rather shy young man came to ask her to dance, she accepted. Not only did she dance with him, she smiled and flirted, too, and soon she was surrounded by an admiring crowd. So it was almost a relief when Lawrence came over to draw her into a quieter corner.

'I'm so glad to get the chance to meet you,' he said. 'Jack has told us that your father was a historian and that now Jack is helping you to complete some task in your father's memory. This must be a very personal and important mission for you. I hope you succeed—and it might help you to know that I would trust Jack with my life.'

Matty was shaken to her core again. *But he's on the run!* she wanted to cry out. Clearly it was no good asking this man to reveal Jack's dark side. But there must be one. There *must.*

After Lawrence had moved on, Matty was swiftly approached by other men hoping for a dance, but she refused, because she'd just thought of something. And this time, it had nothing to do with Jack. Cold fingers were starting to trail down her spine—because she'd suddenly remembered that man earlier, the one she'd guessed might be following her. He'd looked familiar. And now she was sure why—he was the boatman Jack had thrown into the canal for trying to push his barge in front of hers in the queue for the lock.

So he was in this neighbourhood and he was up to no good, she was sure of it. And there was no one to guard *The Wild Rose.*

She hurried to rejoin Susanna once more. 'I'm so sorry. I've loved this evening, but I really need to get back to my boat.'

Susanna looked concerned. 'Of course, my dear. But surely you want Jack to come with you?'

Matty hesitated. The man Bert had been an intimidating figure and if he was up to mischief, she needed help. 'Yes,' she said. 'Yes, I *do* want Jack.'

'Then I think you might find him in the library—Lawrence told me he and Jack were going to look at something in there.'

Matty found the library easily, thanks to Susanna's directions. The door was wide open; candles had been lit, but she couldn't see anyone because at least half the room was hidden from her view by high bookshelves. But as she hesitated in the doorway, she heard voices from the far end. Lawrence and Jack were indeed in there—and they were talking about Charlwood.

She froze. Surely Jack wasn't telling Lawrence about her father's treasure field? He had no right! And why were they speaking in such grave voices? Something was very wrong. Her heart was pounding as she drew closer, still hidden by a tall bookcase. They had their backs to her and were examining some documents laid out on a table.

They were still discussing Charlwood and they were also, she realised, speaking of someone connected to the place in tones of utter contempt. Lawrence was asking, 'Is he still a pompous coward?'

'If anything, he's worse,' she heard Jack answer. 'No different from his army days. He's risen high in government now and has a fine home in Mayfair.'

'Does he visit Charlwood Manor often?'

'Only to gather up the rents from the farms—or so I understand.'

Lawrence appeared to hesitate. 'Does your young friend—Matilda—know of your interest in the place?'

An equal hesitation on Jack's part. Then he said, 'To be honest, I thought it best not to tell her just in case anything goes wrong, you know? It could be dangerous…'

Matty was reeling. What was going on? Why were they talking so intently about the Charlwood estate? She stepped backwards, but in doing so she knocked over a pile of books. There was a crash and the men broke off their conversation. She heard Lawrence's voice: 'What on *earth*…'

Matty was running, out of the library and out of the house, with the men's conversation pounding in her brain.

'Does your young friend—Matilda—know of your interest in the place?'

And Jack's reply—*'To be honest, I thought it best not to tell her just in case anything goes wrong, you know? It could be dangerous…'*

Another lie. One too many. Once she was outside and away from the lights of the house she stood there, feeling dizzy. Nearby, the party was still in full swing, but she moved on swiftly towards the darkness of the gardens.

She needed to be alone. She needed time to collect her thoughts. But first—she had to get to her boat.

Chapter Twenty

She was already calculating the shortest way back to the canal. It was best, she decided, to avoid the main gate and so, running between shrubs and conifers in the darkness, she came at last to the high stone boundary wall where she gripped the top and hauled herself over.

Fresh dismay engulfed her as she heard the sound of her dress catching and ripping at the hem, but what did it matter now? Quickly, she was on her way again. On the far side of the wall were fields which she ran through, causing a flock of sheep to raise their heads in mild alarm. And finally, with a sigh of relief, she saw the canal gleaming ahead of her.

Her boat was still there. But something was wrong.

She'd been right to be afraid. She should never have left it unguarded. She was running again towards it, because the boat was tilting at an odd angle. Climbing aboard, hanging on to the stern rail for balance, she quickly guessed why—it was because the hull had been holed on the far side. She could see, even in the dark, that in the canal there was an unnatural patch of swirling water just below the boat's waterline.

Bert. She suddenly thought she glimpsed a shadowy figure watching her from the bank, but then he was gone. It might have been her imagination, but one thing was definite—if the water continued flowing into her boat like this, it would soon sink.

Clambering down into the cabin, she found that the water there was almost a foot deep. She waded through and found the hole at the far side of the bed. It wasn't more than inches wide, but water was still steadily pouring in.

She hurried up to find the tarpaulin sheet, then descended to the cabin again and tried to push a section of the tarpaulin into place, endeavouring to secure it with anything heavy—her kettle, the flat iron, a big copper cauldron. For the time being the tarpaulin formed a watertight barrier, but then her heart sank again, because her boat was still very much in danger with all that water trapped inside.

She climbed on deck once more, this time to fetch a bucket, then went down into the cabin to fill it, carted the bucket back up the ladder and threw the contents overboard. Over and over again she filled and emptied her bucket until her hands were blistered and she was almost numb with exhaustion.

Can't give up. Mustn't give up.

And then, just as she was starting to think she couldn't do it any more—Jack appeared.

She froze into immobility on the deck, bucket in hand, aware of the water dripping from her dress, her arms, her hands.

'Matty.' He looked tense with shock. 'Matty, I was searching for you everywhere around Lawrence's house. Then I guessed I might find you here. What in God's name has happened?'

'It was Bert.' She put the bucket down wearily. 'Remember? He was the man you threw into the canal. I thought I saw him earlier, before we went to the party. He must have holed my boat while we were away.'

'The low-down, devious wretch...'

She said steadily, 'He's not the only one to be devious. Is he, Jack?'

'What?' He was stepping towards her, his hands outspread. 'Matty, I...'

All of a sudden she felt enormously tired, but she was already picking up her bucket again and saying, 'There's no time to talk about it now. If you truly want to be of any use, then help me bail out the boat. Otherwise you might as well go back to the party and have another dance or two. You're in my way just standing there.'

He looked about to say something, but whatever it was, her expression clearly made him think better of it. He nodded and said, 'I'll help.'

And for every bucket of water she bailed out, he managed two. Soon his clothes were as soaked as hers, but she guessed he didn't even notice. And finally, when no more water was left in the cabin, he looked around and said, 'Right. Everything is wet through, but tomorrow, we can get the mattress and blankets up on deck and start to dry everything out—'

'We?' she broke in. *'We?'*

'I thought,' he said quietly, 'that I could help you. For a start—' and he was glancing at the tarpaulin she'd fixed over the hole '—I can repair that damage properly. Make the boat watertight again.'

She was shaking her head. 'No. Oh, no. I need no more help from you, Jack. Not ever.'

There was a moment's silence. 'Listen, Matty,'

he said, 'I know you were there in the library. I don't know exactly what you heard, but—'

She was holding up her hand in warning. 'Stay away from me,' she was saying. 'I don't want anything more to do with you, do you understand? Because you knew almost from the beginning—didn't you?—that the house I wanted to visit so badly was Charlwood Manor, even though I didn't give you its name. You know the house well, it seems. Yet you never *told* me! And to think I was starting to trust you!'

'Matty,' he said. 'Matty, I grew up at Charlwood Manor.'

'You…?' Sheer shock halted her breathing.

'I grew up there,' he repeated. 'It was my home.'

And suddenly it was too much for her. Her wet dress clung to her, her limbs ached from heaving bucket after bucket of water up the cabin steps. She was exhausted and shivering and just couldn't stop.

'Go,' she whispered to him at last. 'Just go, will you? Back to your friends, back to your *life.*'

But he didn't go anywhere. He simply moved to take her in his arms to cradle her. And it felt so good, so comforting to be held by him, even though his clothes were wet, too, and just for a moment she felt a huge ache rising to her throat.

Only she wouldn't cry. She wouldn't. Not now. Not *ever*.

Jack had found her words just now almost more than he could bear. *'To think I was starting to trust you.'* When he'd called on his old friend Lawrence earlier and Lawrence had invited him to the party, Jack had hesitated in case word got back to Fitz that he was around. But he'd been reassured by the certainty that Lawrence's staff and tenants were fiercely loyal and would guard the privacy of their master's friend against any interloper.

He'd misjudged the main danger, though—that Matty would find out his connection with Charlwood before he had the chance to properly explain. Now she had uncovered his deception, she clearly thought him beneath contempt. And he suddenly realised he was finding that intolerable.

Make an effort to defend yourself, you fool. You must at least try.

'I'm not going anywhere,' he said at last. He'd let go of her and was looking all around. 'Have you got any other blankets? Some dry ones, perhaps, in those cupboards?'

She nodded. 'Up there.' Her voice was muffled. 'In the cupboard above the bed.'

Quickly he went to draw out some folded blankets. 'Right. You go up on deck to get that stove of yours lit and make us some tea. I'll see what I can do about this damage to your boat.'

Really, Jack was thinking that he would give her time. Time to recover from the shock of finding her boat so maliciously damaged and from the shock of realising that he'd been misleading her all along. He wished he could fix her boat right now, but he couldn't even do that because he would need wood and nails to repair the hole properly.

I'll get what I need in the morning, he vowed. *If* she hadn't kicked him out of her life by then.

He climbed up to the deck, half-wondering if he might find Matty armed with a barge pole ready to order him off her boat, but at first he couldn't see her and fresh alarm throbbed through his veins. Where could she have gone? Then he saw her.

She'd been hidden by the cabin roof. She was trying to light the little stove and had pulled on her big coat over that soaked green dress, but she was still shivering badly. Again and again she tried to light the stove, but her hands were shaking too much.

Swiftly he strode over and reached for the tinderbox, noting that she made no effort to acknowledge his presence. He could see that her face was terribly pale, no doubt from cold and the shock of nearly losing her boat. Jack got the stove lit, then somehow he had his arm round her again and was holding her close, saying, 'It's all right, Matty. It will be all right.'

She didn't look up at him, but it gave him a glimmer of hope that at least she hadn't pushed him away. 'I *am* all right,' she said. 'I don't need you, Jack.'

He tightened his arm around her. 'Of course,' he soothed. 'And don't worry. I'll leave here just as soon as you give me the word—but first of all, I want to get a few things straight.' Placing both his hands on her shoulders, he turned her to face him. 'You've not kicked me off your boat yet. Am I to take it as a sign that you're willing at least to talk?'

She looked at him then with her eyes overfull of emotion and he longed to kiss the hurt from them right now. He saw a pulse flickering against the delicate skin of her throat and he wanted nothing more than to press his mouth to that, as well.

Then she spoke and her voice was etched with betrayal. She said, 'I told you everything I knew about Charlwood. The house, the library. You encouraged me. Now I learn you *lived* there. Charlwood Manor was your home. And yet you never saw fit to say anything about this before?'

He'd hurt her. He'd really, truly hurt her. Regret rocked him anew. 'Matty,' he said, 'I didn't mean to humiliate you.'

He heard her make a small, anguished sound at the back of her throat and he went on urgently, 'Please believe me when I say that I really wanted to tell you everything from the start. I genuinely wished to help you get to Charlwood.' She was staring at him now, wide-eyed.

Last chance, Jack.

'You see,' he continued, 'the man who treated your father so badly is my enemy, too. Unfortunately, he also happens to be married to my mother.'

He could see that she'd stopped shivering and for the first time he was beginning to feel a flicker of hope that she might understand. That there might even be some kind of redemption for him. He hadn't realised before just how badly he wanted that. From *her.* Her alone.

He waited, feeling in those few moments as if his life was on hold, until at last she said, 'That man is your stepfather?'

'Yes. May I tell you the full story?'

He saw her hesitate. 'Look,' he said suddenly, 'I've got something better than tea.' Reaching into his deep coat pocket, he pulled out a bottle of wine. 'Lawrence gave me this before I left the party. Perhaps he guessed both of us might need it.'

Her voice was steady now. 'To enable me to swallow yet more of your lies, Jack?'

'No,' he said very quietly. 'To prepare us both for the truth. I'll fetch us two glasses from down below. Shall I?'

'I grew up,' Jack said, 'on the Charlwood estate. That house you visited was my parents' home. My father was an officer in the British army and he died fighting in the American wars when I was seven.'

They were sitting on the deck, their backs against the cabin wall. They were still very close; maybe, he guessed, she was only staying close for the little stove's heat, but he took some comfort in the fact that she hadn't moved away from him. Yet.

Took comfort, too, when she said, very quietly, 'Go on.'

So he did. 'My father was away so often that he was almost a stranger. But to me he was also a hero, and I wanted to follow in his footsteps, so after university I joined the army. Only then, when my regiment was sent to Spain, I encountered an older officer called Sir Henry Fitzroy. You might say it was instant mutual hate. All the soldiers loathed Fitz, and I soon learned the reasons why. He was arrogant, he despised the lower ranks and his military competence was non-existent. For example, during the advance into Spain he ordered a dozen men forward to capture what appeared to be an abandoned gun emplacement at the head of a rock-strewn valley. I objected—I guessed it was a trap—but Fitz threatened to have me court-martialled for questioning his command.'

Jack felt the old rage, the old helplessness surging as he remembered those twelve valiant men heading up the grim, rocky valley. 'My guess proved correct. It was a trap,' he went on, looking straight at Matty. 'They were shot down, one after the other. We all saw it happen. I said to Fitz, "Satisfied now, sir?" and for a moment I thought he was going to hit me—but he didn't.'

Jack shook his head at the memory, at the same time realising that Matty was watching him, her eyes dark and fathomless.

'You see,' he went on, 'Fitz, as well as being an incompetent fool, was a coward. I think the entire regiment cheered when some time later he headed back to London for a comfortable posting with the War Office.' He paused to drink a little of his wine. 'Shortly after that I was captured by enemy troops and ended up a prisoner of war in France for two years. As I told you.'

She still hasn't moved away, he was telling himself. *She's still listening.*

And then she said quietly, 'Were you treated very badly, Jack?'

There was pity in her voice. Not anger, not contempt. He wasn't at all sure he actually wanted her pity, but at least it gave him a chance and he felt hope again.

Letting his eyes crinkle in dark amusement, he said, 'Treated badly? Well, it was hardly feather beds and banquets every night.'

'Was everyone flogged as harshly as you?'

He sighed a little, turning his wine glass in his hand. 'No. I was special.'

'Special?'

'I was picked out because I was the awkward one who kicked up a fuss a bit too often. So I used to be beaten regularly, then thrown into the dungeons to cool off.' He paused and then said in a different voice, 'I used to think about Charlwood often. The sunshine in summer, the crisp snow in winter...' His voice trailed away, then became businesslike again. 'After two years in that gaol some of us were finally released. It turned out that the government had secretly arranged an exchange with some French prisoners and I was shipped back to England. It was my aim to get to Charlwood, of course, but at Dover a letter was waiting for me from my mother. In it she told me not to go to Charlwood but to visit her in London, at an address I didn't know in Mayfair.'

He was shaking his head a little.

'I was puzzled. I was also aware of a feeling of great apprehension. When I got there, a servant answered the door. He said, "Sir Henry Fitzroy is out, sir. But Lady Fitzroy might perhaps see you." Lady Fitzroy? I thought. *Lady Fitzroy?*'

Matty was gazing at him almost in disbelief. 'But Sir Henry Fitzroy was your old army enemy.'

Jack looked straight at her. 'Exactly. And Lady Fitzroy was my mother. While I was a prisoner of war, that bastard had gone and married her.'

'And so by marriage he owns the entire Charlwood estate?'

'That's correct, yes.' He turned to her suddenly. 'But Matty, Charlwood was *not* his when you and your father visited the house two years ago, though it's clear he was already planning to marry my mother and was throwing his weight around. Was reconnoitring the territory, so to speak. And working out how to get his revenge on me.'

'Oh, Jack.'

Just two short words—but the compassion in them warmed him to the very depths of his being. She went on, 'Was it Fitz who accused you of theft and set his men to waylay you?'

'Yes,' he said. 'It's him.'

'So.' She was still looking thoughtful. 'You hate this man because he's married your mother and deprived you of your home.'

He laughed drily. 'Feel free to tell me if you don't think my reasons are good enough.'

'They are *ample*,' she said with surprising, heart-reviving emphasis. 'And I hate this man Fitz, too, for having my father thrown out of

Charlwood—for causing his humiliation and death. Does your mother actually love him?'

'Far from it,' Jack said steadily. 'She was tricked into marrying him.'

'But this man is now your stepfather and owns your home? Jack, if I can help you, I will, I promise.'

Jack felt the most tremendous surge of wanting to hold her, to protect her against everything and everyone. But God, he hadn't done a very good job of it so far, had he? From the start, he'd betrayed her by not telling her the full reasons for his journey. He'd thought that at least he could physically protect her, but he'd been pretty useless at that, too, because if she hadn't come back here when she did, her boat would be lying in the mud at the bottom of the canal.

He'd let her down unforgivably, yet even so all he wanted to do now was to pull her into his arms and kiss those oh-so-sweet lips of hers and banish the anguish in her haunted green eyes. He craved her like nothing he'd ever known.

He could only imagine her acute revulsion if he made any move on her now.

For pity's sake, control your lust, man.

She still looked so desperately intent. 'There

must be a way,' she was saying, 'there just must be, of proving this man Fitz's guilt!'

'There is,' he said quietly. 'Matty, let me explain.'

Chapter Twenty-One

And he told her then. He told her how Fitz had shown his mother a ransom letter demanding five hundred guineas for Jack's freedom. 'My mother,' he explained, 'believed the letter was genuine. But she didn't have that kind of money. Then Fitz said, "If you marry me, I can raise the money on Charlwood." So she married him and, of course, the Charlwood estate became Fitz's.'

'But I thought you told me it was the government that arranged your release!'

'Indeed,' he answered curtly. 'Fitz didn't need to raise any money on the estate—that ransom letter was a fake he concocted, then destroyed. And I believe that you, Matty, have actually seen his attempts to compose it.'

'That letter I saw in a drawer in the library,' she was murmuring. 'In French.'

'Exactly. Now, I could try to contact the War

Office for evidence of the prisoner exchange, but such matters were kept highly secret in wartime. Besides, I don't want all this dragged through the public eye. What I really want is to confront Fitz directly with proof of his fraud. If the document you saw in the library is still there—and I realise it's a big if—it would be exactly what I need to frighten Fitz into admitting his guilt.'

The silence that followed seemed endless to him. He would not have blamed her in the slightest if she'd refused to believe him—indeed, if she wanted nothing more to do with his desperate quest. He prepared himself for it, but he realised, yet again, how it might almost destroy him now to see scorn—disgust, even—in her beautiful eyes.

'What did you do,' she said at last, 'when you realised how Fitz had deceived your mother?'

Relief poured through him. *She believed him.* 'What do you think I did, Matty?'

'I'd guess—I'd hope—that you thumped him.'

He broke into laughter. 'I certainly did. Very hard, as a matter of fact.'

'Good. Then what did he do?'

'Oh, he howled a bit. He said that since I was still technically in the army, he would get me court-martialled. And my mother was sobbing hysterically, so I left his fancy house in Mayfair and vowed revenge.' He paused to drink some more of his wine. 'After that, I'm afraid I went to the bad for a while. I shared lodgings in London with some old soldiers, I drank too much and I made a little money by gambling. I even thought of joining up again, since soldiering seemed to be the only thing I was good for.'

He paused to refill both their glasses with wine. 'But then—*then* I heard how Fitz was wrecking the Charlwood estate. How he was bankrupting the tenant farmers and ruining the land. I couldn't get Charlwood out of my head, though at the time I'd committed myself to an antiques shop in Paddington which—as you know—made hardly any money at all.'

'Because you gave most of your profits away,' she said steadily.

He was surprised. 'How do you know?'

'Susanna told me. She said you sold those relics of the war so you could give the money back to the soldiers they'd belonged to. And there's something else.' She faced him squarely. 'It's about my Roman coin. I remember you tried to say something to me at the auction—*"It's not what you think"*—but I refused to listen. Were you going to give the money from my coin to your soldiers, too?'

He hesitated. 'Since I'd not succeeded in finding you, yes.'

'So you're not quite the complete rogue you pretend to be. Are you, Jack?'

He was silent a moment. 'I'm afraid there's not a lot else I can be proud of. As I said, I'd reached a low ebb.' He reached to take her hand. 'One day, though, this rather exceptional girl came into my life. She had a quest. A mission that she was determined to fulfil, come what may. And I thought, "That's what I should be doing. I should stop making excuses and get on with reclaiming Charlwood."'

'This girl,' he went on, 'lives on a canal boat. She's clever and enterprising. She is also one of the bravest people I've ever met. She offered to help me. She trusted me—even when she knew I was on the run and hadn't been honest enough to tell her why. In a way, that girl *saved* me.'

He was still holding her hand and Matty knew she ought to move away, but she didn't—in fact, she didn't feel she could even breathe. Maybe he wasn't really aware he'd done it, but his touch sent little shivers of longing all through her veins. Something had happened to her as they sat here on the deck. Was it the wine? Was it the night sky above them, warm and sprinkled with a thousand stars? No. It was this man.

He'd come to her rescue when her boat was in peril, but that alone wasn't enough to change her mind about him. What had changed her mind was the look in his eyes when he talked about his past. When he talked about the man who'd married his mother and taken his home.

'You've suffered such injustice, Jack,' she said at last. 'I will do everything I can to help you.'

He'd moved away a little now, letting go of her hand. *Just as well*, she told herself. *Just as well.*

But she felt cold, felt herself growing even colder when he said, 'Matty. There's a question I've been meaning to ask you for some time now. You and your father sound as if you did everything together—were inseparable, in fact. So why weren't you with him on that second visit to Charlwood Manor?'

She told him then about Alexander Corton and Jack didn't interrupt as she talked, but she saw how his eyes darkened and the angles of his face became harder. Was it with disbelief at her gullibility? Her heart flailed and sank, but she pressed on. So be it. He had to know.

'Corton,' she went on, 'came to me when I was alone on the boat and told me he had some information about the lost Roman settlement, so of course I was excited for my father's sake. I asked Corton to wait till the next day, but he said no, he had to leave for Oxford early in the morning. He invited me to see these documents for myself at his hotel in Aylesbury, so I went. But then...'

Then she stopped, because Jack had put his arm around her.

He told himself it was for very obvious reasons. He told himself it was because she'd started shivering again and he wanted to warm her. But he wanted more than that. He wanted to hold her and cherish her until all that damned despair had vanished from her beautiful eyes...

Stop right there, he ordered himself. But he kept his arm around her. No way was he going to stop himself doing that. 'Matty,' he said. 'I think I can guess the rest. You don't have to tell me everything. Not if it upsets you.'

She tilted her chin in that determined way that tightened his heart. 'I want to tell you, Jack. I *want* you to know what a fool I was. Corton led me up to his room at the hotel and of course there were no documents—he knew nothing about the Roman remains and he cared even less. Once I was in his room, he assaulted me.'

'Oh, Matty...'

'No!' She put out her hand. 'I don't want your pity! If he thought I was easy prey, he very quickly regretted it. I slapped him and kicked him where it hurt.' He saw her *almost* smile. 'When I got back to the boat, my father was there.' Her smile had vanished now. 'I realised only then that he'd gone to Charlwood Manor again—this time on his own—and Jack, he looked so very ill! As I've told you, the man he thought was the owner, Fitz, had been there and had ordered the servants to throw him out. I sent for a doctor, but it was too late.'

She looked up at him calmly, but he saw unshed tears in her eyes. 'He died, for which I shall never forgive myself.'

Jack wanted to hold her and never let her go. *Fitz, you bastard.* 'But how on earth can that have been your fault?'

'I was stupid,' she said bitterly. 'I should have realised that Alexander Corton wasn't to be trusted. And I should have been with my father when he went to Charlwood—'

'Matty.' His voice was urgent now. 'Matty,

your mistakes are nothing compared to mine. Listen.' He put his hands on her shoulders, turning her to face him. 'You remember how you believed that those men who attacked the wedding party in London were after *you*?'

She gazed up at him. 'And they weren't?'

'They weren't your enemies, no.' He was desperate to get the words out, get it over with. 'They were Fitz's men, after me, not you, but I never told you. I wouldn't blame you if you can't forgive me, ever, for that.'

Her gaze was steady. 'I do know one thing, Jack,' she said at last. 'Fitz is my enemy, too. So...'

Jack waited.

'So as far as I'm concerned,' she went on, 'we're still in this together. We're still heading for Charlwood. Your home.'

He found himself almost overwhelmed by the flood of sheer relief that poured through him. Then—he couldn't help it—he touched her cheek, caressing her delicate skin with his fingertips, and a miracle happened. Because she reached out to touch his face in return and tremors ran through his whole body as she explored his jaw and trailed her fingers over his sensitive lips. Desire surged through him, hot and hard.

It was with a great effort that he put his hand over hers to stop her and he saw how her face fell. She whispered, 'You don't like me touching you, Jack?'

'I like it.' His voice was almost a groan. 'Too much.'

Her next words were almost a miracle. 'Then please—will you kiss me?'

He attempted to steady his pounding heart. 'No. *No*, Matty. This can only lead to...'

Trouble, he wanted to say. But he didn't say it, because he was already in deep, deep trouble. 'No,' he said again, putting his hands to her waist this time, meaning to ease her away. 'It's not that I don't like you, Matty. I like you very much. But—'

'But what? I'm not fragile, Jack. I won't break. Why won't you kiss me?' Her eyes were wide and yearning.

He said with an effort, 'Your clothes are still wet. You must be cold. You really should change...'

He intended right that very minute to get up and move away. He truly did. But her sweet face was still turned upwards to his and God help him, it was more than he was capable of to resist those tempting, slightly parted lips; especially when she said, 'I'm not cold with you here.'

If he was stunned by that, he was completely amazed by what happened next, because she reached up to clasp her hands around his shoulders and there was a look of such sheer longing in her lovely green eyes that he was just not capable of resisting. *Not cold with you here.* Her words drummed in his head and through his veins and right down to his loins. And he kissed her.

Just a kiss, he told himself, feathering his lips against hers, letting his tongue tease her mouth. *Keep it brief.* Yet when she kissed him back almost shyly, he felt her melt in his arms.

He drew back a little. *Stop, you idiot. Stop this madness now.*

But then she was moving again, arching her neck to press her lips to his again and there came an infinitesimal fraction of time when they *connected*, and he knew what was going to happen and there was nothing he could do to stop it. Somehow, his hands had thrown that blanket across the deck and its soft warmth cushioned them as the kiss deepened.

His thigh sprawled across her legs, his arm encompassed her waist. He could feel that her gown was still faintly damp, but beneath it her body was warm and her small breasts were temptation itself. He could see her nipples through the fabric and gently he used his thumb to caress her there until she gave a soft moan and clamped her hands tighter round him, pulling him close as their legs and arms twined.

He craved her like nothing he'd ever known. He kissed her again, clasping her hard to his chest, and this time she slid her tongue between his lips, exploring him with innocent yet fearless passion. And then he was kissing her back deeply, making love to her fervently; which was, Jack realised with an overwhelming surge of emotion, exactly what he'd wanted to do from the very first day he saw her.

She wrapped her arms around his neck to hold on as if she were in danger of losing her mind if he didn't respond. And there was no earthly chance of him refusing her. They were on the deck of a canal boat, for God's sake, open to the elements—but what could be more elemental, more primitive, more delicious than making love in the open, beneath the stars?

All the time, though, he was anxious not to hurt her, so he made very sure that the blanket beneath them cushioned her at least a little from the wooden planks; although it was obviously she didn't care, since already her hands had found their way under his shirt and were digging into the muscles of his shoulders, while her legs were moving yearningly against his. He fumbled a moment, wrestling with the placket of his damned breeches, because of course he was hard and ready. Then, with his mouth still fused to hers, he reached down to the hem of her frock—*poor crumpled gown, how it had suffered tonight*—and pulled it up and stroked his way along her thighs and straight into her soft, scalding heat.

She moaned his name and arched against his hand and an almost painful wave of desire pounded through him afresh. 'Matty.' His voice was harsh with restrained passion. 'Are you sure?'

She trusts you. Do not get her into trouble, for God's sake.

She was still moving against him and he could feel her heat, her readiness. She was whispering, 'Jack. I want this. Please.' And then he took her innocence, took her virginity, although it was with the utmost tenderness. And her eyes opened very wide as he entered her, caressed her down *there*, while covering her with kisses. 'Are you all right?' he said quietly when he was deep inside her. 'Am I hurting you?'

'No,' she whispered. *'No.'* She lifted her head for his kiss again, which he gave her before bending his head to suckle her breasts, and with that she rose against him and trembled in the throes of her fulfilment. And it was up to him to withdraw and spend himself, while she held him, caressed him.

Afterwards she fell asleep in his arms, curled against his chest while the water lapped a lullaby at the sides of her boat. She'd trusted him. Trusted him in the most complete way possible. And she'd been exquisite.

Rising to his feet, Jack carefully lifted her sleeping weight and carried her down to the cabin. She stirred only slightly and he placed the most delicate of kisses on her lips before laying her on her bed, on a heap of dry blankets he'd managed to pull from one of the lockers. Then he went back up on deck and stretched out on the blanket there, this time to get some rest himself.

But he didn't sleep a wink till long after midnight.

Chapter Twenty-Two

He was wakened by the sound of the dawn chorus in the nearby woods. Rubbing at his eyelids, his limbs cramped from sleeping on the hard deck, he stood up to go hesitantly down to her cabin—and realised that she'd gone.

He felt cold without her. His heart was cold. Had she decided to part with him? He really couldn't blame her, but surely she would never, ever abandon her boat!

Then as he returned to the deck and looked around he saw her in the distance, coming towards the canal with Hercules at her side—she must have gone to fetch him from the stables. He watched her with a full heart, remembering how last night she'd given herself to him with all her body; all her soul, it had seemed. It had been his turn to be the careful one, the cautious one.

He saw her tethering Hercules to a stout post,

twenty yards or so from the boat. Saw, too, that she was dressed in that long coat and boots again—once more she was Matty the canal girl, independent, capable.

She was incredible. He'd never met anyone like her. And he felt the self-rebuke starting to hammer in from all sides. *You careless idiot. What in God's name were you thinking of, dragging her into all your problems?*

Yet Jack had to admit that these last few days of travelling the canals had been the best days of his life, because he'd felt as though the slow but steady progress they'd made each day, with old Hercules at his side, was somehow restoring his body and his mind.

Yes, he'd been made bitter by his years as a prisoner, and that bitterness had been etched even deeper when he returned to find that his old enemy Fitz had moved in on his mother and his family home. To find evidence of that fake letter and to prove Fitz's duplicity would, he'd thought, be a life-changing victory.

But that was before he'd realised what the cost might be.

He'd tricked Matty into thinking that her disguise as a boy had fooled him and he'd kept other secrets from her, told her other lies. But how bitterly he regretted it now, because he wanted her respect—and much, much more.

Over the years many women had held out their lures to Jack, but none had touched his heart like Matty. She was brave and strong-willed, yet completely without vanity or guile. But it wasn't only her character that appealed to him. In that green gown last night, with her cropped hair adorned with those ribbons, she'd looked quite beautiful. Other men had been openly admiring and Jack had felt darts of jealousy. *Hands off. She's mine.*

He'd proved it last night by making love to her. And she'd been utterly exquisite. Ravishingly desirable.

His respect for her this morning was intact, but his guilt lay heavy on his soul. He guessed she didn't trust many people, but she'd given him her trust, even though he had several times almost shattered it. Was she prepared to give him one more chance? He truly didn't know. Yes, this morning she was once more dressed in her boy's attire with her hair thrust under her big hat. But she still looked so lovely that he felt a great wash of emotion. It was as if those months of torment in the prison and Fitz's scheming were all melting away in the face of her fresh, diamond-bright courage.

Having tethered Hercules safely, she was coming towards the boat with a big canvas hold-all over one shoulder. Truth to tell, he wasn't at all sure how to handle this. His prime instinct was to catch her up in his arms and kiss her sweet lips again, but something—maybe the way she looked so businesslike, so purposeful once more—made him hesitate.

In fact, it was she who spoke first. 'Good morning,' she said. And as she stepped on board she opened up her holdall and started drawing out some short lengths of planed timber.

'Good morning.' His response was to raise his eyebrows. 'That wood's for repairing the boat, I assume?'

'I got it from a timber yard just down the way.'

'Presumably you've got nails?'

'Of course.' She was getting out more items. 'I need to seal that hole before setting off again.'

'I'll do it,' he said.

She looked at him steadily. 'So you're still coming with me?'

He moved towards her, his eyes never leaving her face, and he thought he saw just a flicker of fragility in her expression. 'Do you doubt it, Matty?' he said softly.

She shrugged. 'I'm never quite sure of your plans.'

He wanted to kiss her, so much, but her face was shadowed and she'd put up that invisible wall between them again. His heart sank, yet at the same time he gestured lightly to her boat. 'My plan,' he said, 'is to fulfil my side of our bargain and stay with you. Unless, that is, you don't want me to.'

She still looked apprehensive. 'I thought you might have changed your mind. After last night.'

'Never,' he said. 'Never.'

'So we're working partners still, are we?' She had her eyes fixed on those pieces of wood and was arranging them as though they were of the utmost importance—to stop herself having to look at *him*, he supposed.

He looked at her steadily. 'I very much hope so.'

That barrier she'd put up. Why? He felt very bleak all of a sudden, but told himself, *Play it her way. She doesn't trust you yet—and why should she?*

'We're partners,' he went on. 'Shake on it?'

He held her hand for one long moment, then

she pulled away and pointed to the pieces of wood. 'How good are you at repairing holes in boats?'

He grinned. 'Not as good as you, I'd wager, though I'll give it a try.' His expression changed. 'Matty. About last night—'

She broke in before he could go any further. 'Jack. Do you still think Fitz's men might be following you?'

So she didn't even want to talk about last night. 'Yes,' he said. 'It's certainly possible.'

She nodded. That was all. So he picked up the pieces of wood, together with the hammer and nails she'd laid out there, and went below to start mending her boat—*Beautiful Lady*. Beautiful lady indeed. His heart was heavy.

'About last night...' Matty felt those words rolling round and round in her head while she spread out her soaked bedding to dry in the sunshine. What was he about to say? That he regretted everything that had happened? Quite probably.

Her heart was hurting so much, because what she wanted more than anything was for him to kiss her again as he did last night. To make love to her, as he did last night. Had she gone completely mad? How could her body have betrayed her so?

And yet, as she spread out the last blanket on the deck, her memories haunted her. Last night, everything in her world had taken on a magical quality—the stars high above, the gentle sounds of the canal, the wine that had been pounding through her blood. And she'd felt the yearning that she'd felt for days now burning her up inside, felt the sheer longing for him to take her and hold her and much, much more.

Which was why she'd let him touch her where she'd never wanted any man to touch her before. She'd clung to him as if her life depended on it and she'd almost stopped breathing as his lips claimed her and his hands did their work, creating so many wild and intense sensations that everything had melted in that joining of their bodies.

She'd wanted it. She'd almost *demanded* the passion that swept through her like delicious fire and altered everything. Last night, in his arms, it was as if she'd been under some kind of enchantment.

Bess had told her that men were driven by their basic physical urges, but that women felt nothing like the same desire. 'You put up with all that nonsense, lass,' Bess had once said, 'if you love your man.' Bess was wrong, because Jack had offered her pure, thrilling enchantment. What he'd done to her with his lips, his hands and his body had sent such storms of sensation through her that she couldn't ever be the same again.

She tried to squash the memories ruthlessly. *Your fault, Matty. You practically invited him to seduce you.*

What had happened last night must not happen again. She knew that, she accepted it; she must let him think it was a mistake, a one-night-only affair that could be explained away by the tensions they'd both endured during the journey. Her senses had been overwrought, her judgement awry and this morning she must carry on as if none of it had ever happened—but she felt the pain of that denial squeezing her limbs, her heart and her very soul.

She must carry on as she'd begun this morning, keeping him at arm's length. Sensible, practical Matty.

So, while Jack was still below mending her boat, sensible, practical Matty set off to buy a sack of oats from a nearby shop despite her sorely aching heart. On her return she fed Hercules, then saw that Jack had emerged from the boat's hold. He waved to her. 'That hole's all fixed,' he said cheerfully. 'Hungry, Captain Matty?'

She realised he'd already spread out breakfast on the table—bread, cheese and fruit. 'Extremely,' she answered.

But somehow, the food tasted like ashes in her mouth.

It was soon time to set off again and Jack took his place on the towpath at Hercules's side. He felt alert and apprehensive. Today was the final morning of the journey. Today, his whole future might be decided.

He glanced back at Matty, who was by the tiller as usual. If she felt any tension, she wasn't showing it; indeed, she'd made it very clear that she was back in charge and Jack was the deckhand by giving him orders from the very start.

He knew he ought to be relieved by her practicality. There were no sentimental pronouncements on her part, no demands of commitment. She had clearly decided that what happened last night must not happen again, and she was right, surely—so why did he feel an acute sense of loss? The loss of what might have been, the loss of something so very precious?

He tramped on beside Hercules, rebuking himself again and again for his own clumsy handling of the whole situation. Her voice from the boat broke into his self-vilification.

'Watch the rope, Jack,' he heard her calling, 'or it will snap back and break your arm!' And then, only moments later when Hercules had come to an unwarranted stop: 'For heaven's sake, Jack, he's trying to eat ragwort. And it's deadly poison for horses. Keep him away from it, will you?'

She was tough. She was clever. She was independent.

And last night, in his arms, she had been... unforgettable.

It was noon by the time they tied up by a canalside inn, at a place Jack estimated to be only a mile from the Charlwood estate. As he led Hercules to the inn's stable, he was full of mixed emotions.

These were the fields where he used to roam. He remembered every wooded lane, every stream, every pond where trout dabbled. He would get it back, he vowed, whatever it took, whatever it cost him. The trouble was, he hadn't expected it to involve a certain unusual and courageous girl who had put his mind, his heart and pretty much all the rest of him in rather a state of tumult.

Shortly afterwards he entered the alehouse to see that she'd already ordered their meal and was placing drinks and two meat pasties on a table. He watched her chatting easily with some boatmen who sat close by—they clearly recognised her as one of their own.

The canals were her life. *This* was her life, the life she loved; this was a different Matty, not at all the passionate girl he'd made love to last night. The girl who'd surrendered herself to him in a way that had shaken his world.

She looked up calmly as he joined her. 'Well?' she said, pushing his ale and pasty towards him. 'We need to discuss our plan for getting into Charlwood's library and seeing if that letter is still there.'

'Yes,' he said. For the moment he ignored the food and drink. 'We need to talk about Charlwood. But first, Matty—about last night. I wanted to say—'

She leaned forward. 'Jack, you want to get your home back. I want to find my father's treasure field. What happened last night was a distraction, so let's forget it.'

'Right,' said Jack slowly.

Did she mean it? Really, really mean it? Because he was damned if he was going to forget last night and the sweetness of being in her arms! But she was already tucking into her pasty, though after a while she looked up and said, 'First point. How do you know your stepfather won't be at Charlwood Manor? He might well have guessed that you're heading for your home.'

'He won't be there.' He took a swallow of his ale. 'Though you're right to think of it. In fact, I heard from Lawrence that Fitz was planning a visit to Charlwood and had indeed begun the journey by carriage—but this morning, a couple of hours or so after setting off, he'll have received an urgent message demanding his presence back at the War Office in London.'

She frowned. 'How do you know?'

He allowed himself a smile. 'Because Lawrence arranged the fake message. Fitz will be on his way back to London by now and there he'll discover that he was tricked. But it means his arrival at Charlwood—if indeed he decides to try again—will be delayed.'

'You schemer,' was all she said and she tucked into her pasty.

But he saw a glint of approval in her eyes and it cheered him. 'I know. Shameless, aren't I? But it certainly means it will be easier for me to get in the house—'

'Correction.' She sat back in her chair and dusted pastry crumbs from her fingers. 'You're not going in the house—I am. Fitz might have headed back to London, but he'll still have his spies out watching for you.'

'No, Matty!' He almost rose to his feet, then realised they were being watched and sat down again. He said more quietly, '*No.* I'm not even going to discuss this. It could be dangerous for you!'

She watched him calmly. 'You think you're very clever, don't you?'

'Yes—at least on this! I know Fitz, I know Charlwood!'

'Well,' she said, 'you're being pig-headed. At least I stand a chance of success—unlike you. Just think about it. The minute you enter the house, you'll be recognised—you told me there are still servants there from the old days. And if there are any staff there that Fitz has appointed, he'll very likely have given them your description. You'll never get away with it. So it's only going to be *me* entering the house, do you understand? I know exactly where to go and I know what I'm after—I shall collect that old map of the Roman settlement and that draft letter about the Chateau Esperance—if it's still there.'

If was the crucial word. He felt angry and powerless at the same time. He was so close and yet he could still face failure. 'No,' he said again. 'I'll bring back that map for you, if that's what you're worried about. I know you found both items in the library, Matty. All you have to do is tell me exactly where—'

'I won't,' she said calmly.

'What?'

'I won't tell you. And that library is crammed with papers—it could take you all day, longer even, to find anything. So I'm going in by myself and you're not stopping me.'

'I refuse to let you enter the house by yourself!'

She was silent a moment. Then she said, 'Have you got those dice of yours?'

'Yes! But—'

'Give them to me.'

Slowly he retrieved them from his pocket and handed them over.

'Right,' she said. 'The person who throws highest goes into Charlwood Manor. Your turn first.'

Jack threw a three and a four. She threw a six and a five. He groaned inwardly.

'Looks pretty definite to me,' she said.

Her chin was jutting stubbornly. Jack knew when to acknowledge defeat. 'Very well,' he said wearily. 'You're in charge of the campaign, Captain Matty.'

'I'm glad you see it my way,' she said. 'Major Rutherford.'

He pocketed his dice. 'I still think it's crazy! But believe me, I'm grateful.'

She lifted her glass. 'My pleasure.'

My pleasure? Damn, he wanted to give her pleasure like last night, over and over again. He gritted his teeth.

An hour later he watched her as she set off along the path to Charlwood Manor carrying a leather document case she told him had belonged to her father. No green frock or green ribbons this time—in fact, she'd dressed in a drab brown skirt and jacket and wore a rather grim-looking bonnet so she looked exactly like a governess, except that she still had that glint of absolute determination in her eyes.

Just before the path took her out of sight, she turned round and waved to him.

He waved back. And he was missing her already.

As Matty walked up the driveway to Charlwood Manor, she found her footsteps slowing. It seemed incredible to her now that only a short while ago, she'd felt so very certain about everything. She'd thought she knew exactly how she wanted her life to unfold—she would find the site of the Roman settlement for her father, then she would continue to travel the canals in the way she'd always loved. That, she thought, was all she'd ever wished for.

But Jack Rutherford had changed everything—it was no good denying it. He'd changed her hopes, her expectations, even her knowledge of herself, and she was frightened at what she now knew: that she had a heart that was all too vulnerable.

'I'm sorry, Jack,' she whispered aloud. 'I've behaved abominably today, shutting myself off from you, giving you orders. It's because I'm trying to protect myself—and protect you, too.'

Her words fell on empty air, of course. She walked on up the drive and, after hesitating only briefly in front of the imposing front door, she knocked firmly. She *had* to do this, for her father and for Jack.

The door opened and immediately she recognised the kind old servant who'd let herself and her father in two years ago. Bracewell, Jack had called him.

'Ma'am?' Bracewell spoke uncertainly.

'You may not remember me,' Matty said, 'but I called here two years ago with my father, the historian Geoffrey Grey.'

His face cleared. 'Of course I remember! And I was so sorry to hear that your father died soon after his second visit. My sympathies, ma'am.'

'Thank you,' she said quietly, 'my father is very much missed. But I'm trying to continue his unfinished work. And I was wondering if I might be permitted, just briefly, to look in the library again? I remember there was an old map here that might help me greatly...'

Moments later she was in the library. Yes, it had been easy to get inside—too easy. Because she had been in the library scarcely twenty minutes when Bracewell hurried in to her, his face anxious.

'Ma'am. Something unexpected has occurred, I fear...'

Chapter Twenty-Three

Jack had been grooming Hercules, but he put down the brushes quickly when Matty arrived back one hour later. She looked tense and all his fear for her gathered inside him like a dark cloud. 'Whatever's happened?' He was coming swiftly towards her. 'Did something go wrong?'

'You could say so.' She was pulling off her awful hat and her brown governess jacket. 'Your stepfather, Fitz, arrived.'

His face hardened. *'No.'*

'It's very much a *yes*, I'm afraid.'

'But how...?' He was shaking his head. 'It sounds as if Lawrence's message must have gone astray.' His tone sharpened. 'Did Fitz see you?'

'No. Thanks to Bracewell, he didn't. Fortunately we had some warning—Fitz had sent a rider on ahead of his carriage and Bracewell helped me to get out of the house the back way.'

'Matty, I'm sorry! This is why I wanted to go myself. I never wanted to put you in danger—'

Her eyes glinted with determination. 'I keep telling you that I've managed to look after myself for years now—and I still can.' She met his gaze steadily. 'I don't like to fail, Jack.'

He felt the first faint glimmer of hope. 'Then—Matty...'

'I don't like to fail,' she repeated. 'So I've brought you—*this*.'

She opened her father's document case and handed him a sheet of paper. 'Is this what you wanted, Jack?'

He scanned it swiftly.

Jack had never allowed himself to wholly believe that his scheme was possible. After two years, the chances were incredibly slim that the piece of paper she'd spotted in a dusty drawer was still there, but just as she'd promised, this incredibly resourceful girl had brought him what he could see was a rough draft of the ransom letter Fitz had forged. The French was poor, but the content and intention were clear enough. The letter was supposedly from the governor of the French prison—the Chateau Esperance—asking for five hundred guineas for Jack's release.

And it was in Fitz's writing.

'This is it,' Jack said. 'This is exactly what I need. Matty, you're brilliant.' He hugged her.

And slowly but surely she eased herself away, as he suddenly realised, with a jagged tearing at his heart, that he wanted to keep her in his arms. He wanted to hold her tight and cover her beautiful face with kisses and...

She was still smiling, but it was as if she'd deliberately drawn an invisible curtain between the two of them. Protecting herself from him. Who could blame her?

You must sort this, Jack. You must.

'So I'm brilliant, am I?' She raised her eyebrows a little, teasing him. 'Maybe so. But I can't make sense of the ransom, Jack. Fitz really thought he could claim you were worth five hundred guineas?'

'My mother believed it,' Jack said wryly. 'But then, she always was a bit foolish, you know?'

Matty looked more serious. 'Yes. Of course she would want you back at any price.' She lifted her eyes to his. 'So now I suppose you can't wait to start work on reclaiming your family home?'

A week ago, his answer would have been yes, he couldn't wait. But now, suddenly, Jack was gripped by the absolute certainty that he didn't want to leave this girl. Ever.

Careful, he warned himself. *Careful.*

Because he'd realised she was drawing something else from that serviceable case of hers and was spreading it out in front of them.

'While I was in the library,' she said, 'I also found—*this.*' Her voice held a kind of tremulous excitement that he guessed she was trying hard to control. 'It's the map I told you about. A very old map that my father found when we went to the house together. It shows the site of the Roman settlement. Do you see? In the same area where my father found the coin.' She was smoothing the map out almost reverently. 'It existed, Jack. It really did.'

And his heart sank even further.

She led him along a grassy track not far from the canal just as the sun was starting to set and she pointed to the area of rough pastureland marked on that old, faded map. It was inscribed with the name of the man who'd drawn it with such care—*Thomas Dunne*—together with the date: 1653. Matty had it in her hand all the time; Jack wondered if in fact she would sleep with it under her pillow tonight. And now she showed it to him again.

As if he didn't already know every line, every shading of its damnable contents.

Her voice—her sweet, true, *believing* voice—betrayed her excitement, even though she tried her best to keep it steady. 'Here is the stand of pine trees.' She pointed. 'It wasn't far from here that my father found the coin. He'd already guessed there was a Roman site in the area, but he was only working on hearsay, together with some vague references in his history books. Finding the coin lifted my father's hopes, but he couldn't find any other actual evidence. Then he and I saw this map at Charlwood Manor. My father wanted to come back and examine it more closely, to make certain of the area it pointed to and maybe find out more about Thomas Dunne—but you know what happened next.'

Her face clouded. But then she looked around and her eyes lit up again. 'My father's work was all worthwhile. This could be a site of truly great value to historians. Tomorrow I shall begin to explore for myself—I still have my father's tools on board the boat. Maybe soon I'll need more expert help, but I can at least make a start...'

Jack's spirits were as low as they'd ever been in

his life. 'Matty,' he said. 'Matty. There's something you should know.'

As he began to tell her the truth, he saw her beautiful, trusting face grow white and drawn and he felt like the biggest villain on earth. He explained to her that he knew this area well, because as a boy he used to ride his pony out here. He told her that beneath the scrubby bushes and meadow plants lay clay, and over a hundred years ago, all of this area had been dug up for that clay, which was then used to build farm-workers' cottages in the nearby village of Feld-ham.

'All the locals know this was once a clay pit,' he said. 'Of course it became filled in over time and plants and trees began to grow. But if ever there had been a Roman settlement here, any treasure would have been discovered by those clay-pit diggers over a century ago.'

'But what about this map?'

He shook his head. 'Matty, I'm afraid Thomas Dunne was a local eccentric. Yes, there have always been legends that the Romans once settled around here, but there was never any real proof. Thomas Dunne was a fantasist. As well as drawing your map, he wrote many fabricated tales

about times gone by and nobody took him seriously, either in his own lifetime or since. That
would be why your father had never heard of him
and why no one in authority expected to find
any sort of treasure when the clay pit was dug.'

'But my father's coin,' Matty whispered at last.

He hesitated. 'It could have been dropped by
a traveller.'

'As you suggested before we even started this
journey.'

For a few moments after that she stood very
still. And as he saw the light, the hope, die out in
her eyes, he felt her despair twisting his insides.
At last she went on, in a very low voice, 'You
knew this, didn't you? You knew all along that
there couldn't possibly be any Roman remains
here in the place I described—but you didn't tell
me. How could you *not* have told me, straight
away? No—don't trouble to answer, Jack, because I already know what you'll say. It's because you planned all along just to use me. To
bring you to Charlwood, to get those letters for
you, from the library.'

'Matty, please...'

'Listen. Listen to me a moment.' She drew a
deep breath. 'I've always been an outsider, Jack,
wherever I go. I'd grown used to not fitting into

either the Oxford world of my father's friends or the world of the canal folk. I thought I'd learned to accept that I was different—to accept for good that I was on my own. But then you came along and, stupid as I am, I was beginning to think that maybe—just maybe—I could trust you. Even when I found out you were using me to reclaim your family home, I thought, why not? Charlwood is a lovely place, so I couldn't blame you. But now. *This.*'

She looked around, despair clouding her features. 'You knew all along that the place I described to you couldn't hold my father's treasure—but only now do you tell me. Now, when my hopes have been raised so high. Thanks to you, I've been made to feel an absolute fool.'

'Matty,' he said. 'What can I say?'

'Nothing,' she said steadily. 'Absolutely nothing, Jack.'

She was already turning away from him, but he moved to block her way. 'Look,' he said. 'Your father was right—as I told you, there really have always been legends about the Romans in this area and who's to say they're not based on the truth? When Charlwood is mine, we'll search properly. I'll hire experts to comb the whole area for any signs of genuine remains—'

'Do you really expect me to trust you again?' Her voice was bitter now. 'I'm afraid not. You've played games with me several times and I made it rather easy for you, after all. But I cannot forgive you.' She picked up her map and began walking steadily back to the canal and her boat.

'Matty,' he called.

She called back over her shoulder, 'Don't bother saying any more. You're wasting your energy and my time. I'm well aware you still have a few possessions on my boat, so I'll put them out on the bank for you.'

'Please wait. Are you heading back to London? How will you manage on your own?'

'I'll manage perfectly well, just as I managed before *you* appeared. And now the best thing you can do for me is to get out of my life right now. Do you understand?'

The minute she arrived back at her boat, she gathered all his things from the cabin. His spare clothes. And those dice, carved for him in the French prison... Suddenly she felt a huge ache at the back of her throat and her eyes misted, but after blinking hard, she climbed back on deck and dumped them on the towpath. Hercules, tethered close by, watched her and looked puzzled.

She rubbed at her eyes with the back of her hand, feeling more like throwing Jack Rutherford's things in the canal. Stupid man. Stupid *her.* But, oh, she hurt inside, as if every piece of her was damaged beyond repair. She went back inside her cabin, so she wouldn't have to see him when he came to collect his things.

Tomorrow, she would set off on her own again. She would do as she'd done before—earn money by carrying light loads, only a little more often now so she'd have enough income to keep living on her boat. That was her priority. But all her dreams had died: both her dream of finding her father's treasure and her dream of having found someone special.

Time is a healer, she told herself.

What a trite, meaningless phrase. She hurt, she physically hurt—and she didn't think she would ever recover from this betrayal. Yes, life would carry on, but she wouldn't be the same, ever. Couldn't trust anyone with her foolish heart again. She went back to her cabin, listening for his footsteps on the towpath; heard them stop, then go away. She went up a few moments later to find that indeed both Jack and his possessions had disappeared.

Then she noticed a piece of paper pinned to the cabin roof.

Matty,
Please believe that I never meant to hurt you.
J

She nearly cried then. But she didn't, because Hercules needed feeding, and she had to buy some supplies for her journey south the next day. A journey she would be making on her own.

Jack set off on foot for Aylesbury, from where he intended to travel back to London by stage-coach. Deep in his coat pocket, he had the faked ransom letter that would enable him to force the truth out of Fitz. At last, the dark shadows that had lain over him for two long years were beginning to lift and he could see his future ahead.

But the future wasn't nearly as bright as it should have been, because he was haunted by the expression on the face of a beautiful and courageous girl when he'd told her just now that he'd always known her father's dream of finding lost treasure was an impossible one. Yes, it was time to head back to London. It was time to confront Fitz with that fateful sheet of paper he'd so carelessly left at Charlwood and see the fear in his stepfather's eyes when Jack threatened to expose him for the cheating rogue he was. It was time for Jack to claim back his inheritance. Within his actual grasp were the twin goals of revenge on Fitz and the restoration of his lost home.

But all he could think of was—Matty.

Chapter Twenty-Four

Three weeks later

Matty looked around the wharf at Aylesbury and tried to pretend that everything was the same as it always had been.

She was on her own. And wasn't she used to that? Wasn't she coping? Certainly everyone told her so. Thanks to the kindly weather and the help she'd received from other canal folk, she'd sailed her boat here without incident. She'd called round the warehouses close by and secured a contract to carry some cases of pottery to London, which was just the kind of job she needed—light and well paid.

She had, moreover, met by chance with her good friends Bess and Daniel, who had arrived here to pick up a load of wheat. She'd had lunch with them at the alehouse on the quay, but unfortunately they'd wanted to know all about Jack.

'Where's that young fellow you took off with?' Bess had demanded. 'He didn't give you any trouble, did he?'

'No,' Matty said. And changed the subject.

She'd been so terribly naive. *There are no happy endings*, she kept telling herself now as she gazed around the busy wharf. Certainly not with a man like him. The trouble was, she'd just started to believe otherwise.

Those days as she'd travelled with Jack on her boat had been like an idyllic dream. Yes, they'd had disagreements, but they'd had such fun, too. It had seemed so *right*, having Jack with her to tease her out of her anxieties and support her. And now—oh, how she missed him. Poor Hercules missed him, as well—he kept looking around whenever a man approached, as if hoping it might be Jack, but of course it wasn't. Matty tried giving him carrots, but he refused them with a snort.

Nothing was the same without Jack. And Matty didn't see how it ever could be, because he had changed everything. Changed *her*. She'd believed she was impervious to men, but Jack's lightest touch had warned her that here was someone very different and very dangerous; though had she taken heed of that warning? No.

She'd offered only the faintest resistance to his charms.

And when she'd been at her most vulnerable, on the night when she'd almost lost her boat, he'd held her and comforted her and then made love to her—and it had been a revelation. She'd surrendered to desire and to passion, she'd surrendered to the exquisite pleasure she'd always denied herself—leading to an implosion that had rocked her world, with him at its very centre.

She'd fallen in love, but all along he'd kept secrets from her. He'd not told her about his army career and his time as a prisoner of war. All of that she could understand—he was a proud man, after all, and wouldn't want to confess his darkest moments. But he'd not told her about his lost inheritance, either, and instead he'd used her boat to get to his home, so he could find proof of his stepfather's villainy.

And yet she'd forgiven him, time and time again! Only then, on that last day, as she led him to the field with the pine trees where she'd hoped so much that Roman treasure lay, Jack had told her he'd always known there was no historic site around here—because the field had been dug up over a century ago and the man who'd drawn up the old map was a fraud.

Two dreams were shattered at once: her vow to fulfil her father's lifelong mission and her secret, burgeoning hope that, in Jack, she'd found someone special. He was certainly different, since he'd done something she thought was impossible. He'd broken her heart.

She wouldn't be setting off south with her pottery until the next day, so that afternoon she wandered round Aylesbury, finding a quaint area that was full of shops selling prints and books and other curios. Down a back lane she came across a building with a faded sign hanging over the door—*Antiques Bought And Sold*—and when she peered inside, she saw that it was crammed with oddities. Memories of Mr Percival's shop in Paddington suddenly assailed her and her heart screwed up tight inside.

Oh, Jack. She felt a huge pang of longing and of loss.

It was in that moment that a voice came from behind her.

'I've just met up with your friends, Bess and Daniel. They suggested I might find you here.'

She whirled round.

It was Jack, looking ridiculously handsome in his smart London clothes; Jack, gazing at her with such intensity in his blue eyes that it almost stopped her breathing.

Her heart hammered. 'What are you doing here?'

'Searching,' he said. 'For you. May we talk?'

She wanted so much to be strong and say no, but was it strong to run away? Better to stay and listen, surely, and treat him with the scorn he deserved. 'You don't give up easily, Jack,' she said coolly, 'do you? Very well. Since you insist, we'll talk.'

He took her to a tavern that wasn't as noisy as the alehouses near the quay and there he told her how he'd been to London to confront his stepfather in his Grosvenor Square mansion and had shown him the letter Matty had found.

'What did your stepfather say?'

Keep cool. Keep calm, Matty.

She saw Jack give a grim smile. 'It was pretty much as I expected. He blustered and he lied. I told him that unless he immediately made over the Charlwood estate to me, I would reveal him to the world as a fraudster and a charlatan. So I've got Charlwood back.' He paused a moment, gazing into the fire glowing in the nearby hearth. Then he looked directly at her.

His blue gaze was like a sensual onslaught.

Her lungs suddenly ached with the need for air. And he went on, 'If it wasn't for you, Matty, none of this—*none* of it—would have been possible.'

'Well,' she said with false brightness, 'I'm glad I was of some use to you, Jack.'

'You've been much more than that.' His voice was low and intense. 'So much more.'

'I do hope you're not thinking of offering me some kind of reward?' She was already rising to her feet and the sound of her own chair grating across the floorboards was harsh in her ears. 'Don't forget that you deceived me from the very first day we met. You were clever, though, pretending all the time to believe my story about the Roman site. If you've come here hoping to salve your conscience by saying sorry, you're just a little late, I'm afraid.'

She moved to go, but he was on his feet, too, and was grabbing her hand. 'Stop. *Please*. Matty, I've moved into Charlwood Manor now...'

'Good for you. No doubt the house and estate will keep you busy.'

'That can all wait. The real reason I wanted to find you is *this*.' He reached into his pocket and pulled out a folded document. 'My first task, when I returned to Charlwood, was to look again through all the old plans of the estate. And look what I found.'

He'd spread the document on the table between them. 'This,' he went on, 'is a much older map than the one you found. And it shows the site of some Roman remains—not where you thought they were, but a quarter of a mile away, do you see? So I'm here to ask you—will you come with me to examine this new site?'

'So that you can claim the treasure, you mean?' Her blood was heating up because of the way he was looking at her, but she fought down any expectation that things might have changed—until he put his hand, warm and strong, over hers.

She felt his gaze burning into her as he said, 'I haven't even *thought* about claiming the treasure. Come with me, I beg you. I've brought you a horse. It's waiting outside, with mine.'

She looked at him. 'You assumed I would come, then?'

'Yes,' he said. 'I *prayed* you would come. Shall I lead the way?'

Jack had been through many hellish situations in his life; but this time, he had to admit he'd never been so damned scared in all his life. She'd come to mean so much to him, this girl, in so short a time. She was independent, courageous and knowledgeable—and so damned lovely, he wanted to take her in his arms and kiss her, right now.

It was raining slightly by the time they got to the site shown on his map and the air was chilly, but something in her eyes as she looked around warmed him to his core, because they shone with new-found hope. 'This must have been pasture-land for centuries,' she was saying as she dismounted. 'Do you agree?'

He tethered both their horses to a nearby tree. 'It's been used occasionally for sheep, that's all. I checked the estate's records.'

She was moving forward as carefully as if she was on sacred ground. 'There are some ridges here that *could* just be the outline of a villa— they would be about the right size, the right shape. And over there are more raised areas that could have been barns or stables—' She broke off suddenly. 'Of course, I realise that anything here of value is yours, Jack. You're the owner of the land.'

He stepped forward and his heart was thundering. He took her hand and kissed it; then he said, steady and clear, 'If you marry me, Matty, it will be yours, as well.'

Her eyes were wide. 'Jack?' she whispered. But she didn't pull away and that gave him the strength to persevere.

'Marry me,' he repeated. 'There's no one else for me.'

'You can't mean it.'

'I've never been so sure of anything in my whole life. I love you, Matty, so I'm not going to waste time arguing. Instead I'm going to kiss you, which I wanted to do on the first day I met you, when you pulled down that shelf full of Ming vases on my attackers.'

'But they weren't—'

'Yes, I know.' He chuckled. 'They were nothing like Ming vases. But even if they were, I would still have forgiven you—a thousand times over.'

He pulled her to him and he kissed her as if he would never let her go. And when he felt her slender arms twining around his shoulders, he thrilled to her touch and kissed her again; he kissed her out there in the field until she was clinging to him like a vine, arching her hips against him. And he was able to hope again, though then he held her away, just a little.

Why have you stopped? her look said. As if

she was thinking, *Are you going to let me down again?*

Oh, no. Oh, God, no. He bent his head to kiss the delicate tip of her nose and said softly, 'Matty, I love you. In fact, I adore you—but it's raining. You might have noticed that, actually, it's pouring down.'

She began to laugh. 'We're crazy,' she said. And suddenly he was laughing, too, at the sheer, amazing absurdity of it all, their passionate embrace here in the middle of the rain-soaked field. He took her hands and swung her up in his arms—she was his new-found treasure and, by God, he wasn't going to let her go.

He put her down at last, but still held her hand as he said, 'Back to my house. Yes?'

She nodded, still breathless. 'Yes. Back to Charlwood. And, Jack—I love you, too. Of *course* I do.'

He had to kiss her again after that. But then he suddenly remembered. 'Your boat. And Hercules, back at the wharf...'

She wagged her finger, smiling. 'Remember me? Capable Matty? I asked Bess and Daniel to look after them for me. They told me to take as long as I need.'

'Good,' he said softly. 'Because it's going to

take me quite a while to say—and do—everything I want to this time, believe me.'

She was a little afraid of what the staff might
think as Jack led her through the front door, but
somehow all the servants had miraculously disappeared. Knowing Jack as she did, Matty did
wonder if he had sent advance orders.

*Out of my way. I'm arriving soon with a very
special guest.*

A rather rain-soaked guest, as it happened;
but she wasn't cold in the least, because he had
his arm around her as they hurried up the staircase to his room—what a lovely room, with huge
windows looking out over the park! In there a
fire was burning, making the air toasty warm.

She hadn't ever believed in fairy tales. But
for now she had to as she stood there dripping
water on his expensive carpet like a drowned
thing and he came up to her and began firmly
yet with the utmost tenderness to strip her wet
clothes from her, then wrap her in a huge fluffy
towel and settle her, very firmly again, on his
vast bed with its heaps of pillows.

And then he was stripping off his own wet
clothes and was striding towards her stark naked

and... *Oh, my*, Matty thought. She had never seen a more glorious sight in all her life.

His blue eyes glittered darkly as he eased her into the centre of the bed, then he began to kiss her everywhere: her lips, the tender tips of her breasts, until all of her body was exposed and aching for him. He kissed her down *there*, in her most secret place, taking his time until she was writhing with need; then he came back to reclaim her mouth and he slid that hard, proud length that was the very essence of his male-ness into the heart of her. He was touching her down there, too, a knowing touch; she felt the wave of need swell and roar as he drove into her and, when she started to fall apart in shattering pleasure, she felt him join with her and cry out her name.

She woke in his arms an hour later. They were both still deliciously naked, but he'd covered them with a crisp linen sheet. She stirred sleepily—and then she remembered. She was a canal girl. He was wealthy. All this, the beauti-ful house, its farms and land, belonged to him.

He'd propped himself up on one elbow and was watching her, his mouth curling in gentle amusement. 'What are you worried about this time, darling Matty?'

She struggled for the words. *You. Regretting this. Me. I shouldn't be here...*

'The servants,' she blurted out. 'They might think—'

'Let them think what the hell they like,' he said lazily. He moved slightly so he was positioned over her, that stunning body of his stretched out so exquisitely that it started off the familiar pulse of need. 'They'll be perfectly content to be told you're going to be my wife. I'm sure they think it's time I settled down and became respectable.'

His wife. There. He'd said it again! But still she couldn't quite believe it. 'Jack. Jack, I don't want you to do something you might regret. We've not known each other for long, after all. Only a matter of weeks.'

'Is that all?' He was studying her with a small frown on his face, then he reached to kiss the corner of her chin; a delicate kiss that nevertheless set her heart racing. 'Do you know, I feel as though we've known one another for much longer than that. I love you, darling Matty. And I've been waiting for you all my life.'

She drew away from him a little and he felt his breathing stop. He'd found the ultimate treasure in her, and if she didn't want him, then his inheritance could go hang because it would be meaningless without her.

'There's one condition, Jack.' She turned back to him. Her face was solemn and his heart sank. If she was going to ask something impossible, how would he cope?

Then he saw those mischievous dimples playing around the corners of her adorable mouth. And she said, 'Can I keep Hercules?'

He gave a shout of laughter then pulled her to him, and she was every bit as eager for the kiss as he was. He heard her whispering, 'I love you, Jack, so much. I'm yours. All yours,' and he knew, then, that she truly was.

Epilogue

Oxford—one year later

As Matty hurried out of the museum she heard the church bells striking midday. *Oh, no.* She hadn't meant to be so late. But looking around the museum's new display of recently discovered Roman antiquities had taken a little longer than she'd thought.

She'd been invited especially by the museum's curators, because this exhibition would be going on show to the public within days. In it were all the finds made in the last few months at the site near Charlwood that her father had always dreamed of uncovering. And everything in the display was perfect. The staff had arranged it all exactly as Matty had wanted, with a brass dedication plate in the centre of the room.

This display is in honour of the distinguished historian Geoffrey Grey, who was the first to realise the existence of these unique remains of Roman life.

The experts who had come out to explore the site had found treasure indeed—not only the remains of a palatial Roman villa buried deep beneath the soil, but other buildings along with artefacts—urns, vases, coins and jewellery. Matty had insisted it all go to the Oxford Museum. Though the curators there had tried to convince her there ought to be a reward, she wanted none. She'd kept her promise to her father and that was reward enough.

She speeded her steps because she was almost at the quayside now. Once there, she spotted Jack straight away. He hadn't seen her yet, so she was able to study him at leisure—and her heart gave a little leap.

He was standing on the deck of *Beautiful Lady*, leaning one arm casually on the cabin roof while he chatted to the owner of a neighbouring boat. Matty almost had to laugh, because no doubt he'd be talking about locks and tonnage and tillers just as earnestly as someone who'd lived on the canals all his life. And something—some emotion that was almost overpowering—caught in her throat, filling her with disbelief and joy.

He's mine. Yes, Jack was her husband now. At present he was dressed like any other bargeman in boots and breeches, loose shirt and waistcoat. Apparently unaware of her approach, he was still talking to the boatman—only then his eyes caught hers as she drew near.

He tapped his watch, but there was a twinkle in his eye. 'Do you realise you're a little late, Mrs Rutherford?'

She stepped on deck and handed him the catalogue she'd been carrying. 'All in a good cause,' she told him firmly. 'The exhibition is *excellent.*'

He nodded. 'Then it's time we were heading north, before the queue starts to build for the next lock.'

Matty grinned. 'My, aren't we the eager sailor?'

'It's you I caught it from.' He pretended to sigh. 'My life just hasn't been the same since you arrived.'

For answer, she put her hands on his shoulders and pressed her lips to his cheek before murmuring, 'Are you saying you're sorry?'

He pulled her towards him and kissed her on

the lips, very thoroughly. Then he said softly, 'Have you heard one word of complaint?'

They'd married at Charlwood Manor within weeks of Jack's proposal. His mother had been at the ceremony, of course, together with Lawrence and Susanna and other old friends, and there had been many neighbours and tenants who had all expressed heartfelt relief that Jack rather than Sir Henry Fitzroy was back in charge.

There was plenty of work to be done on the estate, which had been drained of cash during Fitz's brief ownership. Jack had tackled that in his usual forthright way—he'd told Fitz that unless he paid back the money he'd taken, his forged ransom scheme would be made public. Fitz paid up.

Jack's mother moved with great happiness into the Dower House on the Charlwood estate. She was completely charmed by Matty and her canal boat—and by Hercules. 'Oh, what a dear horse he is!' she'd exclaimed. 'And how clever you are, Matilda darling, to have sailed along the waterways, all by yourself!'

Hercules was retired and he lived a pampered life in Charlwood's stables. But Matty bought another horse called Robbie and every month or so she and Jack would sail the canals in *Beautiful Lady*, often heading north to Braunston Lock, then down the new canal to Oxford.

It had taken some time for the remains of the Roman settlement to be completely uncovered by specialists and Matty was involved at every stage, just as her father would have been. But now the finds were safe in the museum, so her task was complete.

As they stood on the boat together, she leaned into Jack's strong shoulder and sighed contentedly. He smiled down at her and said, 'Next decision. Are you going to walk ahead along the towpath with Robbie or am I? We need to be on our way, as I said, or—'

'Or we might have to queue for the lock,' she chimed in. 'Yes, I know. I'll walk with Robbie, shall I?'

'Very well.' Then he frowned a little. 'Though I don't want you overtired. Remember what the doctor said. He said—'

'That fresh air and gentle exercise would be *excellent*, for both me and my baby.'

His arms tightened around her. '*Our* baby.' And she felt a fresh wave of joy and delight in her new life.

At first, she'd been frightened of letting Jack down. Frightened also that he might turn out to be different from the man she'd got to know on that memorable canal journey, now that he had the duties of the estate to keep him busy. But there was fun as well, because there had been parties celebrating Christmas and Easter and harvest time. At night he was still her tender lover and the exquisite intimacy of those shared hours made the bond between them complete.

Now she eased herself away from him, intending to go to Robbie, who was waiting patiently on the towpath. But Jack caught her to him once more and whispered in her ear, 'Thank you, Matty.'

She was bewildered. 'For what, Jack?'

'Thank you,' he said, 'for showing me the way home.'

In his expressive blue eyes, she knew she could read everything his heart felt. She reached up to kiss him. 'It's been my pleasure,' she said softly.

* * * * *

LET'S TALK

Romance

For exclusive extracts, competitions
and special offers, find us online:

- facebook.com/millsandboon
- @millsandboonuk
- @millsandboon

Or get in touch on 0844 844 1351*

For all the latest titles coming soon,
visit millsandboon.co.uk/nextmonth